MAGICALAMITY

Also by Kate Saunders

Beswitched

The Whizz Pop Chocolate Shop

MAGICALAMITY

Kate Saunders

A YEARLING BOOK

Text copyright © 2011 by Kate Saunders
Cover art copyright © 2012 by Brandon Dorman

All rights reserved. Published in the United States by Yearling, an imprint of Random House Children's Books, a division of Random House LLC, a Penguin Random House Company, New York. Originally published in hardcover in the United States by Delacorte Press, an imprint of Random House Children's Books, New York, in 2012.

Yearling and the jumping horse design are registered trademarks of Random House LLC.

Visit us on the Web! randomhouse.com/kids

Educators and librarians, for a variety of teaching tools, visit us at RHTeachersLibrarians.com

The Library of Congress has cataloged the hardcover edition of this work as follows:
Saunders, Kate.
Magicalamity / Kate Saunders. — 1st ed.
p. cm.
Summary: Eleven-year-old Tom is shocked to learn that he is a demisprite, half fairy and half mortal, and that he, aided by three fairy godmothers, must save his father, who is hiding in the fairy Realm, while safeguarding his mortal mother.
ISBN 978-0-385-74077-7 (hardcover) — ISBN 978-0-375-98968-1 (glb) — ISBN 978-0-375-98928-5 (ebook) [1. Fairy godmothers—Fiction. 2. Fairies—Fiction. 3. Magic—Fiction. 4. England—Fiction.] I. Title.
PZ7.S2539 Mag 2012
[Fic]—dc23
2011041882

ISBN 978-0-385-74078-4 (pbk.)

Printed in the United States of America
10 9 8 7 6 5 4 3 2 1
First Yearling Edition 2013

For Max

Contents

1

Demisprite

On the morning everything changed, Tom Harding opened his eyes to find his old white cat sitting on his duvet.

"Hi, Elvis," he said blearily. "How did you get in?" He could have sworn he had shut his bedroom door last night. He sat up in bed with a loud yawn—he had slept very deeply, and his head felt foggy. His bedroom looked perfectly normal, but there was an odd silence in the house. Sunlight blazed through the curtains. Then he caught sight of his alarm clock.

Eleven-thirty? That couldn't be right. Mum always woke him up early on weekdays, even during the summer holidays—Tom's parents, Jonas and Sophie Harding, owned a delicatessen and coffee shop, and he had to be up before they opened at half past eight.

The Harding family lived in a flat above the deli, and there should have been plenty of noise downstairs at this time of the morning—the coffee machine hissing, babies wailing, people talking at the tables outside on the pavement. And yet the strange silence stretched on and on, and Elvis's green eyes stared at Tom gravely, as if he were trying to say something important.

"Mum?" Tom called. "Mum, are you there? Dad?"

No reply.

Something was wrong. Tom scrambled out of bed, quickly put on yesterday's clothes and hurried downstairs to the deli. It was gloomy and deserted. The thick green night blinds were still drawn over the big windows, and the CLOSED sign was up in the door. He looked round at the polished wooden counters and the shelves filled with bottles and packets of fancy food. Beside the till, Dad had made a little pyramid of jars of sun-dried tomatoes, and Tom noticed that the top jar was missing. That was the only change he could put his finger on, but everything felt strange.

He dashed back upstairs to the flat. "Mum? Dad?"

"Good morning!" a voice called from the kitchen.

It was a deep, rough voice that didn't belong to either of his parents. Cautiously, Tom looked round the kitchen door and saw a very large bottom bent over in front of the open fridge. The owner of the bottom stood up and turned round, and Tom saw that she was a tough-looking lady, with a wrinkled brown face and short gray hair, dressed in a blue jumpsuit and heavy boots.

"So you're Tom," she said.

"Er—hello. What's going on? Have you seen my parents?"

"The name's Mustard," the tough lady said cheerfully. "Lorna Mustard. I expect your dad's mentioned me."

A single jar of rich red sun-dried tomatoes stood on the draining board. Lorna Mustard picked it up carefully and put it on the top shelf.

"No," Tom said, "I'm pretty sure he's never mentioned anyone called Mustard. Do you know where my parents have gone? Why's the deli shut?"

"Let's not fly into a panic," Lorna said in her gruff voice. "Have some eggs and bacon."

"Did they go out somewhere?"

"You could say that."

"Why didn't they tell me?"

"Hmm. How old are you now?"

"Eleven," Tom said. "Why didn't they say anything?"

"There wasn't time—your dad just managed to summon me. Now I'm here to take care of you."

Tom decided she must be crazy. "I don't need a babysitter, thanks."

"I'm not a babysitter," Lorna said. "I'm your fairy godmother."

"Sorry?" He wondered if he should call the police, or maybe an ambulance.

"Before you ask any more questions, you'd better see this." Lorna snapped her fingers at the small television on the kitchen counter. The screen flickered, and a face appeared.

"Dad?" Tom gasped.

"Hi, Tom." Dad was speaking from some dark, murky place, and he looked scared. "If you're watching this, it means I've been forced into hiding. I can't explain it all now, but I've been keeping a secret. A big secret. I'm very sorry, Tom—there's no easy way to say this—but I'm a fairy."

"WHAT?" Tom's heart was thudding uncomfortably. "Look, what's going on?"

"I thought I could leave my fairy side behind," the recording of Dad went on. "I thought I could open a deli in Primrose Hill and live like a normal human being. I didn't tell you or your mother because I wanted to protect you. But they've found me, and now there's a warrant out for my arrest."

"But that's stupid!" Tom cried. "He's not a criminal!"

"Inside the Realm," Dad said, "I'm wanted for illegal marriage and murder. That's why I had to go into hiding. It's true that my marriage to your mother isn't legal

4

here—but please believe this, Tom"—Tom had never seen Dad so serious—"I did not kill Milly Falconer! The charge is complete nonsense—but there's no time to explain. Whatever you do, don't let anyone lure you into the Realm! Not even if they kidnap Mum and hold her hostage."

"Mum! What's he talking about?" This was a nightmare. "Where is she?"

"She's only a mortal," Dad said. "I'm trusting you to protect her. Tell her I'm sorry about being a secret fairy. I hate leaving you both, but you'll be safer if you don't know where I am. I've summoned your three fairy godmothers, and they'll tell you what to do—their names are Iris Moth, Dahlia Pease-Blossom and Lorna Mustard." In the background there was distant shouting, and what sounded like a gunshot. Dad looked frightened. Very quickly he added, "No more time! Trust your godmothers, Tom—they're our only hope!"

"This is some kind of trick," Tom said faintly.

On the television, something strange and dreadful was happening to Dad. His chin melted like wax, his nose stretched into a point, his face turned black and hairy, his mouth filled with fangs, and before Tom's horrified eyes he changed into a bat. The screen went blank.

Tom collapsed into one of the kitchen chairs.

Maybe I'm still asleep, he thought, and this is a really weird dream.

But the kitchen tap dripped, which it didn't in dreams, and this lady with the big bum—his "fairy godmother"—was only too solid.

"I came the minute I got the summons," Lorna Mustard said. "I don't know what's happened to the other two godmothers—lazy old bags—but I know my duty."

"Mum!" Tom sprang out of his chair. "He said they'd kidnap her! Where is she?" It was horrible to think of his pretty, laughing mother being kidnapped—maybe tied up, or blindfolded.

"Calm down, boy!" Lorna clamped a big hand on his shoulder and pushed him back. "I'm way ahead of you, and I hid your mother the minute I got here."

Tom breathed a little easier. Lorna had a very confident way of talking, and Dad had told him to trust her. For some reason—though she was a total stranger and hardly seemed normal—he did. "Is she OK? When can I see her?"

"I'm afraid you can't see her just yet, because it might put her in danger. But please don't be anxious about her." For the first time Lorna's craggy old face was kind. "She's absolutely fine, and I give you my solemn word that I'm guarding her with my life. Now you'd better have some bacon and eggs—you look shocked."

"I am shocked."

"Did you really not know your dad was a fairy?"

"No! I had no idea!" Tom's best friend, Charlie, had

once been sent out of class for calling someone a fairy. What would Charlie say if he heard about this? Once or twice lately he'd made fun of Tom for wearing a "girly" apron when he helped out at the deli on Saturday mornings. It hadn't done any good telling him it was a man's apron. Charlie would definitely think being a fairy was girly.

"In the mortal world, the word 'fairy' is sometimes used as an insult." Lorna put the big frying pan on the stove and slapped in six slices of bacon. "Little mortal girls think they're dressing up as fairies when they wear pink wings and puffy pink skirts. They think fairy godmothers only exist in stories. Mortals have never really understood us."

"I'm a mortal," Tom reminded her.

"Oh, you're not a mortal."

"Yes, I am!"

Lorna flipped the bacon in the pan. "You're not, you know."

"I'm a normal human boy!"

"Well, you're a boy," Lorna said cheerfully. "But you're not entirely human—and you're definitely not normal."

Tom was a little scared, but also interested. "What am I, then?"

"You're a demisprite."

"A—what?"

His fairy godmother held four eggs in her big hand and broke them into the frying pan all at once. "A demi-sprite is half fairy and half mortal. You're very rare and special because you're not supposed to exist. Fairies aren't allowed to mate with mortals."

"Why not?"

"It makes a puncture in the membrane, and magic leaks out."

"What membrane?"

"Oh dear, it's complicated. It's the thin layer between this world and the Realm."

"Can a demisprite get into the Realm?"

"Certainly not legally."

"So—when my dad married my mum, he was really committing a crime? Wow!" Tom was impressed. Dad was a small, smiling man with curly hair, who wore an apron and spent his days making coffee and slicing salami. But if all this fairy stuff was true, he was secretly as brave and romantic as someone in a film.

"We all tried to warn him," Lorna said, shaking her head. "But nothing beats the power of true love. It doesn't matter how many laws they make—there have always been a few demisprites. They often have amazing talents that make them stand out in the mortal world. Shakespeare and Mozart were demis. So was Stalin—the power shows up in all sorts of ways."

"Wow," Tom said again. "I'm a demisprite!" He tried

out the sound of the word and decided it was weird but glamorous, and not necessarily girly. "Does that mean I have superpowers?" He was starting a new school in September, and was already worried that Charlie would avoid him for not being cool enough. A superpower or two would come in very handy.

"We shall have to find out about your powers." Lorna put two plates of bacon and eggs on the table and sat down. "What skills would you like?"

"I don't know—flying would be good." He'd always had secret fantasies about being able to fly.

"Can't you fly?" She tossed a fried egg into her mouth and gulped it down whole. "No, of course not. Well, you must have some lessons."

"Flying lessons? Seriously?"

"I've never been more serious."

"Can my dad fly?"

"Oh, of course—and he's jolly good at it. He was on the flying hockey team when we were in college."

"Is that where you met him? He never talks about his college." It was incredible to think that his easygoing dad, who had gray hair and a rather round stomach, had been hiding the fact that he could fly—actually *fly*. And he'd thought he knew Dad so well.

Lorna said, "Eat your food before it gets cold."

Tom realized he was hungry and began to eat his bacon and eggs, watching Lorna.

She hasn't done anything magical yet, he thought, except that thing with the television—Cinderella's fairy godmother was a lot more useful. Lorna had cooked the food herself; a proper fairy would just have conjured it out of nothing.

"Ms. Mustard . . ."

"Call me Lorna."

"Lorna, can you help my dad?"

She sighed. "I hope so, but I dropped out of the Realm years ago—I own a scrap-metal business these days."

"Oh." Tom hadn't expected this. It didn't sound very fairylike.

"My magic's a bit rusty. You probably know more than I do."

His heart sank. If his fairy godmother couldn't get him out of this mess, who could? "You couldn't know less magic than me," he said gloomily, "because I don't know any."

"What—none at all? Did Jonas really teach you nothing?"

"I told you, he never told me anything, and certainly not about magic."

"That's a nuisance."

"Don't you use magic anymore?"

Lorna sighed again. "There's not much call for it in the scrap-metal trade. I only used the spells that would make my business successful."

"Could you change yourself into a bat, like my dad did?"

"I could, but I'd have to look it up—and all my spell-books are in a box somewhere."

"Oh." Tom had decided he liked Lorna, but he couldn't help being disappointed.

"To tell the truth, when I agreed to be your god-mother, I didn't think I'd actually have to do anything. I just signed the parchment and sent you a christening present."

This was interesting. Tom tried to remember some of the old fairy tales Mum had read to him when he was little, where godmothers gave wonderful magical gifts. "What was it?"

His godmother grinned suddenly, making her stern face look younger and nicer. "You're good at math, aren't you?"

"Well . . . yes." Tom was very good at math. The head-mistress of his primary school had told his parents he was "exceptional."

"That was my present—math talent."

"Thanks," Tom said politely, though he couldn't help wishing it had been a football talent instead; being great at math didn't exactly make you popular—Charlie said only nerds were good at math.

"I nearly got you a talent for keeping your bedroom tidy," Lorna went on, "but math was only a few pounds

11

more and the postage was included, so I thought, What the heck? I always liked Jonas."

"What about the other godmothers? Did they give me presents?"

"Oh yes, it's the custom. Dahlia Pease-Blossom got you a handsome-token—she was too mean to fork out for full beauty."

"Actually, handsome is fine," Tom said. "I mean, it's really nice." His face turned hot. He was a tall, skinny boy with dark brown hair and blue eyes—and apparently he was handsome, which was nice to know, but a bit embarrassing.

"And Iris Moth sent you a whole hour of invisibility, which is very expensive. She's a nasty old bag in some ways, but she's not as tightfisted as Dahlia—and she's a great one for keeping up the old customs. For instance, she still goes back to the Realm twice a year for the nude dancing at the solstices. I haven't bothered for ages."

"The Realm is where my dad's hiding, isn't it?"

"Yes." Lorna was very serious.

"So we need to go there and look for him."

"No, no—you can't come into the Realm. It's too dangerous. I have to hide you in this world. You see, the Falconers will be looking for you this very minute. We'd better get out as soon as possible."

"The . . . Falconers?"

"They're the ruling family in the Realm. I'll give you

12

the background later. All you need to know now is that they're highly dangerous—and, for some reason I don't understand, they want Jonas dead."

Tom put down his knife and fork, feeling slightly sick. "Is it because of Milly Falconer?"

"Well remembered, boy—we'll make a fairy out of you yet. Yes, Milly was a Falconer, and they still blame Jonas for her death. But there's more to it, I'll be bound." Lorna picked up the dirty plates and took them to the sink. "If only he'd kept to the old law and invited Dolores Falconer to your christening!"

"This is like the play I went to at Christmas," Tom said. "She's the Bad Fairy, right?"

"It's even more complicated than that. She's your aunt."

Another bombshell—Tom was almost getting used to them. What else had Dad been keeping from him? "I didn't know I had any aunts."

"She's your dad's older sister—a complete cow, and always was." Lorna quickly washed the plates under the tap. "All you need to know now is that she wants to use you and your mum as bait—she knows Jonas will come out of hiding to save you. Her people are after you, and we have to get out as fast as possible."

Downstairs, there was loud knocking at the door.

2

Basic Flying

Lorna froze. "Who's that?"

"I don't know—probably a delivery. We get them all the time." Tom was trying to sound confident, but his heart was beating hard. Did this mean the Falconers had come to kidnap him? Would his godmother be able to save him if they had? "Shall I go down?"

"Yes, we should try to look as normal as possible. But I'll come with you." She led the way down the stairs to the deli.

Through the glass door Tom saw the untidy blond hair of his best friend.

"Charlie!" He almost laughed aloud with relief.

"Hey, Tom!" Charlie called from the other side of the door. "Why are you closed? Let me in!"

"Just a minute. . . ."

"Wait!" Lorna grabbed Tom's arm before he could unlock the door. "Do you know him?"

"Oh yes. His name's Charlie Evans. I've known him for years."

"Are you expecting him?"

The question made Tom remember that he was not. "Well, no. I thought he was away in Turkey."

"Hmm, that sounds dodgy. Are you sure it's him?"

"Of course it's him!"

"Look at him again." Lorna's grip on his arm tightened. "You mortals never use your eyes properly. Never mind what you EXPECT to see—what do you REALLY see? Is there anything different about him?"

Tom looked carefully at his best friend's face. As soon as he did, he noticed that Charlie's hair was a little darker than usual—and his upper lip was a slightly different shape—and the expression in his eyes was all wrong. Once again Tom had the sick feeling in the pit of his stomach—it had been horrible seeing Dad turn into a bat, but this poor imitation of Charlie was worse.

"That's not him," he whispered.

"I knew it!" Lorna shoved Tom behind her and banged angrily on the glass. "BOG OFF!"

The boy who was not Charlie suddenly sneezed violently and changed into a tall young man with untidy dark hair and a big turned-up nose. And then he vanished.

"Well, it's started," said Lorna. "Best foot forward, boy!" She marched back upstairs, dragging Tom behind her. "Here's what we'll do. You're coming back to my place, which is still hidden from the Falconers. We can't use any kind of mortal transport—far too risky—so we'll be flying."

"OK," Tom said faintly. He was still shaking from the very creepy sight of someone suddenly vanishing into thin air.

"You go and pack a few clothes while I set up my wings."

"Right." He went into his bedroom and hastily stuffed all the clean clothes he could find, plus his iPod, into his school backpack.

In the kitchen, Lorna was pulling a lot of flimsy, dirty-looking white material out of a shopping bag. She gave it a couple of shakes, and Tom saw that it was a leather waistcoat with two long, droopy white shapes attached to the back.

"My wings," Lorna said briskly.

"Oh."

She chuckled. "I know they don't look like much—

wait till you see them spread in full flight. Are you ready?"

"Yes, but—are you sure they still work?"

"Fairy wings never wear out." She took the jar of sun-dried tomatoes from the shelf, wrapped it carefully in two tea towels and stuffed it into Tom's backpack.

"Do we have to take that?" he asked. "What if it breaks? I don't want oily tomatoes all over my stuff."

"I'm very fond of sun-dried tomatoes—don't you dare take it out, do you hear? Ooof! Give me a hand with this harness, boy—it seems to have shrunk!"

The waistcoat part of Lorna's wings had been made for a slimmer fairy, and it took a lot of heaving and huffing before she was safely strapped in.

"Thanks, Tom—by the way, before I forget, Elvis says goodbye and good luck."

"Elvis! I'd forgotten all about him. I can't leave him here by himself!"

"He'll be fine," Lorna said. "He's gone to stay with his other family."

"What are you talking about? He's our cat!"

"I hate to give you yet another shock—but your cat has been two-timing you with the Atkinsons on the next street. They think they own him."

"Well, of all the—that little furry—wait a sec, how do you know? Can you talk to animals?"

Lorna fanned out her long wings behind her. "Yes, fairies can understand all mammals."

The ability to talk to animals, like Dr. Dolittle, was another superpower Tom had always secretly wanted, and thinking about it distracted him from Elvis's dreadful disloyalty. "Could a demisprite learn to do that?"

"Questions later! Grab the holding loop on my back—it's designed for passengers—and we'll jump out of the window." She jerked open the window behind the sink.

"Hang on. . . ." Tom took a step back. They were up on the second floor, and though he was convinced Lorna was genuinely on his side, he was not quite sure about her magic. "Aren't you going to practice first?"

"Practice? My dear Tom, this is the most ordinary magic! I don't need to practice!"

"But if you haven't done it for a while . . ."

She sighed loudly. "All right! Just to convince you, I'll give you a quick demo of basic flying. First, I climb out of the window and perch, ready for takeoff." She scrambled over the sink and crouched on the sill. "Now I say these simple words: *bish, bash, bosh, borum*—two magic finger-snaps—jump . . . OW!"

Lorna toppled off the windowsill and dropped straight down into the rosebush below.

"Lorna?" Tom gasped, stretching over the sink to look out of the window. "Are you OK?"

"Drat and double drat!" She was thrashing about

18

furiously in a tangle of spiky branches and useless white wings. "I could've SWORN . . . How could I forget that stupid spell?"

Tom dashed downstairs and out into the garden, very worried that his fairy godmother had hurt herself— should he call an ordinary ambulance? She was a sturdy woman, however, and falling out of an upstairs window had only given her a few bruises.

"OW! These thorns are sticking right in my— I'm sorry, Tom, you were quite right—I certainly do need to practice! I'll start indoors next time."

They went back upstairs to the flat. Lorna decided to try for a short test flight in the sitting room, which was bigger than the kitchen. She stood in the middle of the carpet and muttered spell after spell—and still nothing happened.

It took such a long time that Tom forgot they were in a hurry. He got himself a Coke from the deli fridge and sat down on the sofa to watch comfortably. Some magic was coming back to his fairy godmother, but it was always the wrong magic. One spell closed the curtains, another set off every single car alarm in the street—it was very entertaining. The nearest she came to flying was when her left wing suddenly started flapping all by itself, and she started to whiz round in midair like a Catherine wheel.

"This is very embarrassing," Lorna said breathlessly

when she had managed to stop spinning. "I thought flying would be just like riding a bicycle. OK—*flitch, flatch, flotch, flarum*—two stamps of the foot—AARGH!"

There was a flash of bright light. Tom nearly dropped his drink. Lorna's empty clothes collapsed, and a little brown mouse ran out of the heap. He knelt down on the rug beside it. "Lorna? Is that you?"

The mouse looked at him with beady little eyes and squeaked, "Knickers!"

Tom burst out laughing, and so did the mouse—which looked and sounded so funny that he laughed even harder.

He was still giggling when Lorna reversed the spell and leapt back into her clothes, but she was downcast. "I'm sorry about this, boy—a fine fairy godmother I turned out to be!"

"You're OK." She looked so miserable that Tom wanted to cheer her up. "The other two didn't even come."

"That's very decent of you, but it doesn't solve the problem. How on earth am I going to get you to my place if we can't fly?"

"Where is your place?"

"Just outside Glasgow."

"Oh." This was a very long way away. "Well, we could take the train, or a plane—"

"No, no, that's too risky."

"If you can't fly and you can't use ordinary transport, how did you get here?"

"I used a dissolving and relocating spell," Lorna said gloomily. "But that wouldn't do for you. Your molecules would never stand it—you're too human."

"OK. Well, why can't you hide me in the same place you hid my mother?"

"Sorry—you're not human enough for that."

"Oh."

Lorna began to unfasten her wings. "There's nothing else for it, I'm afraid. I'll just have to swallow my pride and ask Abdul."

"Who?"

She was stern. "Are we near Kentish Town Road?"

"Pretty near, yes."

"Good. We've got to find a cafe called The Casbah—next door to a twenty-four-hour supermarket and just by the bus stop."

"I think I know that cafe," Tom said, surprised. "It always has steamy windows. And it's always full of little fat brown guys."

"They're not little fat brown guys," Lorna said shortly. "They're genies. And one of them is my ex-husband."

3

Abdul

"He was incredibly handsome," Lorna said. "With a devilish charm that could sweep a young fairy off her feet." She had decided to risk a short journey on mortal transport and they were on the bus, surrounded by her plastic bags. She couldn't stop talking about her ex-husband the genie. Tom hoped he didn't run into anyone from school. "And he was the first man I'd ever met who had his own flying carpet. I just lost my head. By the time I found out he shared the carpet with his useless brother, it was too late."

"We get off in a minute. It's the next stop." Tom was liking his godmother more and more, but she didn't seem to be much of a fairy. Her magic was too patchy to carry them to Abdul's cafe, and she had forgotten to bring any mortal money with her for bus fares. Luckily Tom often went swimming in Kentish Town, so he had taken charge. He borrowed his mum's transit card and got Lorna and her bags on the right buses.

"And whenever my mother came to visit he'd turn himself into a puff of smoke and sulk inside a lamp for days. Once I got so mad at him, 1 threw the lamp in the garbage." The bus slowed down, and Lorna stood up, grabbing all her bags, including the one with her wings. "Don't forget your backpack, will you?"

"You don't have to keep telling me. It's still on my back."

"Splendid."

They got off the bus beside a row of shops. The Casbah, squeezed between a twenty-four-hour supermarket and a dry cleaner's, was smaller and shabbier than Tom remembered. On a quiet afternoon in the summer holidays it looked disappointingly unmagical. He couldn't see how anything here could help him to save his parents.

"Are you sure this is the right cafe? It's so . . . well . . . ordinary."

"Oh, this is it," Lorna said grimly. She stepped up to the steamy window. "And there's Abdul—sexy as ever!"

Tom peered through the dim glass. Inside the cafe,

five short, fat men with pointy black beards sat at rickety plastic tables. "Which one is he?"

"Isn't it obvious?" groaned Lorna. "The handsome one!"

"Er—sorry, they all look the same amount of handsome to me."

"He's behind the counter—the cafe belongs to him. Come on."

She pushed open the glass door and Tom followed her in. Despite being so worried about Mum and Dad, he was very curious to see real genies, if that was truly what they were. The men in the cafe—all staring at him with big dark eyes—wore normal, everyday clothes and were nothing like the genie from *Aladdin*. When he looked closely at the pictures on the walls, however, he saw that they were all photographs of traditional genies doing genie-ish things in puffs of colored smoke—one of them seemed to be a picture of a whole genie football team posing on a flying carpet.

The genie behind the counter gasped. "Lorna!"

"Hello, Abdul."

"Lorna! Good grief, it's been—how long? What on earth are you doing here?"

"I'm sorry to barge in like this," Lorna said stiffly. "I didn't know where else to go—this is an emergency."

The genie sitting nearest to Tom pointed a finger at him. "Demisprite!"

She put her hand on Tom's shoulder. "This is my godson, Tom Harding."

"That's the demisprite the Falconers are looking for," another genie said. "I heard it on the fairy news."

The cafe was hot, but Tom suddenly felt cold. This was getting seriously scary. In the other world, where his dad came from, he was being hunted like a criminal.

"Don't worry." Lorna gave his shoulder a reassuring squeeze. "You're among friends here—they're all exiles, and several are being hunted themselves. Nobody will betray you."

Abdul came out from behind the counter and shook Tom's hand. "Tom Harding—Jonas's boy! Well, well!" He was nothing like the sexy rascal described by Lorna. He looked kind and rather cuddly, and his rosy brown face was as round and smiling as a clock on a nursery wall.

"You know my dad?"

"Oh yes. I haven't seen him for years, but he was part of the gang in college—those were the days!"

"I wonder why he's never mentioned you. We live quite near here, and we must've passed this place a hundred times."

"He couldn't risk any magical contact," Abdul said. "He was in hiding. So are we—nearly all of us are being hunted."

"By the Falconers?"

"Yes—mostly because we managed to annoy their house genie, Ali Kazoum."

(All the genies in the cafe muttered angrily, and one spat on the floor.)

"Oh." Tom was fascinated. His father came from an extraordinary world, where characters in fairy tales were real and dangerous—and it was partly his world too.

"Jonas didn't tell Tom about his true background," Lorna said, "which is very awkward, because it means we have to rely on my magic—and I've forgotten how to fly. So we're hoping we can bum a ride to my place near Glasgow." She frowned. "I hate asking, but as I said, it's an emergency."

"I'm delighted you asked me," Abdul declared. "All that is mine is yours, my flower! Wait a little while, and Hussein will be back with the carpet. You remember my brother, Hussein?"

"I certainly do." Lorna's frown deepened. "Still taking the carpet for joyrides, is he?"

Abdul's sweet, fat face was dignified. "Actually, these days we use it to run a magical minicab service—but of course we won't charge you. It's a pleasure to help Jonas's son. Let's go into the back room, where we can talk." He took off his apron and handed it to the nearest genie. "Cassim, you take over—look out for Falconer agents, and bring us a couple of kebabs."

"OK," Cassim said cheerfully.

26

Abdul led them through a door behind the counter to a small, hot back room with no window. There was a tall rack of glass bottles of all shapes and sizes, a fridge-freezer, a table and some chairs. Abdul took three cans of fizzy water from the fridge, and they all sat down. Lorna immediately launched into the whole story of the summons, the problem of rescuing Jonas and her rusty magic powers.

Cassim came in with a big tray of kebabs. It had been hours since the eggs and bacon, and Tom and Lorna pounced on them hungrily. Tom was glad to see that Lorna had stopped frowning at Abdul. She was relaxed and smiling, and he thought she was glad to see him again.

"This is very decent of you, Abdul," she said through a mouthful of shredded lettuce. "Tom will be safe at the scrapyard, and I'll do my best to teach him a bit of magic—but I'm blowed if I know what to do for poor old Jonas."

Tom's heart sank. "There must be some way to save him!"

"Of course we can save him." Abdul patted his arm kindly. "Jonas was always terrific at magic. And even before the business with Milly Falconer, he was smart enough to make friends with a few animals—always a good idea if you suddenly need to drop out of sight. I bet that's where he's hiding."

"You're quite right," Lorna said. "He's probably with some bats."

Tom had a moment of unreality. This time yesterday he'd been watching television in the kitchen at home, listening to Mum and Dad chatting and laughing downstairs while they closed up the deli. Now his mother had vanished and his father was living undercover as a bat. The world had turned inside out.

"Of course—there was that bat he shared a flat with in college," Abdul said. "He used to bring him to the pub."

"I remember!" Lorna exclaimed. "What a bore he was—always droning on about animal rights—but I'm glad I was nice to him. They'll never find Jonas among a colony of bats."

Suddenly there was a flash of white light, and one of the bottles on the top shelf of the rack poured out a fountain of thick purple smoke.

Tom jumped out of his chair—was this a bomb? Some kind of purple fire?

"Don't worry," Abdul said comfortably, "it's only Hussein."

This had to be one of the weirdest sights Tom had seen all day. The purple smoke formed itself into a shape and became the silhouette of a man. Twenty seconds later, the smoke had gone and another exiled genie stood in the small room. He was short and round, like Abdul, dressed in an ordinary shirt and trousers—and a pair of huge sparkling earrings.

"Lorna Mustard!" He was shocked. "Blimey, Abdul—what's your ex-wife doing here?"

"Hello, Hussein," Lorna said. "Relax—for once I'm not here to call you a good-for-nothing. I came to get a lift on the carpet. To make a long story short, this demi-sprite boy is Jonas Harding's son, Tom, and I'm his god-mother."

Hussein did not know Tom's dad, but he was also (once he had recovered from the shock of seeing Lorna) very welcoming. He shook Tom's hand and gave him a Mars Bar ice cream from the freezer. "Any friend of Abdul's is a friend of mine—especially if he's an enemy of the Falconers."

"Thanks," Tom said. He was starting to feel more hopeful. These people could do amazing things, and he didn't even know what powers he had himself. They were bound to find a way to help his parents.

"The carpet's warm, and I vacuumed it this morning," Hussein said. "Good luck!"

"Ahem!" Abdul said, pointing to a notice on the back of the door: STOP! HAVE YOU REMOVED ALL YOUR JEWELS?

"What? Oh—silly me." Hussein took off his earrings. "Nice to meet you, Tom. And . . . er . . . Lorna—nice to . . . er— Bye!" He scuttled out of the room.

Abdul said, "He really has changed, you know."

29

"Hmm," said Lorna. "I'll believe it when I see it. Are we ready to go?"

Tom's spirits lifted. He was about to ride on a flying carpet. Who did that? If he hadn't been so worried about his parents, he would have been incredibly excited.

The other genies smiled at him kindly as he went back into the cafe to use the toilet. When he returned to the room behind the counter he found Lorna rummaging in his backpack.

"I'm just giving the jar of tomatoes to Abdul," she told him. "You always liked sun-dried tomatoes, didn't you?"

"Oh—yes—" Abdul carefully took the jar. "Rest assured, I will guard them with my life."

"You won't let your useless brother get hold of them?"

"I swear." Abdul was very serious. "Nothing and nobody shall take this jar of tomatoes from me."

"Well, that's a weight off my mind!"

"I don't know why you're making such a big deal about a jar of tomatoes," Tom said impatiently. "They're very easy to get. Where do we go now? Is the carpet here?"

"Yes, we keep it in the yard." Abdul held up the jar of tomatoes with one hand and snapped his fingers, dissolving the jar into a cloud of pink smoke. "I'll just get changed."

He snapped his fingers again, and there was another puff of smoke—blue this time.

When it cleared Tom cried, "Hey, Abdul—you look fantastic!"

For the first time, Abdul looked like a real genie from the *Arabian Nights*. He was magnificent in a purple turban with a huge jewel pinned to the front. On his feet were gold slippers that curled up at the toes. His round stomach strained against a tunic and trousers of orange satin. He smiled shyly. "You are very kind."

Lorna stared at him in silence. After a few moments, she said, "You've still got it, Abdul."

His round cheeks turned pink. "You too, Lorna."

(They seemed very fond of each other for people who were divorced; Tom made a mental note to ask Lorna what had happened.)

Abdul opened a door beside the rack of bottles and led Tom and Lorna out into a small, sooty backyard, with a child's sandpit in the middle of the flagstones. Tom watched Abdul take a roll of carpet from a small wooden shed. The back of it was like the underside of any old carpet. When he unrolled it over the sandpit, however, Tom caught his breath—the colors were amazing, like a beautiful stained-glass window with the sun behind it. The magic carpet hovered in midair for a few seconds and then sank slowly onto the sand.

"Shoes off, please," Abdul said. "Lorna, you sit in the back with the bags. We'll let Tom enjoy the view from the front."

Tom took off his sneakers, put them in his backpack and (feeling silly, because he couldn't imagine this working) sat cross-legged on the carpet. Abdul put on a pair of pink gloves and sat down next to Tom.

The exiled genie folded his arms and muttered something under his breath. It took Tom a couple of minutes to realize they were rising slowly off the ground. The carpet rose as far as the top of the garden wall. Tom clung to the edge, terrified of falling off—how was he meant to fly to Glasgow on this thing?

"Please relax—imagine you are on the rug beside the fire at home," Abdul said. "You won't fall."

In the warm, still summer afternoon, the carpet soared away above the houses and shops. Tom dared to glance down at Kentish Town Road, far below. The tiny cars and people fell away behind them, and they were shooting across the city like an arrow.

At first it was very scary. Tom clenched his fists and screwed up his eyes, expecting to be blown off the carpet at any moment. But the air was soft and fresh on his face, and Abdul was humming a tune beside him. Tom slowly opened his eyes, bracing himself for the shock.

The view was wonderful. The country was spread out at his feet—swaths of green, glittering stretches of water, buildings like Lego models. The sun was setting, and the carpet sped through banks of pink cloud. This was better than the best carnival ride in the world.

"Lovely, isn't it?" said Abdul. "Such a nice, quiet little country when you see it from up here!"

"It's amazing! But why haven't we been stopped? Don't the army try to shoot you down?"

"We're invisible at the moment—to both mortals and fairies. And we're going the long way round, over Wales, because the Falconers will have invisibility sensors along all the main fairy flight paths."

It was interesting, and a bit unsettling, to think of these invisible flight paths; mortal pilots had no idea they shared the air with fairies and genies and goodness knew what else.

They were traveling faster than the wind. Towns rushed past beneath them. The sky was now a darker blue, and the carpet began to slow down. The evening air was growing chilly. Below them, a great city started to twinkle with lights.

Lorna had nodded off. She woke up with a snort. "Hummph, are we here already? Go about forty-five degrees to the right."

The carpet was losing height, and soon Tom could see the main roads, then the buses, then the faces of the people on the buses. It was extraordinary that nobody could see them. They sailed over suburban streets and back gardens, over disused factories and grim industrial estates. Lower and lower they went, until they were circling slowly over a vast yard filled with twisted lumps of metal and heaps of old tyres. Tom glimpsed a big wooden sign: MUSTARD'S METAL CRUSHING—YOU'LL THINK IT'S MAGIC!

"Here we are!" Lorna said happily. "Abdul, I can't thank you enough. You can drop us in front of the office—that little hut under the crane. What do you think, Tom?"

"Very nice," Tom said politely.

It looked like a cemetery for junked trucks. It was horrible.

4

Mustard Manor

The carpet landed beside a drab little shed with two small, dark windows. A tall crane loomed above it. All around them, as far as the eye could see, were grotesque fragments that had once been trucks and cars. Tom stood up, shivering in his T-shirt. He didn't want to hurt Lorna's feelings, but he was suddenly desperate to be at home again, in the flat above the deli, eating supper with his parents. Never in his life had he felt so lonely.

"Let's not fall out of touch again," Abdul said. "It has been wonderful seeing you, Lorna. I'd love to take you out to dinner, and maybe a wrestling match afterwards—just like we used to."

"It's been good to see you, Abdul," Lorna said gruffly. "And it would be jolly nice to do dinner and a fight someday. But right now all I can think about is this poor little demisprite. He must be exhausted!"

Her voice was strong and kind, and Tom felt ashamed of not liking her scrapyard. She had proved herself a good and loyal godmother, and he was lucky to have her. He didn't want her to think of him as some wimpy little boy. "I'm OK. Thanks very much for the ride, Abdul. It was great—and the kebab."

"My dear boy, the pleasure was all—argh!" Abdul shrieked suddenly and tried to duck behind Tom.

A huge Rottweiler was bounding across the yard towards them, barking and growling.

"Hector, STOP!" yelled Lorna. She broke into a series of snarls and barks (they sounded very strange coming out of a human mouth), and the dog was still. "This is Hector, my guard dog—I've told him to protect you, Tom. And I've also warned him about possible Falconer agents—like that one at your deli this morning. Animals are incredibly good at spotting fairies." She added what sounded like "Arr-uff, ruff, arr, arr-ruff!" and the cnormous dog quietly turned round and trotted away. "Abdul, will you stay for a cup of tea?"

"No, thanks." Abdul was eyeing the dog nervously. "I must get back to the cafe. Tom, say hello to your dad when you find him, and feel free to call on me anytime. I will send your mother the gift of some beautiful dreams."

Tom was alarmed. "She . . . She's not ill or something, is she?"

"Good gracious, no!" Lorna cried. "She's absolutely fine. It's just a genie custom—isn't it?"

"What?" Abdul was flustered for a moment. "Oh, yes— we send people dreams instead of bunches of flowers."

"Oh. Thanks."

"It is nothing." Abdul lowered his voice to a whisper. "Tom, you can do me a favor: your godmother is as beautiful as ever—when you get a chance, put in a good word for me!"

"OK, I'll do my best." Tom liked Abdul, and thought Lorna could do a lot worse. It was impressive to watch him rising slowly on his carpet before suddenly vanishing into the darkening sky.

"Phew," said Lorna. "What a day! I can't wait to get that kettle on." She took a bunch of keys from her pocket and opened the door of the dismal little shed. "Welcome to Mustard Manor."

Tom followed her through the door and gasped.

He was standing in what seemed to be a large and comfortable house. There was an imposing staircase, and a door that opened onto a big, cozy kitchen.

But when he looked back over his shoulder, there was the same depressing scrapyard.

"Come in quickly." Lorna pulled him inside and shut the door. "The magic leaks out when you leave the door open too long—and when too much leaks out, the lights stop working."

"This house is made of magic, isn't it? That's why it's invisible from the outside! Did you build it yourself?"

"It was left to me by my father," Lorna said. "I grew up in this house. It's a fairy house. I can take it anywhere I like."

"It's lovely." The house was frayed and shabby, and most things in it looked extremely old, but there was something very friendly about it. Tom felt comfortable and safe here. It was nearly as good as home.

Lorna took him up the big, creaking staircase to a large bedroom. "My uncle Clarence used to sleep here when he was a boy. Those are his old school textbooks on the shelf—a bit old-fashioned, but you might find them useful when we start your magic lessons tomorrow."

"Couldn't we start them now? I'm not tired."

"You might not be," Lorna said, "but I'm shattered. Put your stuff away and then come downstairs. I'll make us some supper and fill you in on some of the stuff I didn't tell you this morning."

After she left the room, Tom put his backpack on the bed and looked around curiously. A pair of giant bat's wings, made of dark brown leather, was spread out on the wall above the fireplace. There were dusty cricket bats and balls, and pictures of old-fashioned sportsmen and racing cars. It was a typical boy's bedroom, but as soon as you looked closely you saw there were all kinds of odd things—maps of islands that didn't exist, a large diagram of a mechanical flying coach, and books about how to make magic bombs and guns.

When he put his clothes away in the chest of drawers, he found that the bottom drawer was full of dusty rifles and what looked like hand grenades. He picked one of these up, scared and thrilled by its weight. This was not a toy. Could it be safe to sleep in a room full of weapons? Surely Lorna wouldn't keep them in her house if they were live?

Holding the grenade very carefully, he took it downstairs. He found Lorna in the big, warm, messy kitchen, which had an open fireplace and a squashy sofa heaped with old newspapers.

She was stirring something on top of the stove. "I'm making us some beans on toast. Oh, you've found one of Uncle Clarence's grenades. I forgot about those—they're quite harmless. He used to make them for the Christmas Explosions."

"The what?"

"One of our fairy customs—throwing bombs on Christmas morning—such a treat for the children."

Tom put the grenade on the table, trying to imagine how Primrose Hill would look after all the local kids had thrown bombs. "Is your uncle still alive?"

"No, he died before I was born—I'll tell you about him one day, but right now you need to be briefed about your dad." She put two steaming plates of beans on toast on the table, and two large metal mugs of tea.

Cooking was obviously not one of Lorna's talents, but it is difficult to spoil baked beans, and the strong, sweet tea was surprisingly refreshing.

Tom said, "Tell me about the Falconers."

"Ah, yes." Lorna took a noisy slurp of tea. "That's a very good place to begin. We'll get nowhere until you understand how important they are."

"You said they were the ruling family. Does that mean they're royal?"

"Not exactly. They're like an enormous family tree, with branches snaking everywhere you look. There are thousands of Falconers, in every walk of life. If you're a Falconer, or you're married to a Falconer, or the friend of a Falconer, you get all sorts of privileges. Fairies without Falconer connections are second-class citizens. And enemies of the Falconers might as well be—I'm sorry, Tom, I didn't mean to worry you."

"You were going to say, they might as well be dead," Tom said. "I want to know the truth. Don't hide anything from me." His own voice sounded brave, and that gave him courage. He was starting to understand that Lorna had taken risks for his sake, and he wanted to show her that he was worth it.

"OK—their enemies might as well be dead, and if they find Jonas, they'll kill him."

"Are you an enemy too?"

"No," Lorna said. "I came to live with the mortals because the Realm had got so awful for non-Falconers—no law and order to speak of—shootings and poisonings every day—and the taxes were crippling."

"If there's no king, who's in charge? There must be some sort of government."

"There is. It's called the Ten."

"Don't tell me—Ten Falconers?"

Lorna grinned suddenly. "Right first time! I must say, you demisprites are fast learners. Yes, they're all Falconers of one kind or another—there are elections, but it's such a farce that nobody bothers to vote anymore."

"You should have a revolution."

"Not me—I like being alive!"

"But wouldn't it be brilliant if we could defeat the Falconers while we're rescuing my dad?" Tom said. He added quickly, "Look, if I'm spending my summer holidays trapped inside a fairy tale, I don't see why I shouldn't act like a person in a story and have some cool adventures."

"Good gracious, boy!" Lorna was startled. "You've only been a fairy for a few hours, and you're already plotting to overthrow the state!" She was looking at him warily. "You didn't touch anything funny in Uncle Clarence's room, did you?"

"What do you mean?"

"Nothing—I'm being silly." She took another slurp of tea. "Let me get on with the story."

"OK." Tom was curious to know what she meant about her uncle Clarence, but he was also impatient to hear the tangled story behind his parents' disappearance. "Tell me about my aunt."

"Oh yes, your aunt Dolores. She's your dad's older sister, and she married no less a person than Tiberius Falconer himself—it caused a sensation at the time, because the Hardings were nobodies. But Dolores was beautiful and as smart as they come, and nothing stood in her way."

"Hang on, who's Tiberius?"

"Head of the Ten, rolling in money and basically the most powerful man in the Realm."

"Do they have any children?"

"Just one—their son, Pindar Falconer; he's a few years older than you."

"And he's my cousin." Tom had always wished he had a brother or a boy cousin. He had wished it so much that sometimes he felt a space in his life, as if he were missing an actual person. "Why does Tiberius want to kill my dad? He's his wife's brother!"

"That wouldn't bother him," Lorna said grimly. "He killed at least two of his own brothers on his way up. I'm afraid a lot of fairies aren't very nice."

"You're nice," Tom said.

"Thanks—there are a few of us, but the nasty ones are very nasty indeed."

An unpleasant thought came to him. "Are my other godmothers nasty fairies?"

Lorna hesitated. "Well . . . you see . . . well, to tell the truth, I don't know."

"Oh." This was not good news.

"It's years since I've seen them, and I've no idea what they've been up to."

"If they're nasty, it's a good thing they didn't answer the summons."

Lorna said, "You don't know our customs, boy—nice or nasty, they signed the godmother parchment and they have to help you."

Tom thought about this. He was afraid of meeting very wicked fairies but it might be OK if they were on his side. "Was Milly Falconer a nasty fairy?"

"Oh, Milly was all right," Lorna said. "A bit spoiled

and whiny, but basically OK. She was Tiberius's little sister—the only one of his huge family he ever really liked. She was one of our college gang too. There was Jonas and me, your other two godmothers, Abdul and Milly. We formed a punk-rock band called Puke."

"You're kidding!" Tom nearly choked on his beans. "My dad—in a punk-rock band?"

"He was our lead singer."

"No way!" This was even more startling than finding out that his dad was a secret fairy. "What did he sing? Did you write your own songs? Did you play many gigs?"

"Tom, forget the band for a minute!" Lorna tried to sound strict, though she was smiling. "The point is that Milly fell in love with Jonas. And his sister, Dolores, decided he should marry her—it would be a very fine addition to her power. Tiberius agreed, the date for the wedding was set . . . but your dad wasn't in love with Milly and he escaped to live with the mortals. The police questioned us all when he disappeared, but nobody ever found out who helped him."

"Oh."

"Milly never got over it. Lots of other men wanted to marry her, but she wouldn't look at any of them. And then she died."

"How is my dad supposed to have killed her? He wasn't even there."

"There's an ancient law that nobody takes any notice of anymore—unless it suits them. And that's the crime of heartbreaking. Milly died of a dodgy crab pastry, but Dolores is now making out that it was because your dad broke her heart. And he's also accused of misbegetting, which means producing a demisprite."

Tom shivered, though the room was warm. "Me."

"You." She looked at him solemnly.

"What's the punishment if they catch him?"

Lorna was quiet for a moment, which was unsettling. Then the lines seemed to fade from her face and she was smiling. "We won't let them catch him."

"It's death, isn't it?"

"Yes, but you have to try not to worry too much. The Falconers aren't as all-powerful as they think." She put down her mug. "You've had quite a day."

This made Tom smile. "I certainly have."

"Let's go to bed. We have a lot of work to do tomorrow."

"OK." Tom had another moment of longing for his bedroom at home, but it was quite cool to be sleeping in Clarence Mustard's mysterious room. He was incredibly tired, and glad that Lorna would be in the same house, with her fierce, fairy-spotting Rottweiler prowling around outside.

"Good night, Tom. Sleep well."

"Thanks," Tom said. He added, "I mean, thanks for everything—for coming to help me."

He could see that Lorna was pleased. "I'm rather a pathetic specimen of a fairy godmother, but I'll brush up on my magic, and then you wait and see what we can do."

5

Lessons

When Tom came downstairs the next morning he found Lorna at the kitchen table, bent over a tattered old book. She looked up. "Hi, Tom. Did you sleep well?"

"Yes, thanks." He had slept extremely well, and had a lovely dream about his mother being on a wonderful holiday at some kind of tropical health spa. It was only a dream, but he had woken up feeling far less worried about her. He wasn't quite so concerned about his dad, who at least had some magic to fight back with. "What're you doing?"

Lorna groaned softly. "This is my old magic textbook from school. I've been up since dawn, trying to get these spells back into my head—I don't remember it being as hard as this! We need to be able to move around quickly and secretly, and the only way to do that is to fly."

"When do I start?" Tom was dying to see if he could fly.

"Hold your horses—you can't start until I've remembered enough to be able to teach you." Lorna sighed heavily and got up to pour the last dribble of coffee from the dented pot on the stove. "I can't believe I've forgotten the spell! When I lived in the Realm I flew every day, without even thinking about it—I even played flying basketball at school. But those blooming words won't stay in my brain."

"I could start by learning the words," Tom offered.

"Good luck to you! I'll make some more coffee and a bit of toast."

Tom sat down at the table and pulled the old schoolbook towards him. The page was creased and covered with scribbles ("Maud Lightfoot is a COW!!!!"), and he had to strain to make out the long list of spell-words underneath. *Ziff, zaff, zoff—zipp, zapp, zopp—flish and wish*—and so on, for four more lines. It sounded babyish and silly, but Tom believed in magic now and had no doubt that it would work. He read the words over and over to himself, trying to memorize the actions, while Lorna made the toast and coffee.

"I'm glad to see you're not afraid of hard work," she

said approvingly. "We might as well get your wings on now, to see if they fit."

"I have wings?" Tom had assumed he would be sharing Lorna's.

"You can use Uncle Clarence's old ones."

"Great—where are they?"

"In your bedroom, of course."

"Oh, you mean the bat's wings above the fireplace!" Those huge leather bat's wings were not the costume wings Tom thought he was getting. They were amazingly cool genuine wings, and if Tom had enough magic, he would be flying with them. He raced back upstairs.

Uncle Clarence's old wings looked a lot more impressive than Lorna's. Tom stood in front of the fireplace staring at them. Fully spread out, they had a wingspan of at least three meters. He climbed up on a chair to take them off the wall. Cautiously, he touched the leather. It was as soft and pliable as velvet, and so light that the wings were fastened to the wall with only four small nails. He picked them out one by one and climbed down very carefully with the wings in his arms.

There were stiff rods inside the leather, like bones. One long strut caught against the back of the chair and Tom's heart jumped into his mouth. He waited for the sickening snap, but it was bendy and surprisingly strong.

These wings did not have a waistcoat part like

Lorna's. Instead there were leather straps, and the belt part had a holster for a gun. There were also leather handles stitched inside the wings, where Tom assumed you were supposed to put your fingers when flying. Tom secretly hoped that he would be allowed to carry a real gun. In this strange new world, anything seemed possible.

Wings.

The straps were adjustable, but when Tom buckled them on they were a perfect fit. He ran back to the kitchen with the soft leather billowing and swishing behind them.

Lorna inspected him gravely. "Excellent. You're begining to look like a fairy."

"Thanks."

"But it takes time, so don't expect to be looping the loop right away. We'll be doing well if we get you off the ground."

She had let out the waistcoat part of her wings so that it fitted her stout figure more comfortably. Once they were both winged, they went outside to practice on the weedy patch of concrete in front of the disguised Mustard Manor. Lorna brought out one of the kitchen chairs for her first jump and Tom's spirits soared. It was a warm, sunny morning, and even the heaps of old engines and twisted fenders looked cheerful.

"I think I've got it now." Lorna climbed onto the chair. "You can have a try in a minute. Watch me carefully."

"OK, I'm watching."

"You simply say the words, snap your fingers twice—first left, then right—"

"No," Tom said, "it's right first."

"Is it?" She wobbled uncertainly on her chair. "We'd better check in the book."

"I don't need to," Tom said patiently. "I've learned it by heart. I'll talk you through it." He concentrated as hard as he could on the spell. "OK—*ziff, zaff, zoff—zipp, zapp, zopp*—right finger-snap, left finger-snap—" They both snapped their fingers. *"Flish and wish—"* The words seemed to roll off his tongue, line after line, with surprising ease. *"Flash and dash*—oh!"

Something—a muscle he never knew he had—rippled across his shoulders, making his skin tingle. His giant bat's wings suddenly fanned out majestically around him, making an amazing spooky, spiky shadow on the concrete.

"Good grief!" Lorna was pale with astonishment. "I don't believe it!"

Tom couldn't work out why she was so thunderstruck—until he noticed that he was gazing down at her, and his sneakers were floating in midair.

He was flying.

He took a deep breath and slotted his fingers into the leather hand-straps. His wings gently stirred the warm air like giant oars. He thought of going higher, and immediately shot ten meters into the air.

"STOP!" shrieked Lorna.

It was the most brilliant thing that had ever happened to him. He found that if he thought of a direction, he flew that way, as light and free as a leaf on a breeze. When he snapped his fingers—left, right—he halted and hovered. And if he paddled with his feet and made swimming movements with his arms, he flew faster.

"Lorna, look at me—I can fly!"

"Tom, come down! It's not safe! You don't know anything about wind currents!"

He swooped gracefully over the top of the crane. "I'm flying!"

A gust of wind, strong and firm as a giant's arm, suddenly hurled him across the scrapyard. Lorna bellowed, but once the shock had worn off, Tom managed to slip out of the current and put himself back on course with a perfect loop-the-loop.

"It's as good as being a bird!" He landed neatly in front of Lorna. "Sort of like being on a trampoline with a mind of its own—could my dad fly? How could he stand to give it up?"

His fairy godmother plumped down on the chair, wiping her brow with the sleeve of her jumpsuit. "I thought you'd been blown away to kingdom come! I've never seen anything like it! You're a natural."

"Now that I can fly," Tom said, "what do we do next? Can we go and search for my dad?"

"We don't go anywhere until I can fly too—for pity's sake, boy, give me a few tips!"

Tom spent the rest of the morning helping his fairy godmother to relearn her flying skills. After about half an hour she got herself a few meters off the ground. By lunchtime she was doing wobbly circuits, with a rope tied round her waist and Tom pulling her along like an enormous balloon. Finally she managed to fly to the top of the crane with Tom holding her hand. The huge scrapyard was spread beneath them, metal gleaming in the sun. In the distance Tom could see the beginning of a motorway.

"Magnificent!" sighed Lorna. "I'd forgotten how good the world looks from this angle! You can let go of my hand now."

Tom released her hand and she immediately shot up into the air and performed a flashy triple somersault.

"She flies through the air with the greatest of ease!" sang Lorna. "That daring old fairy on the flying trapeze!" She swooped almost to the ground and suddenly shot up again. "I'm really in the swing now! Let's see if I can still make a dainty landing."

She grabbed Tom's hand and the two of them made a perfect landing outside the hut.

"Blimey, Tom!" Lorna said breathlessly. "It's a good thing you learn so fast. Let's stop for now and have something to eat. And then——"

Across the yard, Hector barked sharply.

Lorna's hot red face turned pale. She grabbed Tom's wrist—so hard that it hurt—and dragged him back into the house.

"Hey—what's going on?"

Slamming the door behind them, she bolted it top and bottom and made a quick sign with her fingers. "Someone at the gate—Hector doesn't like the look of him."

Tom was startled to see his tough godmother so agitated. On the hall table there was a kind of round shape covered with black velvet. Lorna whipped the cloth off impatiently, and Tom saw a single headlamp from a very large truck.

"It's a homemade crystal ball," she told him. "An object no fairy can do without. Watch the glass."

The headlamp suddenly glowed with light, so fiercely that Tom had to shut his eyes. The glare died down and he opened them to see a picture in the headlamp—the main gate of the scrapyard with a small hut beside it. A tall, thin postman was knocking at the gate.

"It's OK," Tom said. "It's just the postman."

"Hector says there's something weird about him—watch!"

Outside in the yard, the Rottweiler was barking himself into a frenzy. In the headlamp the tall postman sighed crossly and sneezed twice.

And then he changed into someone else. The postman was gone, and there was now a large, untidy teenager with a huge nose and a mess of black hair.

"Hey, that's the same guy who came to the deli!" Tom cried. "The one who pretended to be Charlie—it's him!"

"I knew it!" Lorna hissed. "They're after me! They've found out that I'm your godmother and they know I've got you!"

In the headlamp, the young man didn't vanish immediately but stood for a moment, looking vacant and scratching his thick mop of black hair.

"What's he doing?" wondered Lorna. "Doesn't this idiot know I have a crystal ball?"

The untidy teenager took something from the pocket of his baggy jacket and began to eat it.

"Well, I'll be blowed!" Lorna said. "It's your cousin Pindar!"

"My cousin?" Tom bent towards the headlamp, trying to get a closer look. His cousin was the son of the two wickedest and most powerful Falconers in the Realm, but he had a very funny, friendly-looking face. His nose was large and turned up at the end like a duck's beak, and he had very big ears that looked even bigger because they stuck out.

"The Fairy Secret Service must be desperate if they took Pindar," Lorna said. "He's always been rather a disappointment to his parents. Your aunt Dolores put him under house arrest once, for being stupid."

"Oh." This cousin of his must be very stupid indeed, if his own mother had locked him up for it.

Pindar finished whatever he was eating, wiped his hands down the front of his jacket, sneezed and vanished. Poor exhausted Hector finally stopped barking.

Lorna puffed heavily, as if she had just run a race. She replaced the black velvet cover on her crystal ball and sat down on the bottom stair. "Let's be calm . . . let's be reasonable." She was muttering almost to herself. "They're looking for anyone with a connection to Jonas. If I was a chief suspect, they wouldn't have trusted the job to a twit like Pindar. That means we have a bit of time. But we can't stay here now."

Tom didn't like the idea of leaving Mustard Manor. "Where shall we go?"

"To tell the truth, I don't know. All I know is that I can't do this job on my own." Lorna heaved herself to her feet. "You have two more fairy godmothers—and it's time those lazy cows started pulling their weight."

6

Crackdown Park

L orna ran the names of the other two godmothers through her headlamp crystal ball. It didn't find them, but she wasn't discouraged. "That only means they've left the Realm, like me. We'll search in the mortal world."

"If you've got a computer," Tom said, "you could Google them."

"Yes, I keep a primitive mortal computer," Lorna said, "to deal with my mortal business—I don't have a fairy broadband connection here, and a good thing too—it would make us far too easy to trace." Her computer was in a small and very messy office next to the kitchen, nearly buried under a heap of papers. She swept these aside, sitting down at the keyboard, and typed "Dahlia Pease-Blossom" into the search engine.

All they got was a list of flower shops and garden centers.

"She's in hiding," Lorna said. "Typical Dahlia! I wonder what she's up to. Never mind, let's try Iris." She keyed in "Iris Moth." "Bingo!"

Tom leaned over her shoulder to look at the screen: "Crackdown Park, Boarding School for Girls Aged 11–18, Headmistress I. C. Moth, MA."

"That's her! The 'C.' stands for 'Clutterbuck'—it was her mother's maiden name."

"Are you sure it's the right one?" Tom couldn't imagine a headmistress who was also a fairy. The headmistress of his old primary school was even less fairylike than Lorna.

"Bet you it is." Lorna clicked on "Crackdown Park," and up came the school website, which showed a huge gray house and a photo of a mean-looking thin-lipped woman. "Yes, that's definitely Iris—I'd know that miserable lizard face anywhere. There was a rumor in college that she had a bit of dinosaur blood. She always did say her family went back a long way."

Tom shivered. Iris had little currant eyes, a tiny nose and a wide, lipless slit for a mouth; she did look a bit like a disapproving *Tyrannosaurus rex*, if you could imagine a T. rex with stiff gray hair and glasses. He had a horrible feeling she was going to be one of the "nasty" fairies.

Lorna browsed through the photos on the Crackdown Park website. They were all of very clean, serious schoolgirls playing cellos and staring into test tubes. The school fees, discreetly listed on a separate page, were enormous.

"Trust old Iris to do well for herself!" Lorna said sourly. "She always had her eyes on the prize."

"Will she know how to help my dad?"

"Don't you worry—she might be on the mean side, but she's fiendishly clever. Go and get your stuff while I give Hector his instructions and show him where the food is. We're on the move again."

Tom went upstairs to repack his belongings. He was sorry to be leaving Uncle Clarence's bedroom before he'd had time to explore it properly—one of the cupboards was filled with rifles, and he longed to investigate the wooden chest that held rows and rows of little silver bottles. Perhaps he could come back someday, when he had found his parents and the nightmarish part of this adventure was over.

Lorna's luggage was six plastic bags, each stuffed to its bursting point. When Tom returned to the kitchen she was tying these around her waist on a piece of string, like a puffy plastic skirt.

He snorted with laughter. "Sorry—it's just—maybe

we shouldn't be flying in broad daylight." This portly flying bag lady was bound to attract attention. "Maybe we should wait till it's dark."

"Oh, nobody will see us," Lorna said happily. "I took this out of your dad's underwear drawer." She held up a tiny tube of bright green glass. "It's the hour of invisibility Iris sent you for your christening. I reckon we'll only need about forty minutes of it."

Once they were both winged and ready, they went outside to take off from the patch of concrete. Lorna unscrewed the top of the glass tube and delicately tipped a little heap of glittering green powder into the palm of her hand. She hurled it into the air and it wrapped them in a pale green mist.

"We're totally invisible now," she said. "To both mortals and fairies."

"Good—I was worried we'd get arrested."

Lorna grimly adjusted her plastic bags. "That, my dear Tom, is the least of our worries."

It was a very fast journey. The speed they were flying at took Tom's breath away—it was like being an arrow, or a bullet. He saw the country below as a speeded-up film—rivers and valleys, busy high streets, gray ribbons of motorway, soft green hills—rushing past beneath him.

Crackdown Park was just outside Cheltenham, a stately gray mansion surrounded by immaculate formal gardens. Tom and Lorna slowed to a hover above it (Tom was already better at speed control than his godmother).

"This place is amazing," Tom said. "Iris Moth must be really rich."

Lorna looked at her watch. "We don't want to run out of invisibility—we need to touch down somewhere."

"How about those bushes by the tennis court?"

"Good idea. Gently does it—don't want to crash. . . ."

They flew down to the clump of bushes. Tom landed neatly on both feet while Lorna collapsed in a heap, with a loud "Ooof!" Luckily the plastic bags cushioned the impact.

Tom shrugged off Uncle Clarence's wings. The bony struts collapsed like telescopes, so that the wings could be folded small enough to stow in his backpack. Lorna crammed her wings into one of her plastic bags. Cautiously they emerged from the bushes.

Tom's summer holidays had started nearly a week ago, but the Crackdown Park girls hadn't broken up yet. They were very quiet, sedate girls. Tom saw them strolling in groups of two and three, or sitting with books on benches under the trees. He and Lorna must have stood out, yet nobody took any notice of them. The girls, elegant in their navy-blue uniforms, walked past them with dreamy faces, barely seeing them.

"This is spooky," Tom muttered. "Why are they all walking about in silence?"

61

"Because they're so refined," Lorna said, scratching her bottom vigorously. "This is a very posh school."

They walked up the imposing stone steps into a huge cool hall with a white marble floor.

"Hello!" called Lorna. The hall was a chamber of echoes and her loud voice sounded like a trumpet fanfare. "Anybody home?"

A girl came out from a door under the stairs. She was a tall, pretty teenager with long blond hair. "Good afternoon. May I help you?" Her voice was flat and dull, and the blankness of her eyes made Tom uneasy—she wouldn't quite look at them, and spoke as if reading from an invisible script.

"Yes," Lorna said, "we've come to see Iris Moth."

"Do you have an appointment?"

"No. This is an emergency."

"If you phone the office you can make an appointment."

"I told you," Lorna snapped, "we're here on very urgent business."

The girl droned, "The headmistress can't see you without an appointment."

"This is ridiculous!" Lorna stamped her boot. "IRIS MOTH!" The echoes bounced and clamored around them. "IRIS CLUTTERBUCK MOTH—COME OUT THIS MINUTE!"

A door burst open—and there stood Iris Moth. Tom

saw at once that this fairy godmother was not kind like Lorna. Her lips had pursed into a thin streak of fury, her little eyes shot sparks and it was impossible not to think of her distant dinosaur ancestors. She clicked across the marble on her high heels and the echoes were like gunshots.

"What is the meaning of this? Who are these people?"

"They don't have an appointment," the girl said.

"Hello, Iris," Lorna said.

Iris Moth looked at her properly, her furious expression changing to one of horror. "Lorna Mustard!"

The two fairy godmothers gawped at each other in silence for a long moment.

"You know why I'm here," Lorna said.

Iris Moth turned her hard little eyes to Tom. "And this . . . this—BOY?"

"This is Jonas's son, Tom Harding." Lorna was stern. "You chose to ignore the summons, but I didn't."

"Thank you, Camilla," Iris said to the blank-faced blond girl. "That will be all."

"Yes, Ms. Moth," said Camilla, drifting away like a sleepwalker.

"You'd better come into my office. Bring this creature." Iris nodded towards Tom. "Jonas's demisprite."

The way she spat out the word made Tom wince. He felt that she hated him for something that was not his fault. The feeling was horrible and it made him clumsy;

he tripped over his feet as they followed Iris's clicking heels into her office.

"Blimey, Iris—this is fancy!" Lorna admired the richly furnished, book-lined office while she untied the string round her waist. The heap of plastic bags slithered to the floor. "That's better! Any chance of a cup of tea?"

"I'm afraid you won't be staying long enough for a cup of tea," Iris said. "Just tell me what you want."

"You know perfectly well! You ignored the godmother-summons."

Iris was shifty. "No, I didn't."

"Yes, you did! It went out two days ago!"

"I'm a very busy woman."

"Haven't you heard the news from the Realm?" Lorna demanded. "Jonas has been charged with murder and misbegetting—he's gone into hiding, and they're hunting for Tom."

"I don't follow the news from the Realm," Iris said coldly. "I live as a law-abiding mortal these days. I haven't practiced magic for years."

"What about that Camilla kid just now?"

"She's very shy."

"Knickers!" said Lorna. "Either she's drugged up to her eyeballs, or she's under a spell."

Iris scowled. "I told you, I don't have anything to do with magic. I run a highly successful mortal school and I'm a thoroughly decent citizen." She shot another toxic glance at Tom. "I'm sure I'd like to help, but there's not much I can do."

Tom was very disappointed, and Lorna was angry. "This is your godson!"

"Well, I'm sorry." Iris did not sound sorry. "I don't dabble in spells anymore. The best I can offer this demi-sprite is a sex change and a free place at the school."

"A sex change!" Tom gasped. "I don't want a sex change!"

"Iris, listen," Lorna said. "I don't like bothering you, but I didn't know where else to turn!"

There was a knock at the door.

"Ah, that's the Year Nine nature ramble coming back." Iris Moth was suddenly brisk and businesslike. "Come in!"

Three girls came into the room. Two of them were lugging plastic bags. They had the same vacant, dreamy look as Camilla. Lorna was right, Tom thought; they had to be under a spell.

Taking no notice of Tom and Lorna, the girls stood in a silent row in front of the headmistress's desk.

"Hello, my dears," Iris said, with a sideways glance at Lorna. "I do hope you had a lovely ramble. Let's see what you've brought back for the nature table."

The first bag contained an elaborate gold clock, several sparkling necklaces and a large vase. "Eighteenth century—what a super specimen. Well done, Hester."

65

"Thank you, Ms. Moth."

"And Catriona, what about you?" Iris eagerly pulled the other bag towards her. "More Rolex watches! You do have such a talent for finding them lying about. Well done, dear."

"Thank you, Ms. Moth."

"And Leonora—surely you haven't come back empty-handed?"

The third girl droned, "No, Ms. Moth." She took something from the pocket of her navy cardigan. It was a wedge of banknotes the size of a brick.

"Crikey!" Lorna squeaked.

Iris glared at her, then smiled at the girl. "Well done—this lovely lot of . . . er . . . specimens will win you a house point, dear."

"It came from the Abbey National," said Leonora.

"Fascinating! Off you go, girls."

The three girls trooped silently out of the room.

The moment the door had shut behind them Lorna burst out, "You steaming old HYPOCRITE! You haven't given up magic at all—far from it! You're using it to turn your girls into zombies who go out stealing for you—and you must need a heck of a lot of magic to keep off the mortal police!"

Iris shrugged crossly. "So what? A fairy has to make a living."

"I manage to make an HONEST one," Lorna said.

"I need the extra cash to give my school the edge—the top of the league."

"So you do know enough magic to help my dad," said Tom.

Iris looked at him, her stubby nose wrinkling with disgust. "No amount of magic can undo his crime."

"Come off it, Iris!" cried Lorna. "Jonas hasn't committed any crime!"

"According to the laws of the Realm, he has," Iris hissed. "Why should I help this creature? His father broke Milly Falconer's heart!"

"POOH!" yelled Lorna. "What do you care?"

"She was my dearest friend!"

"You were just sucking up to her because she was a Falconer and you're a SNOB!"

Iris Moth's lips were so thin they were almost invisible. "I was NOT sucking up! She asked me to be one of her bridesmaids! And then Jonas refused to marry her."

"He didn't refuse," Tom said.

"What did you say?" Iris turned to gape at him in outraged astonishment, as if a slug had suddenly spoken.

Tom's heart thudded, but he had to speak up for Dad. "He didn't refuse to marry her—he never asked her in the first place. It's not his fault that he couldn't fall in love with her."

Iris shuddered. "You mortals really do have the most

67

disgusting way of talking about marriage—this silly mania you have for falling in love first! You probably can't help it, but Jonas should have known better."

"If you thought it was so bad, why did you agree to be my godmother? Why did you send me a christening present?"

The lizard-faced headmistress pursed up her mouth and her cheeks turned a little pink. "I'm a great believer in keeping up traditional fairy customs. And—and I liked your father at one time."

"Don't you still like him just a bit—just enough to help us?"

She was silent for a moment, and then she let out a long sigh. "All right, I know my duty. I suppose I'll help. And I suppose you'd like a cup of tea."

7

The Third Godmother

Iris had cups and saucers and a kettle in one corner of her study. She made them all tea and handed round a plate of chocolate biscuits. Tom relaxed a little. This woman obviously didn't like him much, but she was a very talented fairy, sure to know how to help his dad.

Iris and Lorna began talking about their businesses.

"OK," Lorna said, "I admit I use a bit of magic—but only to clear the drains and stuff like that. I don't use it to commit crimes."

"But it's so easy to bamboozle mortals!" Iris didn't seem to mind being called a criminal—and she didn't seem at all guilty about the schoolgirls she had turned into thieves. "In my opinion a fairy's mad if she doesn't take advantage." She took a small silver flask from the drawer of her desk. "How about a drop of Kaulquappe?"

"You've got Kaulquappe!"

"I take it for my sinuses," Iris said. "It's not for the demisprite, of course."

"His name's Tom."

"Tom," Iris repeated, shooting Tom a suspicious look. "Well? Do you want some Kaulquappe or not?"

"Go on, then—not too much—haven't tasted it in donkey's years." Lorna chuckled suddenly. "It's fairy gin, Tom—ten times as strong as the mortal sort, made by German kobolds. 'Kaulquappe' is German for 'tadpole.' Where on earth did you get it, Iris? Don't tell me you found a fairy liquor store!"

"No such luck," Iris said stiffly, with the pale ghost of a smile. "I still visit the Realm quite often, and I pick up the Kaulquappe in the duty-free." She poured a slug of fairy gin into Lorna's cup, and a larger slug into her own. "Now, let's get down to business. Tell me about Jonas."

Her mouth full of chocolate biscuit, Lorna filled her in on the background. Iris took notes in a little book, like a doctor, and every now and then she said, "I see."

"And when we last heard from him, he was hiding with a colony of bats."

"I see." Iris put down her pen and folded her hands.

"We left in a hurry—we had a visit from Pindar Falconer."

Iris raised the place where her eyebrows should have been. "Pindar! Are you sure?"

"Oh yes." Lorna took a swig of tea. "I'd know him anywhere."

"It was two visits," Tom said. "I think he's following us."

"But Tiberius swore he'd never let Pindar anywhere near an important job ever again! Not after the fiasco with those flying coaches." Iris was thoughtful. "The last I heard, he was working in a circus, cleaning up after the elephants. His mother said that was all he was fit for."

Even though he was the enemy, Tom was starting to feel a little sorry for his cousin Pindar. Aunt Dolores—the Bad Fairy—sounded horrible. He saw why Dad had cut off all contact with her. The clumsy teenager he'd seen in the crystal ball had looked perfectly harmless, and it must be awful to have a mother who kept telling you that you were stupid.

"Of course," Iris went on, "they might have sent Pindar to check up on you because they didn't think it was an important job. I mean—who takes godmothering seriously nowadays?"

"I do."

"You're old-fashioned. Nobody else bothers."

"Please," Tom burst out, "you keep talking as if it's all hopeless—there must be something we can do!"

His two godmothers looked at him in silence.

"It's a challenge," Iris said coldly, "but as I tell my girls, we must see challenges as opportunities. The Realm is ruled by a set of very old laws, and even Falconers must obey them. The first thing we should do is get some really expert legal advice—there has to be some kind of loophole."

Lorna knocked backed the rest of her tea. "I bet Dahlia would know—don't you remember how brilliant she was in college?"

"Of course," Iris mused, "she *is* the demisprite's third godmother. And her subject *was* fairy law. She'd be a judge by now, if she hadn't been so shallow. Have you consulted her?"

"We haven't found her yet," Tom said. "Do you know where she lives?"

Iris's eyes were like little cold gray pebbles. "Not exactly—but I know where to find her."

"Tell us, and we can go and look for her," said Lorna.

"You can't do it without me," Iris said. "Can the demi-sprite fly?"

Tom was sick of being ignored. "You can ask me, you know. I do understand English. Yes, I can fly."

"Oh."

"And we've still got twenty minutes of the invisibility you gave me for my christening."

"Hmm." Iris's expression did not change, but she said, "I'm glad it was useful. For the time being, however, I'll provide invisibility. It's fiendishly expensive—but one of my sixth-formers just made me several million with her math project, which was a stock-market scam. I'll use it to fund the expedition." Her cold face softened, though it might have been a trick of the light. "I owe that much to Jonas."

Lorna was grinning. "You're not such a bad old bat after all, Iris Moth. Where are we headed?"

"Harrods," said Iris.

"Really, Lorna! What frightful wings," Iris complained. "And do you have to festoon yourself with all those bags?"

"What does it matter, if I'm invisible?"

"You're still visible to me."

Tom wished his two godmothers would stop bickering. It hadn't boiled over into a real argument yet, but he could tell they were getting increasingly irritated with each other—Iris produced a pair of sleek, streamlined wings of a dazzling white, and Lorna muttered "La-di-da!" under her breath. The three of them were on the roof of the school, getting ready for takeoff.

Iris saw Tom looking at the wings, and another ghost

of a smile crossed her wintry dinosaur face. "The latest model," she told him smugly. "Sat-nav and up to five hundred miles an hour." She measured out the invisibility very precisely and scattered the powder neatly across them.

Tom was nervous about taking off from this dizzy height. He felt confident about his flying, but he had never had to jump off a roof—if his parents had been able to see what he was doing, they would have had heart failure. His mouth was dry, but he wasn't going to show Iris he was scared. Taking a deep breath, willing himself to stay calm, he muttered the flying spell and floated easily onto a smooth current of summer air.

"Nice takeoff," Iris said behind him. "The demisprite has been well taught."

"For the last time," Lorna snapped, "his name's Tom!"

They were all quiet now, concentrating on the job of skimming across the warm landscape towards London (Tom had one sad moment of wishing he could fly home to his parents). The built-in sat-nav on Iris's wings guided them to Harrods. They landed on the pavement outside the famous shop. Iris performed a textbook landing, with pointed toes and graceful arms. Lorna accidentally landed with one leg in a rubbish bin, and there was a lot of muttered swearing as she wrestled herself free.

"We're still invisible," Iris said. "We'll stay invisible

74

until we spot Dahlia—if she sees us first, she might try to give us the slip."

"I wouldn't put it past her." Lorna stowed her wings back in their plastic bag and peeled off an ice cream wrapper that was sticking to her jumpsuit. "You'd better lead the way, Iris—I don't know anything about posh shops."

"You astonish me," Iris said sarcastically.

Tom was glad he couldn't be seen as he walked into Harrods. Everything in the shop, including the customers, was gleaming and smart and expensive. He felt like a total scruff in his dusty T-shirt and crumpled jeans. They were walking through the perfume and makeup department. Every few minutes they were assaulted with another brand of perfume, until Tom—who hadn't eaten for hours—felt slightly giddy. Sticking close to Lorna, he dodged through the crowds of shoppers.

"Blimey, all these lipsticks!" exclaimed Lorna. "If they were different colors I could understand it—but they all look exactly the same!"

"There!" Iris hissed, halting in front of a counter that said CHANEL.

Tom saw a very thin, very elegant lady holding a tiny Chihuahua on one arm and browsing among the anti-wrinkle creams. Her hair was smooth and platinum blond. She wore very high heels and very red lipstick, and her fingers sparkled with diamonds. Every now and then she halted and sniffed the air curiously.

"Good grief—Dahlia Pease-Blossom!" whispered Lorna.

"She's holding up very well," Iris whispered. "I know for a fact she's two years older than me."

"What d'you reckon she's had done?"

"Ha! What hasn't she had done? There's enough Botox in there to paralyze a herd of buffalo!"

Both fairy godmothers tittered quietly—being snide about Dahlia had finally brought them together.

Dahlia Pease-Blossom was alone at the Chanel counter, so Lorna and Iris quietly went over and stood on either side of her. At the same moment their invisibility ran out.

"Hello, Dahlia," Lorna said.

"Oh my g—" Dahlia was so shocked that the Chihuahua on her arm suddenly yelped and changed into a poodle. "Lorna Mustard—Iris Thingy! I thought I smelled magic!"

"MOTH!" Iris snapped furiously.

"Yes, of course—what on earth are you doing here?" Dahlia had recovered her glossy smile. "I know—you're arranging a college reunion!"

"Not quite," Lorna said. "This is about the godmother-summons—don't pretend you didn't get it. Jonas Harding is wanted by the Falconers, and they're hunting for his son." She pulled Tom forward. "This is Tom, our godson."

"Tom, darling!" Dahlia bent over to kiss him, wrapping him in a cloud of perfume. "Lovely to meet you! I see you got my handsome-token."

"Hi," Tom said politely.

"I'm sorry I missed the summons—I never take much notice of stuff from the Realm because it's mostly junk mail these days. And I have been frightfully busy."

"Don't tell me," Iris said. "You were having your nails done."

Dahlia arched her perfect eyebrows. "If you must know, I was at my husband's funeral."

"Oh."

"We didn't have long together," Dahlia sighed, "but we were blissfully happy until that coffee machine exploded! And after the funeral I had a lot of meetings with the poor darling's bankers; then I had to sell his fleet of planes and the Impressionist paintings. . . ."

Lorna whistled. "Trust you to marry money!"

"Darling, I ALWAYS marry money." She glanced at her gold watch. "Well, what do you want me to do for this handsome godson of ours?"

"Your duty," said Lorna.

"You mean"—Dahlia looked into all their faces, one by one—"godmother duty?"

Tom's spirits sank. Here was another godmother who

didn't want to help him. Were all fairies except Lorna this unreliable?

Dahlia saw his disappointment and gave him a proper smile that made her tight face more wrinkled and much kinder. "Good gracious, you're the spitting image of your father! I used to go out with him, you know. I think you're going to be even more handsome."

"Don't embarrass the boy," Lorna said. "He needs your help."

Dahlia stopped smiling. "Magic help?"

"Obviously! We can't do anything without magic."

"Frightfully sorry, darling—I'm not involved in that sort of thing these days. I've forgotten every word of it."

"What about the dog?" said Tom.

"What?" Dahlia looked down at her ex-Chihuahua, who was now a poodle. "Oh—I forgot you saw that. But really, it's the only magic I use."

"A likely story!" sniffed Iris. "You were the cleverest student in the whole college. You'd have done great things—if you hadn't also been the prettiest." She sounded rather bitter. "I've had to come out of retirement to do my godmother duty—at great personal inconvenience—and I don't see why you can't too."

"Shhh!" Dahlia was suddenly still and alert. "I can smell something—we're not the only fairies in this perfume department!"

Instantly the two other godmothers were on guard.

Lorna put a protective hand on Tom's shoulder. He looked around at the other shoppers. They were all smartly dressed ladies, examining lipsticks and pots of face cream. Which of them was a Falconer?

"Look!" whispered Dahlia. "Over there—by the rack of exfoliating bath mitts!"

A tall lady in a yellow summer dress was stumbling about very oddly. She gazed around her with a wild, crazed look and suddenly sneezed so hard that she knocked over the rack of bath mitts, tripped and fell to the floor.

When she dragged herself to her feet, Tom burst out laughing—she had changed into Pindar Falconer, and he was still wearing the yellow dress. It was hilarious to see the look on his face when he realized and went bright red.

A second later he vanished, and a young shop assistant fainted.

None of the godmothers was laughing.

"We're not safe here," Dahlia said. "Let's take a taxi to my place."

8

Fairy Fight

Tom was glad they were traveling by ordinary, non-magical taxi. Flying made him very tired, and his stomach gurgled with hunger. It felt like months since he had woken up in Uncle Clarence's bedroom. His godmothers talked anxiously about his cousin Pindar and how dangerous he was, but Tom couldn't be scared of such a clown.

The taxi took them to a large white-painted house in a nice square in Chelsea. Dahlia was behaving like the perfect hostess—"Do come into the drawing room and make yourselves at home!" But Tom noticed that she double-locked the front door, and made the same quick weaving movement with her hands that Lorna had used when she was "sealing" Mustard Manor.

"Cor!" Lorna dropped her plastic bags in a heap and sank into one of the sofas. "This is like something out of Buckingham Palace!"

"Yes, do put your bags down anywhere," Dahlia said. "And do sit down."

It was the grandest room Tom had ever been in. The curtains were pale-green silk. The wallpaper looked hand-painted and there were fat, deep sofas heaped with cushions.

Lorna kicked her shoes off. "Oof! Great to get the weight off my feet!"

"I can see that it must be quite a strain," Dahlia said.

When she looked at Lorna there was a gleam in her eye that Tom didn't quite like   as if she was laughing at her, and not in a kind way.

"Well, very nice," Iris said, in a tight voice, "if a little cluttered."

"Cluttered?" cried Dahlia. "So sorry! Is this better?"

She snapped her fingers and the room was suddenly stark and bare, with plain white walls, no curtains and hardly any furniture.

Lorna shrieked when the sofa vanished under her and she landed on the floor. "Ow! Stop showing off!"

Dahlia smiled and snapped her fingers again. The

room was back to normal—whatever "normal" meant in this house. Tom sat carefully next to Lorna, hoping the sofa wouldn't vanish again.

"Tom, you must be ravenous," Lorna said. "I know I am. Is there anything to eat?"

"Yes, of course," Dahlia said. "I'll call down to the kitchen. Which would you prefer, Tom—Pheasant Bordelaise à la Gaston, or burger and french fries?"

"Burger and french fries, please."

"Make that two," said Lorna. "And tell whoever it is to bring the ketchup."

"Oh, he'll bring everything. I have the most marvelous servants."

Iris said, "I'll have the pheasant—and please do something about that disgusting dog!"

The little dog on Dahlia's arm now had the head of a poodle on the body of a miniature dachshund.

"Whoops, I wasn't concentrating," Dahlia said. The breed-shifting dog vanished, and she took a thin gold phone from her handbag, tapping out a text message with a red thumbnail. After this she served them all drinks from a carved cabinet—fresh orange juice for Tom and Kaulquappe and tonic for the godmothers.

The juice was cold and delicious. Tom leaned back on the soft cushions, looking more closely at the pictures around the room. They all seemed to be of old men in dark suits.

Dahlia saw him staring at a large painting of a gray-haired man with a large bald patch, above the fireplace. "That's Mr. Grisling, my late husband," she told him. "Such a darling man!"

Iris gave one of her disapproving sniffs. "And who are all the other old codgers?"

"My other ten late husbands."

"ALL of them?" choked Lorna. "Did you marry a Welsh choir?"

Dahlia stiffened. "I've had a lot of tragedy in my life. Every time I get married, some hideous accident comes along and kills my poor husband. Before Mr. Grisling there was Mr. Fortescue—I begged him not to use that lawn mower! That's him, on the little table beside you."

Lorna peered at the small photograph of what looked like an egg with glasses. "I can see why you only keep a tiny picture of this one."

"Looks aren't everything," Dahlia said coldly. "Mr. Trent—who came before Mr. Fortescue—wasn't what you'd call classically handsome, but he had a beautiful nature. We had three wonderful weeks together before the hang-gliding disaster. I didn't stop crying all the time I was selling his factories."

Tom was starting to be uncomfortable, and he could see that Lorna and Iris felt the same way. Lorna was scowling, and Iris's lipless dinosaur mouth was as jagged as barbed wire. It was impossible not to think that there was something rather suspicious about the way Dahlia kept losing her husbands and gaining their money. What had she done to them?

There was a knock at the door and a gray-haired man in a white jacket wheeled in a trolley laden with food. Very quickly and quietly he set out supper on the coffee table—two elegant plates of Pheasant Bordelaise à la Gaston for Dahlia and Iris, and two magnificent plates of burger and fries for Lorna and Tom.

Tom was a little disturbed to notice the strange blankness in the servant's eyes. It reminded him of the way Iris's girls had looked at Crackdown Park.

The man bowed and silently left the room. Tom started to eat the burger, which was fantastic, as Lorna fell on her fries with a groan of happiness. Her jumpsuit was soon decorated with blobs of ketchup.

"Very tasty," said Iris. "I must say, I can't fault the food."

Dahlia still smiled, but there was a dangerous glint in her eye. "I'm sure you can fault something, Iris—it's coming back to me now. You always did love to criticize."

"I speak as I find," Iris said. "And if you've given up magic, I'll eat my wings."

"Of course I dabble a bit." Dahlia shrugged crossly. "Don't we all?"

"I don't use magic to marry people and then MURDER them, thank you very much!"

Tom put down his burger. The word had been said, and he couldn't look at Dahlia.

She was as cool as a cucumber. "Murder? Oh, darling— don't be silly."

"What REALLY happened to your husbands? And don't give me any rubbish about exploding coffee machines," said Iris.

"If you murdered them," Lorna said, "that's a major violation of the fairy code."

"Oh, pooh!" snapped Dahlia. "For the last time, I haven't murdered anyone! Darling, I couldn't murder a fly!"

Tom glanced at the portrait of Mr. Grisling above the fireplace. "Hey!" He'd shouted it out before he knew what he was doing. All three godmothers turned to look at him. He pointed at the portrait. "That's the same guy who brought the food!"

"Good grief, he's right!" cried Lorna. "The late Mr. Grisling isn't late at all! She's found a way of turning him into a slave and nicking all his money!"

Dahlia looked sulky. "You make it sound so vulgar." She caught Tom's eye. "It's really not as bad as that, darling—I don't want you to think I'm the wrong sort of fairy."

Lorna chuckled with her mouth full. "How many slaves have you got, then?"

"Eleven," Dahlia said.

"I thought you'd had twelve husbands," Iris said. "Where's the other one?"

"He wasn't a mortal. Don't you remember? My first husband was a Cornish piskie—Sir George Trebonkers. Looking at a picture of him would be too painful. After our divorce he went back to his ghastly castle in the Realm. The last I heard he was shacked up with some goblin or other. So much for love!" Dahlia sighed.

"Ha! I could imagine so when its interchangeable with slave labor," said Iris.

Lorna chuckled unkindly. "That's a bit rich coming from you!"

"What's that supposed to mean?"

"You cast spells on children and make them steal for you."

"Does she indeed?" snapped Dahlia. "She goes all goody-goody about my husbands, and she's Fagin in a cardigan! Don't you preach at me, Iris Thingy!"

Iris's face flushed a dull red. "It's MOTH, thank you very much! I use the money I get for the benefit of the school! It pays for scholarships for poor girls! I don't use my magic to turn a lot of decent men into slaves!"

"No—because it takes a bit more than magic—and you never had the right equipment!"

"Pooh!" shouted Iris. "At least I'm not a wrinkled old tart full of Botox!"

Dahlia hissed, "You still haven't forgiven me, have you? I had Jonas and you didn't—and you can't get over it!"

Iris's blush deepened until her face was nearly magenta. "He wasn't in love with you!"

"Maybe not," Dahlia said. "But he wasn't in love with Milly, either! And you know it, Iris Wasp!"

"MOTH!" shrieked Iris.

"Hey!" Lorna cried out sharply, her mouth full of burger. "The boy!" She glanced at Tom. "How d'you think he likes hearing about his dad's love life?"

For a split second Dahlia was confused. If her forehead hadn't been so tight she would have scowled. "All right, we won't rake up the past."

"It's just silly," Lorna said, "now that we're all old."

"Speak for yourself!" snapped Dahlia. "You look NINETY and your bum's so big it has its own POST-CODE!"

Lorna's face became thunderous—Tom had never seen her so angry. She sprang to her feet. "I like having a big bum! You should try it sometime!"

She gabbled a few words, and Dahlia let out a blood-curdling scream—"ARRGHH!" There was a ripping sound. Her bum had grown so huge that it had burst right out of her tight black skirt. Lorna and Iris both broke into howls of laughter.

"Oh, very funny!" Dahlia magicked back her slender figure and quickly checked her reflection in the big mirror. "If you want to behave like a cow, Lorna Mustard, you can BE a cow!" She raised her arm.

"NO!" shouted Tom. "Stop it! Stop fighting!" He was suddenly furious—his dad was being hunted and all they could do was squabble like little girls. "Dahlia—don't you DARE turn Lorna into a cow! She's been great to me when you and Iris didn't want to know! And she's a much nicer fairy—she doesn't cast spells on humans to make money! You both say you loved my dad—but Lorna was the only one who kept her promise to him!"

There was silence, and the three fairies stared at their godson.

"Thanks, Tom," Lorna said gruffly. "Sorry I lost my temper."

"The demisprite is right to stand by his true friends." Iris said.

"Tom, darling!" Dahlia swooped down to kiss his cheek. "You're Jonas all over again—he always used to break up our little arguments. You're right—we should be thinking about how to help him. You'd better stay here, I suppose—I'll get one of the husbands to make up the beds."

"Does this mean you're going to help us?" Iris asked.

"My dear Iris, I don't have any choice, and neither do you. We each signed that godmother parchment in blood. If we ignore our duty, Tom has the right to take us to court. Goodness knows I've bent a few fairy laws, but I was always very careful not to break them."

"I don't like staying in this house while you're keeping all those slaves," Iris said, "but since you ARE keeping them, tell one of them to bring me a pot of strong tea. And I'd prefer a bedroom with a garden view."

"I'll sleep anywhere," said Lorna, who had started eating again. "But it's not right, Dahlia. You'll have to set those poor chaps free."

Tom was glad she had spoken up for the enslaved husbands; it made him very uneasy to be waited on by these millionaires and captains of industry. "There must be people who are sad because they think your husbands are dead," he said impulsively. "It's mean to let them go on being sad."

For the very first time Dahlia looked seriously startled. She stared at Tom and her tight cheeks turned a little red. "You really are so like your father! And you make me wonder what he'd think of me if he were here—perhaps I have been a tad strict with my staff. Perhaps I should let them out into the garden sometimes."

Tom and Lorna looked at each other. "You're not getting the point," Lorna said. "Jonas would say you were breaking the spirit of the law by being cruel to mortals. We're not supposed to exploit them."

"Oh, everyone does it!" Dahlia shrugged impatiently.

"And I'm not being cruel to them—they have luxurious quarters downstairs, and they don't have all the worry of thinking for themselves. Come along, Tom—I'll show you up to your bedroom."

Tom had the feeling she was using him as an excuse not to talk about her enslaved husbands. He could tell that Dahlia was the leading fairy of the three godmothers. The other two respected her cleverness and were slightly afraid of her. Was he afraid of Dahlia? He tried to make up his mind as he walked up the stairs behind her. It was obvious, from the way she treated the husbands, that she didn't give a toot about mortals. Unlike Iris, however, she didn't seem to mind demisprites.

And she had once been in love with his dad. So had Iris, and Milly Falconer. Tom didn't like thinking about this; it was embarrassing and made him feel he didn't know his own father. Did his mother (who sometimes giggled at Dad's paunch, and said his gray hair was like an old nest) have any idea about his past life as a pinup and punk rocker?

"This will be your bedroom while you're staying here." Dahlia opened a door and led him into a room lined with posters of singers and bands Tom had never heard of. Three electric guitars hung above the fireplace, and there was a drum kit in the bay window. A notice board near the door was covered with old school timetables and blurry photos of groups of boys making faces. It was one of the coolest bedrooms Tom had ever seen.

"It belonged to my son, Justinian," Dahlia said. "When he was a teenager."

"Your son?" It was hard to picture this elegant, rather wicked fairy as anyone's mother.

She smiled. "He's grown up now, of course. You won't have heard of him, but in the Realm he's a rock star—Jay Trebonkers."

"A rock star!" Tom was impressed. "What kind of music does he play? What was his last big hit?"

"He's got a number one at the moment, called 'Old Fairies Suck.'" She pointed to the notice board. "That's Justinian—the one with the pointed ears."

It was fascinating to see photos of this boy who had large pointed ears—in real life, too, not in some sci-fi drama.

"The old piskie families all have those ears," Dahlia said. "Anyway, if there's anything you need, ring the bell on the mantelpiece and one of the husbands will come." In the doorway, halfway out of the room, she halted and turned round sharply. "You know, we're idiots."

"Are we?"

"We've overlooked the most important question."

"What do you mean?"

"Your aunt, Dolores Falconer—it all comes back to her. She wants Jonas dead. Why?"

"Why?" Tom echoed. "We know why—because he broke Milly Falconer's heart and had an illegal demi-sprite."

"Oh, I know all the official reasons," Dahlia said, "but I'm prepared to bet this isn't about Milly Falconer, or the illegal breeding. Mark my words, Dolores is after something else!"

9

Intruder

Justinian's old room had a bathroom, and Tom took a hot shower. He couldn't get Dahlia's question out of his mind—why did his aunt Dolores want to kill her own brother? It was becoming less and less surprising that Dad hadn't told him anything about the Realm. How ironic that he'd been worried about getting bored during the holidays; Charlie would never believe a word of this.

After the shower, feeling clean and very tired, Tom went back downstairs to find his godmothers. He heard loud voices, but not because they had started another fight. The three of them were in the drawing room, drinking coffee and chatting about their old college days.

"Ah, there you are, darling," Dahlia said. "We were just about to check the fairy headlines on the laptop." Her laptop, encrusted with diamonds, was open on the low table in front of her.

Tom had never seen a laptop covered with jewels before. "Do fairies have a different cyberspace?"

"Totally different," Iris Moth said. "The Realm Wide Web, or fairy Internet, exists in another dimension."

Dahlia's scarlet nails clicked busily on the keyboard. The light that streamed from the screen was whiter and brighter than the light that came from computers in the mortal world. The colors had that special stained-glass radiance Tom had seen in Abdul's flying carpet.

"Oh, you're on Abracadabra," Iris said. "I use FOL." Catching Tom's eye, she added, "That's Fairies Online— it's a very good package."

Dahlia clicked on "Headlines" and the screen filled with a picture of a sulky young man with long red hair and pointed ears. TREBONKERS'S TANTRUM DESTROYS STADIUM.

"It's that son of yours," Lorna said. "What's he done now?"

"It says he had a fight with the drummer in his band," said Tom, reading the screen over Dahlia's shoulder.

"They started throwing grenades at each other, and the concert had to be canceled—the place was reduced to rubble—wow!" Mortal rock stars often destroyed hotel rooms and guitars; this was rock-star bad behavior on another scale.

"Naughty boy," Dahlia said comfortably. "That's the second stadium he's destroyed this year! Last time it was because they brought him the wrong sandwich. I sometimes wonder if I spoiled him."

The next news story flashed up, and Tom forgot all about rock stars.

The headline said: POLICE HUNT GENIE TERRORIST. The picture was of a stout man with a black beard, wearing a pale blue turban and sunglasses.

"Hussein!" gasped Lorna. "Look, Tom—it's my useless ex-brother-in-law!"

It certainly was Abdul's brother—Tom recognized his earrings. Impatiently he skimmed through the story.

This is the face of the terrorist who broke into the palace of the Falconers' house genie ALI KAZOUM yesterday and turned it into an enormous puff of smoke. Nobody was injured, but everything vanished, including the clothes of the Kazoums and their staff. "One minute I was eating breakfast in my dressing gown," Mr. Kazoum said later, "the next I was standing stark naked on a patch of scorched earth. If I ever catch the rascals who did this I will feed their entrails to the vultures! This is just another stupid bid to frighten the Falconers— and it won't work! We stopped Clarence Mustard, and we will CRUSH his followers!" Police are searching for a tall, well-built genie captured on a neighbor's crystal ball shortly before the attack.

"I don't believe it! I just don't believe it!" Lorna was flabbergasted. "That layabout—a militant anti-Falconer!"

"What does he mean about your uncle Clarence?" Tom asked eagerly—he had known there was something exciting about this character; he had sensed it when he wore his wings.

Lorna exchanged doubtful looks with the other two godmothers. "It's not a good idea to talk about him, but I suppose you might as well know. Years and years ago, before any of us old bags were born, my uncle Clarence led a famous uprising against the Falconers. To make a long story short, they crushed the uprising by killing everybody involved—including Clarence. He's a bit of a legend. Sort of like a fairy version of Robin Hood. He robbed from the Falconers to give to the poor. "

"He never had a chance," Dahlia said. "Everyone knows the end of their power has to come from the inside—that's what it says in the old legend. Just one decent Falconer—from the proper line of Falconers—

would do it. But there hasn't been a decent Falconer for a thousand years." She added to Tom, "I qualified as a fairy lawyer, darling, specializing in old law, so I know what I'm talking about."

Lorna was pale and frowning. "I hope Abdul's not involved—there were some shady-looking genies hanging round his cafe!"

"He'll be OK," Tom said, wanting to cheer her up. "Abdul's . . . well, he's too sensible." He'd nearly said "too much of a wimp," but didn't want to be rude.

"That's true," Lorna said. "He's more than just a handsome face."

The next headline flashed onto the screen: TREBONKERS SPLITS WITH KAULQUAPPE HEIRESS. "That's the last story," Dahlia said. "Nothing about Jonas, thank goodness; just more celebrity gossip about my naughty son."

Lorna looked at her watch. "Nearly midnight! Tom, you'd better go to bed."

"OK." He was goofy with tiredness.

"Wait—take this and put it under your pillow."

Lorna put something hard, heavy and cold into his hand, and Tom was suddenly wide awake. She had given him a gun. "Is it—loaded?"

"I loaded it myself," Lorna said. "You won't be dealing with mortal intruders, boy. If anyone breaks into your room, shoot first and ask questions later."

Tom's heart was beating hard; this was frightening but strangely exciting. "Will they be trying to kill me?"

"Yes," Iris said (sounding rather pleased, Tom couldn't help thinking). "Or they might keep you alive just long enough to trap your father. Don't wait to find out. Shoot to kill."

"OK," he said breathlessly—though he was sure he could never fire this thing at anyone. And what if it went off by mistake when it was under his pillow? Holding it very carefully, Tom said good night to his godmothers and went up to Justinian's room. He tried putting the gun under his pillow, but he knew he would never get to sleep while it was there, so he put it on the bedside table and fell asleep.

There was someone in the room. Tom heard a scratching sound, over by the big window.

Not moving a muscle, he was suddenly wide awake and listening hard.

His godmothers were still carousing downstairs; he heard Lorna laughing loudly, and then a Christmassy shout, as if they were all drinking a toast.

Should he yell for help? Or would the intruder destroy him before his godmothers could come to his aid? Straining to keep his breathing soft, Tom listened.

The scratching sound was there again—something was definitely moving near the window.

He opened his eyes and in the darkness he saw the outline of the big bay window, and Justinian's drum kit.

The cymbal clashed all by itself and one of the drums thumped, as if it had been hit with something soft. Tom sat bolt upright in bed, his heart walloping in his chest. In the shadows he saw the black outline of the gun on the bedside table, and he grabbed it.

"I know you're there!" His own voice sounded scared and stupid, and he made an effort to toughen it. "Come out and show yourself!"

The silence went on, but now he was certain he had company. He switched on the lamp beside the bed and looked around the room. Everything was quiet and still. Sliding out of bed, he crept across the floor, holding the cold, heavy gun in front of him in what felt like a bad imitation of James Bond. When he got to the drum kit he almost laughed aloud with relief.

A small, round dark-brown mouse sat in the middle of the snare drum; it must have bounced off the cymbal.

"You gave me a fright," Tom told it. "This house is owned by a fairy—so you'd better find somewhere else to infest."

Unless, of course, this mouse was a fairy in disguise; he had seen Lorna turn herself into a mouse. He bent down to examine it more closely. It looked like any old mouse, and Tom was starting to feel rather stupid pointing a gun at it—when it suddenly sneezed.

Tom cried, "I know who you are! You're Pindar Falconer!"

The mouse let out an "Eeek!" of alarm and tried to climb over the rim of the drum.

"I'm armed—don't try to run away—look, I don't want to shoot a mouse, but I will if I have to!"

The mouse took a reckless dive off the drum, and suddenly there was Pindar Falconer, sprawled across the floor, holding his hands up. "Wait! Don't kill me!"

"Well—" It was impossible to be frightened of Pindar; there was something so honest and friendly about his funny pink face with its huge turned-up nose. "How do I know you won't kill me?"

"I don't want to kill you—honestly!"

"In that case, why have you been following me?"

Pindar was crestfallen. "You spotted me?"

"Are you serious?" Tom moved to the mantelpiece and carefully put down the gun (which was a huge relief; carrying one of these things in real life was nothing like a computer game). "The whole of Harrods spotted you!"

"Oh, bum." Pindar's cheeks turned red. "You saw me in the dress, right?"

"Yes—it was really funny."

"It's the disguising spell, you see—I'm allergic to it. It makes me sneeze and then everything goes wrong. I'm allergic to a lot of spells."

Tom took his first proper look at his cousin. Pindar

was a tall, gangly teenager, with flyaway arms and legs, huge feet and an untidy shock of dark hair. He was wearing jeans, and a T-shirt that said OLD FAIRIES SUCK. He scrambled to his feet, and the two cousins stared curiously into each other's faces.

"Do you work for the Fairy Secret Service?" Tom asked.

"No. I was going to, but I failed the exam for the spying academy."

This wasn't surprising. "I heard you were working in a circus," said Tom.

"Oh, that was a bit of a disaster," Pindar said. "I got fired—I killed one of the lions."

"Did it attack you?"

"Oh no." Pindar sighed. "It was the same as Harrods—I sneezed suddenly and it had a heart attack. I'm pretty useless at everything, you see."

"Sneezing a couple of times doesn't make you useless," Tom said; this boy was supposed to be his mortal enemy, yet he had a strange desire to cheer him up. "It wasn't your fault."

"That's not what my father said." Pindar frowned and stood up straighter. "I'm sure you've heard of my father. His name's Tiberius Falconer—and I hate him! I hate my mother, too." His voice wobbled. "That's why I'm here—I've run away."

"Oh." Tom hadn't been expecting this.

101

"My father said I'm not a true Falconer—and I said I was GLAD because I didn't want to be any kind of Falconer. I want to join the other side—whatever that is."

"You ran away? Where from?" asked Tom.

"Falconer Palace, in the Realm. I was sent back there after the circus fired me. My parents were furious to see me again, and my mother said I had to work in the laundry. So I escaped."

"You make it sound like a prison!"

"It might as well be," Pindar said. A darkness crossed his face, and for a moment he looked older. "They never liked me, and I thought it was because I wasn't worth liking and took after the ugly side of the family. But then I saw how mean they could be to perfectly nice people—they had my tutor sent to the salt mines, and my father openly boasts about murdering two of his own brothers."

"Where did you go? I mean, where have you been staying?"

"Nowhere," Pindar said sadly. "I've been sleeping in people's window boxes."

"Aren't they a bit small?"

"I'm a fairy, aren't I? I can shrink myself. But it's not very comfortable. A snail oozed right across my face last night."

"Gross!"

"You don't want to know what a snail's bum looks like that close up."

Both boys laughed.

"But I don't care," said Pindar. "I'm not going back to that place until my mother and father have been locked up." He was sad again. "I saw your parents, Tom, while I was spying on you."

"When were you spying on me?"

"Just for a couple of days, before your dad disappeared—and I can't imagine having parents as nice as that. Your mother's always singing and smiling; your father's always making jokes. It must be great."

"Yes, it's pretty good," Tom said. "I haven't got them at the moment, though," he added. "My dad's in hiding, and my mum—well, she's being hidden somewhere. I'm staying with my fairy godmothers."

"They seem OK," Pindar said, "for old ladies."

"They've been really kind to me." Tom suddenly saw how true this was; they were all taking a risk because of the promise they had made to Jonas. "I'm sure they'll let you stay here—if you've really changed sides." In a way the two of them were in the same situation, he thought—two boys without parents. But poor old Pindar had left his parents because they were hateful, and he had no godmothers to take care of him. "Are you hungry?"

"Starving!" Pindar said it so loudly that they both smiled again. "I've been eating stuff I found in dustbins—do you have any food?"

"Not up here, but I'm sure my godmothers will give you something—come downstairs." Tom didn't like the idea of summoning one of Dahlia's enslaved husbands, and he also thought it would be a good idea to have fairy backup while there was a Falconer in the house—even an unwilling one.

"OK," Pindar said. "I'm so hungry that I don't even care if this is a trap."

"Relax—I swear it's not a trap." Tom decided he trusted his cousin. He pulled on his jeans and they went downstairs to the drawing room.

The door opened onto a scene of chaos. The three fairies lay across armchairs and sofas. There was a mess of smeared glasses, empty bottles and old potato chip bags.

Lorna raised her head from the sofa. "H'llo, Tom—wassup?" She noticed Pindar and roared, "Arrrrgh! Falconer!" She pulled something out of her pocket and aimed it at the intruder.

"You can't shoot anything with that, darling," Dahlia said. "It's an old bagel."

"Oh—so it is—crikey, it's gone hard as a rock. Well—put your hands up and wait till I find my blooming gun!"

104

"Please don't shoot Pindar," said Tom. "He's run away from his parents."

All three godmothers stared at Pindar until his face was as red as a tomato.

"Why on earth should we believe him?" demanded Iris. "This is some slippery Falconer trick!"

"I'm positive he's telling the truth!"

Lorna struggled into an upright position, shaking her head several times, and took a long, hard look at Pindar. "Why did you run away?"

"Because I couldn't stand them anymore," Pindar said. "It's really horrible having parents who're evil."

"I think we should kill him, just to be on the safe side," said Iris.

"No!" Tom shouted. "I won't let you—he's my cousin! You'll have to kill me first!"

Iris's little dinosaur eyes narrowed to pinpricks. "Do you think this Falconer would do the same for you? Look at him! What on earth is the meaning of that disgraceful T-shirt?"

"Oh, don't be such an old poop," Dahlia said. "'Old Fairies Suck' is my son's latest hit—all the young people in the Realm are wearing those." She gave the bewildered Pindar a dazzling smile. "You can tell us the whole story, but I'm sure you'd like something to eat first. Boys are always hungry."

"Yes, please!"

Out came the gold phone. "I'll tell my staff to bring up a nourishing lamb casserole with roast potatoes and French beans, and a steamed syrup pudding."

"Cor!" Lorna said. "Make that two—with custard!"

"My dear Lorna—how can you possibly eat anything else without exploding?"

"I still vote we kill him," Iris said.

Dahlia gave Pindar another smile. "Did you hear that, darling? She doesn't believe you. I'm afraid you'll have to convince her by wearing a truth-globe."

"Ha!" shouted Iris. "Nice move, Dahlia—he'll never DARE to wear one of those!"

"What's a truth-globe?" Tom was suspicious, in case they were planning something that might hurt his cousin.

"You wear one round your neck and it changes color and gives you an electric shock if you're lying," said Pindar. "Don't worry, Tom—I don't mind wearing one, because I'm going to tell the truth."

"Good for you!" Lorna said. "He must be on the level—unless he fancies being grilled like a sausage!"

Dahlia took a miniature gold key off her bracelet and opened a small walnut cabinet. Very carefully she took out a shabby leather box. From this she pulled a ball of clear glass on a long gold chain. It didn't look like much to Tom, but the other two godmothers gasped in admiration.

"What a lovely piece!" Iris cried. "It must have cost a fortune!"

"It was my mother's," Dahlia said. "It's a wonder she managed to leave it to me—my father was constantly trying to break it." She hung the globe around Pindar's neck. "How does it feel?"

Pindar blushed again. "Fine."

"Let's test it," Iris said. "How old are you?"

"Fourteen."

"Have you been following us?"

"Yes."

"Who's working with you?"

"Nobody."

"Nonsense!"

"He's telling the truth," Lorna said. "The globe isn't even cloudy. Do you really mean to tell us that nobody else is after us?"

"Yes," Pindar said. "My tutor left a list of names—I think they were his old college friends. The first name was Jonas Harding. I was spying on him in the mortal world just before he was arrested and Lorna came."

"Does anyone else know we're Tom's godmothers?"

"Oh, but—I wasn't looking for Tom."

Tom and the godmothers looked at each other, suddenly confused.

"Well, for goodness' sake," Dahlia said, "who are you looking for?"

"The contact," Pindar said. "I'm trying to join the followers of Clarence Mustard."

"What rubbish!" interrupted Iris. "No such group exists!"

"The globe's still clear." Lorna's rugged brow was furrowed. "How did you get to hear about it?"

"My tutor told me. I think he was one of them."

"Clarence Mustard was my uncle," Lorna said, "but if you think I know anything about his so-called followers—well, you've come to the wrong fairy. Sorry."

"No, I haven't," Pindar said. "I was looking for the group coordinator."

"Darling, don't be silly!" cried Dahlia. "You won't find that sort of troublemaker in my house!"

Pindar looked as if he wanted to argue, but he was distracted by the arrival of the food. Mr. Grisling pushed in a trolley laden with steaming plates of casserole and roast potatoes, and Pindar sighed with joy. He shoveled it in ravenously, trying not to get blobs of sauce on the valuable globe around his neck.

"This is fantastic," he said shyly to Dahlia. "Thanks."

"Pindar's been living rough," Tom said. "He needs somewhere to stay."

"Well, he can't stay here!" snapped Iris. "It would be far too risky! If he's run away they'll be searching for him, and we'll be swarming with Falconers in a second!"

"They're not searching for me," Pindar said, his mouth

full of syrup pudding. "They're glad to get rid of me—they don't know I know what I know!"

"And what's that?" Dahlia asked.

"Sorry, I'm afraid I can't tell you," Pindar said politely. "I can only tell the contact." He looked up at the three fairies. "Which of you is Iris Moth?"

10

Hopping Hill

There was an astonished silence. Lorna's mouth dropped open. Dahlia's face was too stiff with Botox to show much emotion, but her eyes widened.

"Iris? Are you sure?" asked Tom.

"Oh yes," Pindar said. "That was the name my tutor gave me, before my parents sent him to the mines."

"Well, he must've got his wires crossed," Lorna said. "Iris Moth is the LAST person to get mixed up with anti-Falconers."

"He said Iris Moth." Pindar was polite but stubborn.

Tom, Dahlia and Lorna looked doubtfully at Iris. She was shiftily avoiding meeting their eyes. "Nonsense! I'm far too respectable."

"My tutor said you'd put me in touch with the followers of Clarence Mustard."

"That's just ridiculous," Lorna said. "My uncle Clarence is dead!"

"Oh no. He's pretty old, but he's still alive. My tutor met him. He's hiding out on Hopping Hill with his followers."

"Alive?" Tom was excited; using Clarence's outgrown wings had given him a feeling that he knew this legendary fairy version of Robin Hood.

"Well, blimey!" Lorna gasped. "It's a good thing my father isn't around—he disowned Clarence after the affair at Quong." She looked at Tom. "I didn't tell you about that, did I? It was his worst act of terrorism. Clarence managed to gate-crash the annual nude ball at the summer solstice. He exploded a terrible transforming spell—twenty Falconers were permanently changed into dung beetles."

Tom laughed. "Cool!"

"It was no laughing matter!" Iris Moth said fiercely. "It was the first serious challenge to their power! Thanks to him, two members of the Ten are still living in a sandbox!"

"My dear Iris," Dahlia said, "you are indeed a dark old dinosaur! There you were, posing as a crashing snob and Milly Falconer's best friend—and all the time you were plotting their downfall!"

"I had you all fooled!" Iris said triumphantly. "I've been anti-Falconer since before this demisprite was born! I ignored the godmother summons at first because I didn't want to blow my cover."

"So what's he like, then—my uncle Clarence?" Lorna asked. "My father said he was incredibly cheeky, when he mentioned him at all."

"He's very old, but still very strong," Iris said. "And he still loves a joke—you'll have noticed how all the biggest terrorist attacks have his trademark wit."

"Ah, yes!" sighed Dahlia. "The toffee bombs! And who can forget the melting toilets? The Falconers do so hate being laughed at!"

"He sounds brilliant," Tom said. He turned to Iris. "If you tell Pindar where to find him, can I go too?" It would be incredibly exciting to meet the legendary Clarence Mustard in person.

"You?" she sniffed. "A demisprite?"

"I might be a demisprite, but I can still be anti-Falconer—can't I?"

"Hmmm." The little dinosaur eyes were pinpricks. "You do seem quite intelligent. We'll see."

"If they took Hussein," said Lorna, "they'll take anyone!"

Iris was smug. "As a matter of fact, you're wrong about your ex-brother-in-law. He's been Clarence's top genie

112

operative for years. Remember the jelly flood at last year's boat race? That was Hussein."

"Blimey!" Lorna's craggy face was pale. "And I called him a layabout!" She glanced at her watch. "No wonder my brain feels like cotton wool—it's two in the morning! And we haven't decided what we're going to do with this runaway Falconer."

Pindar was in the middle of a yawn. He tried to look alert while the fairy godmothers considered him.

"I think he should stay." Tom couldn't bear to think of Pindar spending another night in someone's window box. "He can sleep in my bedroom."

"You haven't asked me what I know," Pindar said. "I brought some useful information. While I was sneaking out of the palace I heard my parents talking."

Iris looked at him sharply, giving him her full attention. "Well?"

"They've found gold on Hopping Hill," said Pindar.

There was another stunned silence and Tom tried to read his godmothers' faces.

"Have they?" Iris said slowly. "Have they, indeed? Thank you, Pindar; that explains a lot. In fact, it explains everything."

"What do you mean?" Tom asked. "What is Hopping Hill, anyway? If Clarence Mustard's hiding there, does that mean it's like Sherwood Forest?"

"Hopping Hill is a mountain in the middle of the Realm," Iris said. "It's very big and very high and covered with thick forest, and that makes it a perfect hideout for anyone on the wrong side of the Falconers—it's the last wild place in the Realm, and a refuge for outlaws of every kind. They're constantly sending in spies and raiding parties, but they never catch anybody. Once upon a time, in the dark ages, it was an active volcano and several dragons lived inside it. There's a legend that when one good Falconer comes along, the dragons and the volcano will wake again—nonsense, of course. I happen to know Hopping Hill rather well, and it's completely dead. Tiberius knows it's riddled with terrorists. He's been dying to blow the whole thing up for years— but it's not Falconer property." She gazed round dramatically. "Since the dawn of time, Hopping Hill has belonged to the Hardings."

"To . . . my dad's family?" Even after all the surprises he'd had recently, it was fascinating to discover that his dad owned a volcano.

"Yes, it belongs to Jonas. That's the main reason Dolores wanted him to marry Milly—to bring Hopping Hill into the family. And that was before they found gold there! Don't you see?" Iris stamped her foot impatiently. "Dolores can't get the gold unless she kills Jonas and inherits the mountain. That's why she won't rest until she's found him."

Tom felt as if he'd swallowed an ice cube; suddenly the danger of Dad being killed felt real and terrifying. "My dad doesn't want it—why does she have to hunt him down and sentence him to death? He should just give her Hopping Hill, and we could go home."

"Impossible!" Iris said. "He would never betray the Hoppers—which is what the people of Hopping Hill are called. And in any case, the law says Dolores can't have it unless Jonas is dead."

"Wouldn't I inherit it? I'm his son!"

"Demisprites don't count."

"The Falconers don't care about a bit of gold!" protested Lorna. "They're ROLLING in the stuff!"

"Actually, they're not." Pindar's round cheeks reddened again as they all looked at him. But he spoke very confidently. "My parents are totally broke—that's the other thing I wasn't supposed to hear."

Tom saw that this information had a big effect on his three godmothers.

"Well, well, well!" Dahlia said with a wicked smile. "The Falconers are fortuneless! Is that just your parents, darling—or the whole boiling lot of them?"

"All of them," said Pindar. "Their debts are huge, and they're penniless—my mother's sold half the castles, and my father keeps putting up the taxes. My father's two brothers that he never managed to kill have both

115

gone bankrupt. They can't keep it secret for long. Shop-keepers have started asking for their money. Or else they break in and steal back their stuff."

Iris's little eyes glittered with excitement. "At last, something we can use against them! This boy might be the best informer we ever had!" She looked at Pindar. "If your father knew what you'd told us, he wouldn't rest until he'd had you killed."

"I know," Pindar said sadly. "I can't ever go back."

"This proves you're on our side," Iris said. "I vote Pindar stays."

"Me too!" Tom grinned at his cousin—it was something to win over sniffy old Iris.

"And me!" cried Lorna. "Pindar's one of us now!"

Dahlia gave him another radiant smile. "Stay here as long as you like, darling!" She took the truth-globe from his neck. "We don't need this anymore."

"Thanks." Pindar ducked his face away shyly, and Tom suddenly knew that he wasn't used to being praised, or having nice things said to him.

Dahlia yawned. "It's ridiculously late—you boys had better go to bed. Pindar will have to sleep on the floor tonight, I'm afraid. I'm simply too partied out to summon any husbands."

The two boys said good night to the godmothers and went back upstairs to Justinian's bedroom.

"I'm glad you're staying," Tom said. He wanted to say

he felt happier now that his cousin was with him, but that would sound silly.

"This is the best place I've been in since the circus."

"Did you like the circus?"

"It was OK." Pindar took off his dusty sneakers. "The elephants were really nice to me."

"Oh, I forgot, you fairies can talk to animals—I'd so like to do that. Do you think a demisprite would be able to learn?"

"Dunno," Pindar said, with a gusty yawn. "But it's not that hard. There are spells for it."

There was only one bed, but plenty of pillows and blankets, and they made Pindar a comfortable place on the floor.

He took off his jeans (revealing underwear with a picture of Jay Trebonkers on the back) and lay down at once. "Thanks, Tom; this feels fantastic."

"Are you sure it's soft enough? You can have the bed if you like."

"No, really—I'm fine here." Pindar pulled the blanket up to his shoulders with a contented sigh. "After that last window box, it feels like the Ritz. And it's so nice to belong somewhere."

Tom got into bed and switched off the bedside lamp. He should have been tired, but he was wakeful and curious, and he knew Pindar felt the same. They looked at each other through the net of shadows.

117

"Do you miss your parents?" asked Tom.

"No. I never felt I belonged with them. They didn't like me."

Tom tried to imagine having parents who didn't like him, and couldn't. However annoying your parents were, you always assumed they were basically on your side. "Are they strict?"

"Yes," Pindar said. "But I wouldn't mind that if I thought they cared about me. They couldn't have kids for years, though they tried every spell in the book. And then I came along. But they didn't like me, and nothing I do is good enough for them. I've spent most of my time in my own wing of the palace, with a couple of servants and my tutor, Terence Banshee."

"You liked him."

"Yes, Terence is great." Pindar's voice was sad. "They banished him to the mines. He had a copy of Clarence Mustard's *Anti-Falconer Handbook*. Just before his arrest he told me about Iris Moth. But I wasn't brave enough to run away until last week."

If Mum had been here, Tom thought, her kind heart would have bled for Pindar. She would've said nice things to him, given him cake and perhaps kissed him good night. Tom couldn't do any of this, but he did want to make his cousin feel he had at least one good friend.

"I'm glad you did run away," he said.

"Thanks—me too."

It should have been rather weird to share a room with this stranger, yet it felt oddly comfortable, as if he had known his newly discovered cousin all his life. "Good night, Pindar—nice to meet you."

"Good night, Tom—nice to meet you, too."

11

The Message

Almost at once, Tom fell into a dream. He was on a beautiful white beach—he knew he was dreaming, but at the same time it seemed incredibly real. He felt the heavy heat of the sun and the soft sand under his feet, and heard the sighing of the waves.

His mother was lying under a big umbrella, holding a red drink full of fruit. She wore a bikini and looked very happy.

In the dream she wasn't surprised to see him. "Tom! Isn't this lovely?"

"Fantastic." If this had been real life, Tom would have hugged her and bombarded her with questions, but in the dream, he was quite casual. He sat down in the shade beside her. "What've you been up to, Mum?"

"Oh, just lazing about and having fun," Mum said. "I've started pottery classes."

"Great."

She sipped her drink. "And I do a lot of thinking. I see everything from here. Before I forget, I must tell you something very interesting I know about Pindar."

"Pindar?" Even in the middle of his dream, Tom was startled to hear his cousin's name.

"He thinks his mother didn't love him— but he's wrong. She loved him very much, Tom, every bit as much as I love you." She lay back on her sun lounger. "And when you see your dad, tell him it's just like Snow White."

Tom was awake, in a sunlit bedroom, with his mother's voice ringing in his ears. It was on the tip of his tongue to ask her what she meant. When he was little he had loved the Disney film, but now he couldn't remember anything about it except the dwarfs. And what was all that about Pindar?

Things that appear hugely important in dreams often seem very silly when you're properly awake. Tom shook the whole thing out of his head and sat up in bed.

Pindar came out of the bathroom rubbing his head with a towel. "Morning, Tom—d'you think there's any breakfast? You won't believe it, but I'm starving again."

Tom decided not to tell him about the dream. From everything he'd heard about Pindar's mother, it didn't sound likely that she loved him so much. And his cousin had reminded him that he was also very hungry. "Me too—it must be something about staying up late. Let's go downstairs and see if there's any food."

They found the fairy godmothers in the drawing room—or what had been the drawing room and now looked like a futuristic beauty clinic. The three fairies lay on couches, wearing nothing but white towels, while three of Dahlia's enslaved husbands rubbed cream into their faces.

"Look, here are the boys," Lorna said through her cream. "Can we stop now?"

"No," Dahlia said firmly. "Your skin's in a shocking state."

"It's not right, that's all—this man used to own an airline! He shouldn't be giving beauty treatments to old fairies!"

"Nonsense, he loves it—don't you, Mr. Bates?"

"Yes, madam," the husband droned.

Dahlia raised her head. "Go across the hall into the dining room, you two, and have something to eat. I'm giving Iris and Lorna a makeover."

The two boys went across the hall to a comfortable, red-painted dining room, where a long, polished table was crowded with a feast of bacon, eggs, sausages, fried onions, toast, muffins, jam and croissants.

"Cool!" said Pindar, sitting down and loading his plate with sausages. "Ms. Pease-Blossom's really good at food."

"Dahlia's good at everything," Tom said. "Lorna can't do magic food, but she's a lot nicer than my other two godmothers. She doesn't enslave mortals, for a start. Fairies don't think much of mortals, do they?"

"Well—no, to be honest." Pindar reached out for a muffin. "We make a lot of jokes about how thick mortals are, and all the silly stuff they believe in. Like gravity."

"Gravity! Of course we believe in gravity!"

"It's only half the story," Pindar said. "What mortals know as gravity is actually caused by the existence of the Realm. It wraps the whole earth like a big invisible duvet. Without us, you'd all float away into space."

"But—but—the atmosphere . . . Oh, never mind." Tom decided to forget about this as quickly as possible. If he ever managed to get to his middle school in the mortal world, he didn't fancy telling his science teacher that gravity was caused by fairies.

"Isaac Newton was a demisprite," Pindar said. "My tutor told me about him—in secret, because we're not meant to know about them. You're the first demisprite I've ever met. What's your special thing?"

"My—what?"

"You demisprites usually have something you're very good at. You know—like Mozart with his music, Shakespeare with his writing—Stalin with his murdering."

"Oh. I'm good at math, I suppose."

Pindar dolloped strawberry jam on his muffin. "I wish I could find something I was really good at."

"You must be good at something," Tom said. "My mum says everyone in the world has a talent for something—even if it's only burping the alphabet, like my friend Charlie."

"The whole alphabet? That's pretty good for a mortal."

"Tom—" Lorna put her head round the door. Her face, still slathered with cream, was deadly serious. "You'd better take a look at the fairy news. You'll need to brace yourself. It's not good."

Tom felt sick. "Is it Dad? Have they—have they killed him?"

"No, he's alive and well, but they've caught him—there was a massive raid on Hopping Hill last night. Come and read it for yourself."

Dad wasn't dead. Tom took a deep breath and felt less horrible. He wasn't dead, that was the main thing. In the drawing room Iris and Dahlia (still in their towels and face cream) bent anxiously over the jeweled laptop. MILLY'S KILLER CAUGHT! screamed the headline.

The hunt for JONAS HARDING, illegal breeder and killer of Milly Falconer, ended dramatically last night when police carried out a surprise raid on Hopping Hill. Harding, found hiding with a colony of bats, will face a public trial next week.

Half the screen was taken up with a photograph of a bat, its claws bound together with a pair of tiny handcuffs.

"He doesn't look well," Iris said, shaking her head.

"Don't frighten the boy," said Lorna. "Nobody looks their best when they're disguised as a bat."

It was incredibly strange that this handcuffed bat was Dad. "What'll they do to him? Where have they taken him?"

"They'll take him to the Falconer Fortress," Pindar said. "It's the highest-security prison in the Realm."

"They won't torture him, will they?"

"Not with so many people watching," Dahlia said briskly. "This is a high-profile case, darling—the eyes of the fairy world are upon him. Tiberius wouldn't dare."

"What about the raid?" asked Pindar. "Did they capture Clarence Mustard, too?"

"Ha! They don't know he's still alive!" snapped Iris. "They burned down his HQ, but Clarence and most of his followers escaped into the forest."

Tom looked at the other photograph on the screen—a

small mug shot of what was either a pink chimp with no fur or a very ugly bald human being. The caption underneath said: "TOM HARDING the demisprite." "Hey—is that supposed to be me?"

"They try to make all demisprites look like that," Pindar said. "Really thick and hideous—to put fairies off marrying mortals."

"What's their problem with fairies marrying mortals, anyway?" It was insulting to see his name under the face of the bald, pink, blubbery monster.

"Without getting too technical," Dahlia said, "it makes power leak out of the fairy Realm into the mortal world. And certain Falconers want to keep all the magical power for themselves."

"So what would happen if lots of fairies had demisprites?" Tom was curious. "Would fairies be less magical?"

"Yes," said Lorna. "And mortals would be more magical. They'd finally get clever enough to cure all their illnesses and stop global warming. And fairies wouldn't be able to take advantage of them. The two worlds would eventually mix together. Some of us think that wouldn't be a bad thing."

"And some of us would be RUINED!" Dahlia shuddered. "We HAVE to be able to take advantage of the mortals! I've never held with such mad ideas. And in any case, all that matters now is Jonas."

126

Tom looked hard at the photo of the bat, trying and failing to see a trace of his dad's face there. "Can't we— I don't know—break into the prison and rescue him?"

Iris snorted. "Impossible! It'd be easier to steal Dolores Falconer's moon-diamonds."

"She sold them," said Pindar. "But Ms. Moth's right, Tom—we can't break into the Fortress. Honestly, they'd kill us all."

"We'll do the one thing they don't expect," Dahlia announced. She was suddenly wearing a smart suit and the black gown and stiff wig of a barrister—which looked a bit strange because she had forgotten to remove the face cream. "We'll PROVE his innocence! We'll make such a brilliant case that even a crooked Falconer jury has to let Jonas off—or get torn to pieces by an angry mob from Hopping Hill!"

This sounded hopeful, and Tom's spirits rose a little.

"I'd like to join that angry mob," Pindar said. "It sounds like a great mob to be in."

"All well and good, Dahlia," Iris said huffily. "But just HOW are we going to prove Jonas is innocent?"

"I don't know—to tell the truth, I thought Jonas would be more of a help, and he hasn't even sent us a message." Dahlia put her hand up to her face. "Whoops!" The face cream disappeared, and her lips were suddenly coated with brilliant scarlet lipstick. "He hasn't even sent a dream! I paid very careful attention to my dreams last night, and all I got was a silly anxiety dream about wearing clothes at a grand nude ball. Nothing that could've come from Jonas."

"I think I dreamt about trucks," Lorna said.

"He didn't send me any dream-messages either," Iris said. "I just had my normal dreams, which are always about money."

"Well, there's a surprise," Dahlia said sarcastically.

Iris shot her a poisonous glance, and Tom hoped they weren't going to start arguing again.

"I had a dream," he said loudly. "It was about my mother."

"Ha! A mortal?" Iris sneered. "Who cares about some stupid mortal?"

"She's not stupid!" snapped Tom. "She's just as clever as you are—even if she can't do magic!"

Dahlia was alert. "Yes, quite right—shut up, Iris—did your mother say anything?"

"She said to tell Dad it was just like Snow White."

"And?"

"That's it." Tom's face was hot; it sounded extremely lame when he said it aloud.

There was a long silence.

"Snow White," said Iris. "Well, that's a big help—a bit of waffle about one of those silly fairy stories the mortals take so seriously. Personally I blame those Grimm brothers." She added, "Demisprites, of course. Trouble-makers."

"Iris Moth," Dahlia said, "shut that dinosaur trap of yours! You're an old FOOL—and so am I! We've just been utterly shown up by a MORTAL!" She let out a triumphant burst of laughter. "Tom, darling, your mother's smarter than the lot of us put together!"

Iris was furious. "A fool? What on earth are you talking about?"

"It was staring us in the face, and we missed it!"

Tom exchanged bewildered looks with Lorna and Pindar, both obviously as confused as he was. "What does Snow White have to do with my dad?"

"More than you think," Dahlia said. Her face was alight with excitement. "Mr. Bates, bring up the case of lightning-guns. We're going on a mission."

"Where to? Can I come?" Tom caught her excitement, longing to do something instead of just waiting and hiding. "What's a lightning-gun? Can I have one?"

"Steady on," Lorna said. "I'm not sure your parents would want you to mess about with this gun. Dahlia, stop cackling and tell us what this is about."

Dahlia took off her barrister's wig. "We're off to fetch the one piece of evidence that will save Jonas."

"She's been at the fairy gin again." Iris was still cross about being called a fool. "There's no such thing."

Dahlia turned back to Mr. Bates. "Fetch my Chanel wings and the matching handbag."

"Yes, madam."

"Blimey," Lorna said, vigorously rubbing the cream off her face with a towel, "Chanel makes wings?"

"Yes—Coco Chanel was a demisprite, and she did some classic designs for fairies." Dahlia looked at Lorna and sighed. "I wish you'd let me put those auburn streaks in your hair! Trust me, darling—you'd be an absolute genie magnet!"

Iris hissed, "What is this evidence? And what's it supposed to do for Jonas?"

"We have to go into the Realm," Dahlia said, "and kidnap the dead body of Milly Falconer."

12

Fatherland

A few minutes later the last lump of plaster fell from the ceiling, and Tom and Pindar dared to come out from behind the sofa. The echoes of Iris's terrible scream slowly died away. She had unleashed a scream so loud that it had broken the windows and cracked the plaster—the room looked like a battle zone.

Dahlia brushed lumps of plaster off her shoulders. "Next time you disagree with me, Iris, could you make it quieter?" She muttered a long spell to herself, weaving her hands about. The room was restored to tidiness, and Pindar burst into a fit of sneezing.

After about twenty sneezes, he flopped down on the

sofa. "Sorry," he said foggily. "That's one of the spells that brings on my allergy."

"This is an OUTRAGE! This is MADNESS! It's the stupidest idea I've ever heard!" spat Iris.

"It certainly does sound loopy," Lorna said. She was back in her jumpsuit now, and there must have been something magical in the face cream, because she definitely looked a little less craggy. "How do you suggest we kidnap a dead body?"

Now that his ears had stopped ringing from the noise of Iris's scream, Tom could think properly about Dahlia's amazing suggestion. "It'll be tough if she's buried a long way down—it would take a lot of digging."

The three fairies looked at one another.

"Of course, this demisprite boy doesn't know," said Iris.

Tom didn't like the way Iris always looked pleased when he didn't know something. "So tell me!"

"Milly's body isn't buried," Lorna said. "Her brother was so grief-stricken when she died that he had her sealed up in a glass coffin."

"Oh—like Snow White! That's what Mum meant!" Tom remembered the end of the Disney film.

"Tiberius built a special chapel for the coffin," Lorna went on, "and all the sorrowful young men who wanted to marry Milly formed themselves into a group called the Adorers."

"A bit like an order of monks in your mortal world," Dahlia said. "The Adorers spend all their time weeping over Milly and guarding her body. At one time the Chapel of Milly was quite a tourist attraction in the Realm. People used to queue up to have their picture taken next to the corpse."

"A lot of the Adorers got bored after a few years and went off to marry other people," Lorna said thoughtfully, "so the coffin won't be as well guarded as it used to be—though I'm blowed if I know why you want it."

"Don't you see?" Tom cried out impatiently. "They thought Snow White was dead, but she had a bit of poisoned apple stuck in her throat! The Prince dislodged it when he kissed her!" When he was little Mum had always cried at the bit when the dwarfs gathered round Snow White's glass coffin. And he had always been surprised—didn't she remember the happy ending? But Mum said she couldn't help crying, because the dwarfs were so sad.

Suddenly he missed her a lot. Dad sometimes laughed at Mum for being softhearted. Tom didn't think these fairies (except maybe Lorna) knew much about soft hearts.

"Exactly!" Dahlia clapped her hands. "What an intelligent boy you are, Tom—and I'm beginning to think you might owe some of it to your mortal side."

Lorna was thunderstruck. "But Milly died! There wasn't any poisoned apple!"

"Wasn't there? What about that crab pastry? Oh, we've been blind—blind! Milly Falconer was murdered, all right—but not by Jonas!" To everyone's surprise, Dahlia turned a somersault in midair and let out a wild laugh. "I can't WAIT to see the looks on their faces!" She was suddenly businesslike. "Now listen, everyone. This is going to be a very tricky heist to pull off. Snatching the coffin is going to be a heavy job, and we can't use magic to carry it out of the chapel or we'll set off the alarms—so we need every pair of hands. Somehow, we have to sneak Tom and Pindar into the Realm."

"Can Tom get into the Realm?" Lorna asked. "He's a demi."

"Oh, he'll be fine," Dahlia said brashly. "There are more important things to worry about. Once we've all got ourselves into the Realm without arousing suspicion, we have to carry out a large glass case that contains quite a hefty corpse." She gazed round at all of them. "Make no mistake, we'll be taking an enormous risk. If we're caught, it'll mean death for us old fairies and exile to somewhere ghastly for the boys."

There was a silence. Death or exile. Tom tried to look brave, but he was cold with fear. The mortal world had never seemed so far away.

"Count me in," Lorna said. "My magic's a bit patchy,

134

but I can fight—I didn't win those Golden Boxing Gloves in college for nothing!"

"What must be done must be done," Iris said, cold and brisk. "Dolores holds her grand nude ball today, and I have an invitation. That'll be a perfect excuse for me to be in the Realm."

"Good thinking," said Dahlia. "I'll say I'm visiting the Realm to see Justinian. He has a big concert today—as long as he manages not to blow up the stadium."

"I haven't been back for donkey's years," Lorna said. "It's going to look dodgy if I suddenly show up now. The boys and I need to get in without being seen."

Dahlia waved her hands airily. "I have a brilliant idea to cover that. Here's what we do. . . ."

They gathered for takeoff in Dahlia's back garden. It was another sunny day, and Tom listened to the normal noises of children playing and cars in the square beyond. He was frightened, excited and so incredibly curious that he almost didn't care about the danger. The Realm was where his dad had grown up. It was part of his history, and he couldn't imagine what it would be like. When people talked about "Fairyland" they normally meant a pink, sugary kind of place, full of ponies and unicorns, like the covers of comics for little girls. Yet the land his godmothers spoke of was full of guns and explosions.

Dahlia threw out a cloud of pale-green invisibility powder.

Pindar burst out sneezing. "Sorry—achoo!"

"You seem to be allergic to magic," Lorna said. "Jolly awkward for a fairy—where on earth did you get it from?"

"It runs in his family," said Iris. "Clover Falconer was just the same."

"Who? Oh, that poor-relation cousin—yes, of course! Poor old Clover—how could I forget her? She came to visit Milly during college Nude Week. And she couldn't do the simplest spells without sneezing her head off."

"You seem to do a lot of nude stuff in the Realm," Tom said. "We won't have to take our clothes off, will we?"

"Certainly not. Only the grandest fairy occasions are nude," Iris said. She was wearing a raincoat, rubber boots and a diamond necklace. "I'm stark naked under this coat."

"Oh." Tom heard a snort of stifled laughter from Pindar and tried hard not to smile. He totally did not want to think about what Iris looked like naked.

Iris proudly took a stiff white card from her pocket and showed it to Tom.

Tiberius and Dolores of the House of Falconer
Command the Attendance of
Iris of Clutterbuck and Moth
At a Grand Nude Ball

The letters were of thick gold. In the bottom right-hand corner it said: *Dress: none.*

"Love the necklace, darling," Dahlia said, busily unfolding a pair of shiny black-and-gold wings. "Isn't that one of the Cartier pieces that went missing?"

"Yes, one of my girls brought it back from a school outing to Bond Street." Iris was looking beadily at Dahlia's Chanel wings. "Very chic, I'm sure. Personally I prefer efficiency."

Tom put on Uncle Clarence's wings. They were comfortable and familiar, and he felt braver when he was wearing them. Maybe I'm imagining it, he thought; but that doesn't matter if it makes me stronger.

Pindar pulled something out of his back pocket, muttered a spell—sneezed—and shook out the folds of a pair of leather wings a lot like Tom's.

Lorna's wings looked tattier than ever.

Dahlia wrinkled her nose. "It's a shame you can't use this trip to buy yourself some new fliers, darling. Lightfoot's sale started yesterday." She opened a polished wooden case that one of the husbands had carried out into the garden.

"Wow," breathed Tom.

The case was lined with scarlet velvet. Against the cloth gleamed five beautiful silver pistols.

"Standard lightning-guns," Iris said stiffly. "Very nice, I must say." (She didn't enjoy paying compliments.)

137

"They don't fire bullets," Dahlia said to Tom. "Watch."

She pointed one of the guns at a small bush in the corner of the garden. There was a white flash, like lightning, and the leaves and branches of the bush turned fiery orange, then fell to the ground in a heap of black ash.

Tom's mouth was dry. "Does it do the same to people?"

"Of course!" said Iris. "And no corpses to dispose of afterwards—such a TIDY weapon!"

Dahlia handed the pistol to Tom. "The trigger automatically sparks the magic. If anyone attacks, fire this right at them. You'd better take a practice shot."

"OK." Tom handled the gun very carefully. It was much lighter than the old revolver Lorna had lent him. "What shall I shoot?"

"That cat on the wall."

"No!" The cat slinking along the garden wall was white, like Elvis. "I don't want to kill anything!"

"He isn't a nice cat," Dahlia assured him. "He has a very bad attitude to fairies, and he shouts insults through my letter box. Aim for his head."

"NO!"

"Oh, all right! Shoot at that." She pointed across the lawn at a wooden bench.

Tom took aim and pulled the trigger. The bench turned to flame for a moment, as if made of hot embers, before falling on the grass in a heap of ash. It felt very satisfying, and he would have loved to shoot something else, but instead he put the lightning-gun into the holster on his wings, where it fitted exactly.

Dahlia handed the guns around to the other godmothers and Pindar. It was time for takeoff. Tom concentrated on the spell, trying to ignore poor Pindar's sneezes, and shot into the air. This time there was no flying over countryside. They flew up and up, through the clouds, through what seemed like miles of pale-blue sky. The white summer sun was hot and Tom had to screw up his eyes to see Lorna's stout form ahead of him. Dahlia had put on a pair of sunglasses that matched her wings.

The air cooled on his cheeks as they flew towards a bank of thick white cloud. Tom was confused—hadn't they already left the clouds far below them?

It wasn't a cloud. As they came nearer, Tom realized that they were approaching what looked like a border, or a customs point. He saw low buildings and a row of little booths where people were queuing with pieces of paper. He noticed—with a jolt of shock—that there were other fairies flying alongside them. They looked like ordinary mortals, carrying suitcases, briefcases and shopping bags and dressed in ordinary mortal clothes. One was a policeman.

Somehow (Tom wasn't quite sure how he had come to be standing on solid ground) they had landed. He took a deep breath and gazed around. This was the uttermost edge of the fairy Realm. He had left the mortal world and was actually in another dimension. It felt different, in a way he couldn't pinpoint—the feel of the air on his skin, the strange, soft, bright glow of the light.

They were in the entrance of a gigantic hall with a vaulted roof of cloud, like a cross between a cathedral and a busy airport. All around them, fairies were briskly landing, shrugging off their wings and heading for the queues. Tom noticed them clutching pieces of card that had a faint glow, like weak lightbulbs. He guessed these were fairy passports—did his dad have one?

"Synchronize watches," said Dahlia. She had taken charge, and the other two fairies accepted her authority. "Tom, your mortal watch won't be any use. We're on fairy time up here. I make it two thousand past moon—got that?"

Lorna, Iris and Pindar fiddled with their watches. Tom added "fairy time" to the long list of things to ask his dad about—if he ever saw him again.

"Our invisibility runs out in five minutes," Dahlia said. "Iris—you go on ahead. We'll meet you at the Chapel of Milly at moon two-eighty—got that?"

"Moon two-eighty. Got it."

To Tom's total horror, Iris took off her raincoat and stood in front of them wearing nothing but wellies and a diamond necklace. It was amazingly embarrassing; he

140

couldn't look up until Iris had walked away into the crowd.

"Make for the collection shed over there." Dahlia pointed to a very large wooden shed. A notice said: MORTAL GOODS COLLECTION POINT.

Outside the entrance was a little hut like an observation post. At first Tom thought there was a small child inside it—until he saw, with a slight shock, that it was a tiny man. He knew there were tiny people in the mortal world, but this man did not look human. His light brown skin was like leather. His nose and ears were pointed. He was a magical creature from a story—a pixie, or a goblin. How incredible that the stories were real. And how even more incredible to see a pixie or whatever working as a security guard.

There was no time to stare. The four of them dashed past the observation post into the gloomy shed just before their invisibility ran out. All around them stretched long lanes of metal shelves, piled with boxes and parcels.

"So far so good!" Dahlia took a piece of paper from her handbag. "This is where all the stuff fairies have ordered from the mortal world comes to be scanned on entry into the Realm. You'd be surprised how many useful things are mortal made. My boxes contain mortal drums, ordered by my son because fairy drums aren't loud enough. They're in Aisle P, number eight hundred and thirty-four." She bustled off through the tunnels of boxes and the others hurried after her. "Stop! Found them!"

She pointed at two large wooden boxes labeled TREBONKERS. Tom, Lorna and Pindar helped her drag them off the shelf. Tom's heart was beating hard, but so far, it was all going to plan.

Lorna curled up inside a kettledrum. "Blimey, this is a tight fit! Can't I shrink myself?"

"No," Dahlia said. "You've forgotten the rules, darling—all enchantments must be removed before going through customs. You'd only give us away."

Tom and Pindar were each sealed up inside a large drum, which was then shut inside the wooden box (Dahlia was amazingly strong).

"Tom, can you hear me?"

"Yes," Tom said—though it was hard to speak when he was curled up like a prawn.

"Can you breathe?"

"Just about!"

"I should just mention," Dahlia said, "that as you're a demisprite, there's a teeny-weeny chance that when you go through the scanner you'll disintegrate."

"WHAT?"

"Well, it's too late to do anything about it now. We'll just have to wait and see."

13

Rock Star

When you've just been told you might be about to disintegrate, it's hard to concentrate on anything else. Tom curled up in his cramped, dark hiding place, listening to the confused noises he heard outside and praying Dahlia was wrong.

They were moving—Dahlia had found some helpers to put the boxes on a trolley. They didn't know there were people inside the drums, and Tom felt himself being hurled and heaved and slammed down, until he literally didn't know whether he was on his head or his heels.

"They're drums for my son, Jay Trebonkers," he heard

Dahlia explaining. "He's waiting for them at the Tiberius Stadium—do let us through quickly, please!"

"Right you are, Lady Trebonkers," a man's voice said. "Never mind the paperwork. My two girls are going to that concert, and if I do anything to hold it up I'll never hear the last of it!"

Tom's box rocked violently. Searing white light poured into the darkness, and he could suddenly see the knees of his jeans a few centimeters in front of his nose. He nearly gasped aloud—it felt as if a cool breeze had shot through his entire body and somebody had filled the core of his bones with toothpaste. And though it wasn't exactly painful, it felt extremely peculiar. It was a relief to be plunged back into warm darkness.

"Tom," Dahlia's voice said, close to the box, "have you disintegrated?"

"I . . . I don't think so."

"Good. We're safely through customs now."

"Can we get out?"

"Not yet, but it won't be long."

He was being moved again—loaded into the back of a truck, as far as Tom could guess from the confusion of shouts and jolts. The engine juddered into life and they were off.

I'm inside the Realm, he thought; I'm in a place where fairy tales are real.

There was a thunderstorm raging—no, those explosions were not thunder—was that gunfire? One sound started to drown out all the others. At first Tom thought he could hear a huge flock of starlings. It got louder and louder, until he realized they were driving through the middle of a screaming crowd. The truck had slowed down, and Tom heard a girl's voice shrieking, "I love you, Jay!"

They had reached the stadium where Jay Trebonkers was performing. The noise of the crowd was deafening, and Tom wished he could move enough to put his hands over his ears. Suddenly, the screams were muffled, and he guessed they were now inside the stadium. Finally he felt his box being dropped on a floor.

The drum seemed to burst open and Tom fell out of it, dazzled by the light.

Lorna grabbed his hand, heaving him to his feet. "Are you all right, boy? My heart was in my mouth when we went through customs. I was terrified you'd disintegrate and I'd never be able to fit all your molecules together in the right order!"

They were in a plain white room lined with lighted mirrors, and there were costumes hanging on a rail— this must be the dressing room of Dahlia's rock-star son. A lanky young man with large pointed ears and bright red hair was sprawled on a chair. Tom had never met any kind of rock star before. He was impressed, and a bit shy, and he could see that Pindar was even more shy. Pindar thought Jay Trebonkers was wonderful.

When the rock star saw his mother, however, he reacted like any other son—he looked startled and guilty and tried to hide what he was drinking. "Mum! What're you doing here? You hate my gigs!"

"Justinian, sweetie!" Dahlia kissed him. "As you see, I used your drums for a little people-smuggling."

"Oh yeah?" Justinian did not seem surprised. "Well, you picked the right place—I paid Superintendent Falconer a fortune to keep the police off my back today."

"Darling, I knew you'd help us. This is my old college friend Lorna Mustard."

"Cool," said Justinian. "Hi, Lorna."

"Nice to meet you," Lorna said stiffly.

"And this is Tom, the Harding demisprite." Dahlia pulled Tom forward. "He's our godson."

"Cool," said Justinian again. "Hi, Tom. You don't look anything like your 'Wanted' posters."

"Thanks," Tom said, shaking hands with the fairy rock star. Justinian was wearing a bright green bodysuit and heavy boots with yellow wings attached to the heels (Tom couldn't take his eyes off these; they kept fluttering like the wings of live birds), and his pointed ears bristled with metal studs.

"And this is Pindar Falconer."

Justinian stared at Pindar. "But you're dead!"

146

"Dead?" Pindar's face had been red with shyness at meeting his favorite singer, but it now turned white. "I'm not dead!"

"Well, they buried you, mate. I sang at your funeral—and your parents still haven't paid me."

"Hang on," Lorna said. "What are you talking about? If Pindar's dead, why didn't we see it on the news?"

"They wanted it to be low-key." Justinian shrugged. "You know what the Falconers are like. They control what goes out on the news."

"My own parents have had me declared dead because they wanted to get rid of me—I told you they didn't like me," said Pindar. "If they see me again, they'll kill me." He spoke calmly but looked very sad. "It means I don't belong anywhere now."

"You do!" Tom said fiercely. "You're my cousin, and my dad's your uncle—you belong with us!" It was horrible that someone as nice as Pindar should be so lonely and unloved. Tom knew Mum and Dad would never turn their backs on him; they were far too kind. "If we ever get out of this mess, you can come and live in our flat above the deli—we could easily fit another bed in my room."

This struck him as a brilliant idea, and he was glad to see the hope coming back into his cousin's face.

"Thanks, Tom," Pindar said, smiling. "I wouldn't care about being officially dead if I could stay with you."

"Your own parents!" Justinian shook his head thoughtfully. "Heavy! Are you guys staying for the gig?"

"I wish we could—Tom's never heard any of your music." Pindar sighed. "But we're here on a mission."

"We can't tell you anything else," Dahlia said. "You haven't seen us, do you understand?"

"OK. Good luck, then." Justinian grinned at both boys—he was nice, Tom decided, and less scary than his mother. "It's great that you're not dead, Pindar, mate. And Tom, since my mum's your fairy godmother, we're sort of brothers, aren't we? Take care, man!"

"Bye, Jay—great to meet you—I think you're the coolest person in the universe—thanks for singing at my funeral . . . Ow!" Pindar was hustled out of the dressing room by Lorna, who was muttering crossly, "No manners . . . didn't even kiss my hand . . . and that room REEKS of alcohol!"

"Poor Justinian!" Dahlia said. "He's always nervous before a concert—so sensitive!"

Lorna muttered something else—Tom caught the words "lout" and "National Service."

Luckily Dahlia didn't hear this. They were outside the star's dressing room in an empty corridor, and she was crisp and businesslike. "Right, we're right on schedule. Follow me out of the stadium and stick close."

She set off along the corridor, and Tom, Pindar and

Lorna hurried after her. They went down a dank stone staircase to an emergency exit deep in the basement. Dahlia opened it, and they were suddenly on a crowded street.

"Try to blend in," Dahlia said, putting on her sunglasses. "Tom, try to look as un-mortal as possible."

"How am I supposed to do that?"

"Just keep your head down."

Tom didn't want to keep his head down. He wanted to gaze around him, taking in every weird and wonderful detail. This was the Realm, and it was incredible. The sunlight had a silver dazzle to it, like the early morning of a hot day, and the colors were so intense it almost hurt to look at them. A crowd of fairy teenagers in T-shirts like Pindar's poured past them, making for the stadium. Tom and the fairies walked steadily in the opposite direction. Pindar tried to hide his face, but Tom was worried that someone would recognize him and think they'd seen a ghost.

He relaxed a little as they began to leave the mass of screaming teenagers behind. They were walking through a bustling street market now, and Tom could see that it was very pretty, with dinky little stalls and shops straight out of a fairy tale. Beyond the quaint streets a purple-sided mountain rose out of soft green fields. Its steep slopes were covered with thick forest, and Tom was suddenly sure this was Hopping Hill—the reason his aunt Dolores wanted to kill his dad. He hadn't expected it to be so beautiful.

But though the Realm was beautiful, it was also a seedy-looking place. Many of the shops were boarded up; some were blackened ruins. One even had flames shooting out of all the windows, and nobody took the slightest notice. They had to hurry past the entrance of an alley where a gunfight was going on.

A bolt of lightning narrowly missed Lorna's boot. "OI!" she yelled furiously. "Watch where you're pointing that thing!"

"Don't get into a fight!" hissed Dahlia. "Do you want to draw attention to the fact that you're walking beside a demisprite and a Falconer who's officially DEAD? Boys—put your heads down!"

Tom and Pindar focused hard on the pavement as they dodged a crowd of drunken leprechauns outside an Irish bar—it was incredibly strange to see storybook creatures in real life. As they moved away from the stadium and the noise of screaming faded, the sound of explosions grew louder. Tom couldn't see where they were coming from, but the air was sour with gunpowder and his hair was soon filled with brick dust.

"Blimey," Lorna said, "it's even worse than I remembered! Is it always like this?"

"Actually today's pretty quiet," said Pindar.

"Quiet? Tiberius has let the Realm go to rack and ruin—I can't wait to get back to my scrapyard!"

"Oh, how tiresome." Dahlia halted suddenly. "There's a police patrol up ahead." She pointed to a bank of flashing lights at the end of the street. Two police fairies, with dark-blue leather wings and blue helmets, hovered above the crowd like big blue dragonflies.

"Oh, help!" gulped Pindar. "Now what do we do?"

"Run!" Lorna grabbed Tom's arm.

"Hold your nerve!" Dahlia rapped out in a tone of voice that must be obeyed. "If we panic, we're finished!"

"But they'll spot Pindar! There's no way we can hide that blooming great nose of his! I mean—sorry, Pindar."

"No, you're right," Pindar said cheerfully. "It's a really terrible nose. I'd love a magical nose job—but it's the Falconer nose, and my father thinks it's noble."

"I'm glad you're not too attached to it," Dahlia said, with one of her slightly dangerous smiles. "I've had an idea."

"We don't have time!" cried Lorna.

"Nonsense, it won't take a minute. See this chemist's shop?" She raised her eyebrows in the direction of a little shop nearby—nothing like the local chemist near Tom's home, which was stark and white, with shelves full of diapers and cough medicine, but cobwebby and mysterious, its window crammed with dusty bottles.

"I'm going inside—I'll keep the assistant talking for as long as I can to give you and the boys time to nip round to the back of the shop."

"But there's no time," Lorna hissed. "They'll arrest us—we'll never get to the Chapel. Iris can't kidnap Milly's coffin all by herself—and we won't have any defense for Jonas. . . ."

Tom knew they had to stay calm. He looked at Dahlia. "What do we have to do?"

"Yes, Tom, I'd better give the orders to you," Dahlia said. "You may be a demisprite, but you're very clear-headed. This shop is the old-fashioned kind of fairy chemist that makes all its own potions. There'll be a vat of handsome-mixture bubbling away somewhere."

"A vat of what?"

"You remember the handsome-token I gave you for your christening? You buy them at the chemist's. The mixture is very expensive and unstable, and you're only allowed to buy tiny amounts at a time, and it only works on newborn babies. But to make the tokens, they boil the potion up in big vats. Pindar, I want you to break into the back of the shop, dip my handkerchief into the handsome-vat and rub it on your nose—and your ears— well, your entire face. That should be enough to disguise you."

Tom was suspicious. "Won't it be dangerous?"

"Dangerous?"

"You said it was unstable."

Dahlia sighed rather crossly. "All right, if you want to split hairs, the wrong dose can work in reverse and turn you hideously ugly—there's an illness called Ugly Chemist Syndrome that's caused by contact with handsome-mixture."

"You can't make Pindar ugly!" Tom was annoyed by the way Dahlia didn't seem to care about anybody—didn't his cousin have enough troubles?

"I don't care," Pindar said. "Honestly, Tom—I'm not very handsome anyway, and at least I'd be disguised."

Dahlia took a large white lace handkerchief from her handbag and gave it to Pindar. "Go on, then—I'll keep him talking as long as I can." She went into the shop.

Tom, Pindar and Lorna ran down the narrow passage at the side of the chemist's shop. They found another door, which opened into a backyard full of barrels and bottles. Tom was so nervous he could hardly breathe—suppose they were caught? What would those flying police do to them?

"This'll be where he makes his potions." Lorna pointed to a pair of shabby padlocked doors. "They're locked, but I don't see why he bothers—his security's rubbish!" She muttered a few words, waving her fingers around the lock, and it fell open.

Pindar started sneezing helplessly. "Sorry—achoo! It's my allergies—achoo!"

153

"Shh!" Lorna pushed open the big doors. "Good grief, I haven't heard such dreadful sneezing since poor Clover!"

They crept into a cluttered, dark, weird-smelling space like a garage, crammed with test tubes, bottles and heaps of printed labels—SWAIN'S ANTI-SPITE POWDER, SWAIN'S OWN RECIPE WART ENHANCER, SWAIN'S CURSE-REMOVING CREAM. There was a big stove where several cauldrons filled the air with thick steam.

"Aha! That's what we're looking for!" Lorna pointed to a shadowy corner, and Tom saw a huge metal drum, sunk into the ground, giving off an odd, heavy sort of steam that poured down to the floor and hovered there like a low cloud. "OK, Pindar—dip in the hanky, and then we can go."

The vat was sunk so deeply into the floor that Pindar had to kneel on the very edge. "Achoo! Achoo! The potion's a long way down—"

"Careful!" hissed Tom.

"Achoo! Oh no—I dropped the hanky! I'll fish it out—"

"NO!" wailed Lorna, forgetting to be quiet.

Too late. Pindar pulled his arm out of the mixture, and they all stared at it aghast. Tom would've loved to say something positive, but what? This was a disaster. Poor old Pindar's hand and arm up to the elbow had turned wizened and scaly and moldy green, like the claw of a particularly shabby old lizard.

Lorna groaned. "That's ruined it! Now you're more noticeable than ever!"

"ACHOO!" sneezed Pindar.

Tom tried to grab the back of his cousin's shirt, but he wasn't quick enough. Pindar toppled right into the vat of potion, with a loud gulping noise as if he were being swallowed into a swamp.

14

The Adorers

Tom didn't lose his head. "The broom!" he hissed at Lorna.

"What?"

He pushed past her and grabbed a long broom that was leaning against the wall and held it out over the seething gloop in the vat. Pindar took hold of the handle and together Tom and Lorna dragged him out onto the concrete floor.

Tom couldn't see anything at first except a dark shape in a reeking cloud of steam. He watched it fearfully, bracing himself in case Pindar had turned into a hideous lizard—he swore to himself that he'd still like his cousin no matter how ugly he was, but how could Pindar ever come to live in the mortal world if he looked like Godzilla's grandfather?

"Bum!" Lorna cursed softly. "We've made a right mess of this!"

Tom and Lorna stood gaping at Pindar as the steam cleared.

"This is bad, isn't it?" Pindar looked at his arms and legs. The potion had evaporated very fast, leaving his jeans and T-shirt spotlessly clean and dry—they even looked ironed. "I'm not scaly anymore, but tell me the truth—I can take it! How . . . ? How ugly am I?"

Tom caught Lorna's eye—and they both suddenly burst out laughing. When you're not supposed to laugh, it is very hard to stop, and Tom had to put his hands over his mouth to keep quiet. Lorna laughed so hard that she had tears in her eyes.

"Wow, I must be totally repulsive," said Pindar.

"Repulsive?" Tom managed to calm down. He had only laughed because he was so shocked. "You must be kidding! You're really, really HANDSOME!"

"Who, me?"

"Yes, my dear Pindar," Lorna said, wiping her eyes. "You're beautiful!"

And it was true. The old Pindar had had a big nose like a turned-up duck's beak, and great flat ears. The new Pindar had the same friendly, helpful, slightly worried expression, on a face of film-star handsomeness—Tom felt slightly shy of the gorgeous stranger, until his cousin sneezed, turning bright red, and he saw that the essential Pindar was just the same.

"Well, we've done the job," Lorna said. "Nobody will recognize him now—his own parents wouldn't know him." She looked searchingly at Pindar. "Though funnily enough, he looks more like you now, Tom—in fact, he looks just like your father when we were at college. There must be more Harding in him than we thought. Come on, let's get out of here."

The three of them hurried back to the front of the shop, and Tom wondered if the new Pindar really looked like him. Obviously he wasn't as handsome as Pindar, but his cousin did suddenly look like a much younger version of Dad, and he was distracted by another pang of longing for his parents—would he ever see them again?

But there was no time to worry about that now. Dahlia came out of the chemist's shop carrying three heavy bags. "Where have you BEEN? I had to buy all his wretched special offers!" She glanced sharply at Pindar. "Where's Pindar? And why is this gorgeous boy trying to spy on us? Buzz off, you attractive rascal!"

"This is Pindar," Tom said. "It went a bit wrong."

"Pindar? Good gracious!" Dahlia dropped the shopping bags into a nearby litter bin. "I wouldn't say it went wrong! Darling, you're the image of your uncle

158

Jonas! Well, the Harding side is the good-looking side of your family—your father looks like a duck-billed platypus with ears and a mustache."

This wasn't kind, but Pindar snorted with laughter. "He does, actually." His handsome cheeks reddened. "Er—does this stuff wear off?"

"No, darling, you'd better get used to being a pinup. That Falconer hooter is a thing of the past!" She glanced at her watch. "Oh wonderful—we're still in good time for the Afternoon Sobbing."

Tom saw at once that the Chapel of Milly was past its best. It was a small, square building of red brick in the purple shadow of Hopping Hill, set in the middle of a garden—but the buildings all around had been bombed and the garden was full of rubbish. They had traveled to the fringes of the city, through alternating scenes of fairy-tale prettiness and patches of blackened ruins—it had been scary dodging the gunfights and explosions, and Tom's mouth and nose felt gritty with dust.

"There's Iris," Lorna said. "Trust her to be early!"

Iris—thankfully wearing her raincoat—stood in front of the wooden doors of the Chapel. "You're thirty-two flickers late, and—who on earth is this?" Her thin lips turned white.

"It's Pindar," Tom said hastily. "He fell into a vat of handsome-stuff."

"Good heavens—just for a moment I thought—you look so much like . . ."

Tom was curious. The first thing all three godmothers had said about the new handsome Pindar was that he looked like Dad. No wonder they'd all had crushes on him.

"Yes, it's brought out his Harding side," Dahlia said. "How was the nude ball?"

"Magnificent—you'd never know Tiberius is penniless. Dolores had some fabulous buttock-paintings, and there was quite literally a fountain of Kaulquappe." Iris had recovered and was frowning at her watch. "The Adorers will be out in just a few moments. We must pretend to be tourists."

"This doesn't look like much of a tourist attraction," said Tom. "It's a bit of a dump, to be honest. And we're the only people here."

"It used to be a lot more exciting," Pindar said. "A long time ago, when I was little, there were two hundred Adorers—they had a choir, and there were loads of stalls selling food and souvenirs."

"Yes, and people used to come in flying coach parties to have their picture taken with Milly's corpse," Iris said wistfully. "Some of the Adorers used to do juggling acts to entertain the queue. Her memory was properly honored in those days."

Lorna snorted. "That's because Tiberius put former

Adorers on the fast track in the civil service—and who bothers with that nowadays? Times have changed, all right. Nowadays none of the bright young people want a career in the Realm."

A bell started pealing, low and solemn.

"Here they come," Dahlia said. "Bow your heads, everyone."

Tom bowed his head but kept watching avidly out of the tops of his eyes. A large, battered house that was half a ruin stood near the Chapel. The door of this house opened and a line of men (he counted twenty) filed out. They wore long black robes and black hoods that hid half their faces. The Adorer at the front of the line was loudly sobbing. He produced an iron key from the depths of his robes and (still sobbing) unlocked the door of the Chapel.

"Well, I never!" whispered Lorna. "Look, girls—it's poor old Derek Drapton! Now, he really DID adore Milly!"

"She wouldn't look at him," sniffed Iris. "The Draptons are a minor family and his legs were too spindly."

"His legs? Darling, I heard it was because of his tiny—" Dahlia stopped as Derek shuffled past them, sobbing loudly in the depths of his hood.

One by one, the Adorers filed past the boys and the godmothers. Tom's mouth was dry—how on earth were they going to get away with this? Now that they were at

161

the point of carrying out Dahlia's plan, it seemed absolutely crazy. He glanced at Pindar, who was looking more like his old self as Tom got used to the handsomeness. Pindar was as scared as he was, but his face showed a rocklike determination.

Dahlia's scarlet lips moved and her manicured fingers snapped. The last five Adorers in the line silently fell to the ground. "Right—get their robes."

This was one of the parts of the plan that had worried Tom. Fairies are a lot stronger than mortals, and Pindar and the godmothers briskly stripped the black robes off the unconscious Adorers, but Tom found it a real struggle—an unconscious person is amazingly heavy, and by the time the others were in their disguises he had only managed to get the man and the robes into a tangle and Pindar and Lorna had to help him. The robe was like a monk's habit, with a belt made of rope and a deep hood.

They left the stripped Adorers lying on the bald, dirty lawn in their underwear and sandals. Dahlia put a finger to her lips as they entered the Chapel. Tom followed her, then Iris, then Pindar, with Lorna at the back.

Tom made an effort to calm down. It was going like clockwork so far and he was right behind Dahlia—her magic was of a very high quality, even if she did despise mortals and turn them into slaves.

Pindar let out a stifled sneeze and Tom's heart skipped—but none of the Adorers took any notice.

Though his orders were to keep his head bowed to blend in with the other Adorers, he couldn't resist looking round. This place gave him the shivers. It was like a church or a museum. There were rows of chairs, and the walls were covered with pictures of Milly Falconer. The biggest one was life-sized and showed a plump young woman with a round, pink face and fat ringlets of brown hair. She was dressed very grandly in a glittering white gown, gauzy white wings that sparkled with jewels and a small jeweled crown.

Derek Drapton broke into louder sobs. The other Adorers began sobbing too.

"Sob!" Iris hissed, behind him. "Boo-hoo!"

Tom let out a couple of feeble sniffles and immediately wanted to laugh, in spite of the danger; the godmothers were so bad at acting grief-stricken. Luckily, apart from Derek Drapton, the genuine Adorers weren't much better. Tom was amused to see that one of them was listening to an iPod under his hood and another was texting on his phone. For heartbroken lovers, they looked bored.

It was a shock to see Milly Falconer's dead body. The Adorers had formed a circle around her glass coffin and Tom looked as closely as he dared. He'd never seen a dead body before, and Milly had been laid out in the same dress, wings and crown she wore in the life-sized portrait. He'd expected her to be pale like a wax figure, yet she looked amazingly alive—pink and peaceful, as if she were asleep.

Derek Drapton dropped to his knees. "Oh, Milly!" he wailed. "You were so beautiful, so graceful—WHY? WHY?"

"Why?" echoed the other Adorers (rather half-heartedly, Tom thought).

"Milly, the world is a parched desert without you! My only beloved! Woman of my dr—" The weeping Drapton froze midsentence with his mouth open.

Dahlia dropped a tiny glass tube into her handbag. "Hurry up, everyone—we've got exactly ten minutes before they all wake up and raise the alarm."

"Achoo!"

"Oh, Pindar—do stop sneezing!"

"Sorry—achoo!"

Tom knew exactly what he had to do; they had practiced this twice before they left Dahlia's house. He threw off the black robes. His wings were tightly packed into a traveling harness on his back, which he quickly untied. He shook the creases out and took his place at the foot of the coffin.

"I wish I dared to use a bit more magic," Dahlia said.

"But it's just too easy to spot, and the police are trained to investigate any sudden surges." She was rummaging in her handbag, and she suddenly swore. "Drat and double drat! The tube of invisibility has leaked all over the inside of my bag! Now I've got a lot of invisible credit cards! Never mind, we'll just have to hope what's left is enough." She scattered the pale green powder around them (sending Pindar into a storm of sneezes). "Now let's get Milly out—one, two, three, HEAVE!"

With tremendous huffing and groaning, the five of them lifted the glass coffin off its velvet-covered plinth and staggered out of the Chapel into the rubbish-strewn garden.

"Blimey," gasped Lorna. "She was always going on diets—I wish one of them had WORKED!"

The coffin was incredibly heavy, and Tom felt as if his arms were being pulled out of their sockets with the weight. This—and Pindar's sneezing—made it hard to remember the flying spell. Slowly, painfully, they got off the ground with their load. As soon as Tom was properly airborne it felt much lighter. He was able to breathe properly, and to gaze around him at the aerial view of the Realm—spread out beneath them like a beautiful quilt dotted with blackened holes.

"We were just in time," Iris said. "Look down there!"

Far below them, there was movement around the

Chapel. The Adorers had woken up and discovered that Milly had gone, and there was the distant sound of an alarm bell.

"Make for the border," Dahlia said. "Fast as the wind—hold tight, Tom!"

He gripped the coffin as tightly as he could, until his fingers hurt, and a good thing too—this was speed as he had never known it. The ground below was a blur and his ears were almost blown off his head. Holding on took so much concentration that he didn't have time to be frightened.

"Police sirens!" Lorna shrieked over the rushing of the wind. "They're chasing us!"

Tom heard the sirens—distantly at first, and then they were surrounded by flying police with stiff wings of blue leather, helmets with lights on and enormous guns. He felt sick.

"HALT!" a deafening voice roared through a loud-speaker. "YOU HAVE BEEN PICKED UP ON THE INVIS-IBILITY SENSOR—HALT OR WE'LL SHOOT!"

"Keep going!" Lorna yelled desperately. "We can still outrun them—OW!" A bolt of lightning flashed past her shoulder. "They're firing at us!"

A storm of lightning bolts rained around them—Tom felt the heat of one just missing his leg. The coffin jolted and juddered. Iris managed to grab her lightning-pistol with one hand, sending out a volley of shots—Tom saw a police fairy hurtle to the ground with one wing a cloud of glowing ashes.

"GIVE UP THE DEMISPRITE!"

It was Tom they were after. He was about to fall into the hands of the Falconers.

Suddenly something dark came between Tom and the sun. He saw a man with a black mask over his face shooting down the police one by one, as if he were playing a computer game. It was a nightmarish sight—fairies exploding into ash in midair, sometimes right on top of him.

And then came a tremendous WHACK, which swept Tom off the coffin and sent him plunging towards the ground—with his wings in a tangle and no time to say the spell. His head filled with fog, and he was just aware of Pindar swooping down and grabbing his wrist—before he dropped into deep, silent darkness.

15

Old Friends

Out of the darkness came Lorna's voice. "I'll never forgive myself! How can I face Jonas now? He trusted me to take care of his son—and I nearly got him killed!"

Tom tried to tell her he was OK, but he couldn't move. He was trapped in something warm and thick, like a fly in molasses.

"Oh, do stop fussing," said Iris's voice. "He wasn't killed—thanks to Pindar."

"Yes, well done, darling," Dahlia's voice chimed in. "That was a splendid rescue."

It was all coming back to Tom. The last thing he remembered was Pindar's hand grabbing his wrist. He saved my life, he thought; Mum and Dad will have to let him live with us now.

"Where is everybody, anyway?" Lorna asked. "They haven't even offered us a cup of tea!"

Tom made an effort to open his heavy eyelids, and saw dancing flames. He was lying on a smooth carpet of grass, beside the massive trunk of a tree. The godmothers and Pindar were sitting around a crackling campfire.

"He's waking up," said Iris.

"Tom!" Lorna loomed over him. "Can you hear me?"

"Yes."

"Drink some of this," she said, holding a metal cup to his lips.

Tom took a sip of something hot and fierce that spread a feeling of liquid light through his whole body. The fog in his brain cleared and he sat up.

"It's just a drop of Kaulquappe." Lorna drank the rest of it. "Blimey, what a hoo-ha!"

"What happened? Where are we? Pindar—thanks for saving me," said Tom.

His cousin grinned. "That's OK."

"A bolt of lightning knocked you off the coffin and stunned you," Dahlia said.

"Who were the guys in black masks?"

"We were rescued by Clarence Mustard's outlaws," Iris told him proudly. "They've brought us to Hopping Hill."

"This is Hopping Hill?" Tom gazed round curiously. So this was the wild, beautiful fairy mountain owned by his dad. Now that his eyes had got used to the shadows, he saw that they were in a clearing in the middle of dense forest. A short way off, two masked men with machine guns stood on guard. "Where's the coffin? I didn't break it when I fell off, did I?"

"No, it's safe and sound over there." Lorna pointed to a black shape behind the guards. "The chief outlaw covered it with his cloak—he said it was depressing." (Tom knew what he meant; he was glad he didn't have to look at that plump pink corpse.)

"We should never have brought this boy into the Realm," Iris said crossly. "We should've guessed Dolores would come after him."

"What does she want with me?" Tom shuddered; it was horrible to think he was being hunted by his wicked aunt.

"She must've taken legal advice," Dahlia said coolly. "My old professor, Judge Plato Falconer, does all her difficult work. Dolores must be afraid of legal claims on Hopping Hill after she's killed Jonas."

"But . . . but . . ." Tom was confused. "Why would I make a legal claim? You said I couldn't inherit Hopping Hill because I'm a demisprite!"

"You can't—but you can still take her to court. And if

you do that, it could tie up the gold for years. Fairy law is as old as time and ridiculously complicated."

"But—won't she just break the law?"

"No, darling. Fairies are killed if they break the old law. You have to find ways of getting round it."

"Hmm, you'd know all about that." Iris sniffed.

"Sorry to keep you waiting." The leader of the outlaws stepped out of the shadows. He took off his black mask and rubbed his hands through his short gray hair. "These masks are so itchy!"

"Terence!" Pindar gasped. His newly handsome face was pale with joy. "Don't you know me?"

It was Terence Banshee, Pindar's beloved former tutor. He had an odd face, Tom thought; big, bright black eyes, a snouty little nose and a tiny chin. His ears were extremely large, and slightly pointed at the top.

He looked sharply at Pindar. "Why, yes—you must be Jonas Harding's boy—you're the spitting image of him! Though you're on the big side for an eleven-year-old."

Here was somebody else saying Pindar was the image of his dad. "I'm Jonas's son," Tom said, scrambling to his feet. "My name's Tom, and I'm the one who's eleven."

"Good gracious—you're like him too—what's going on?"

"Terence," Pindar said desperately, "don't you recognize me?"

171

Tom felt sorry for his cousin; his old tutor was the only person who had ever really loved him, and now the man didn't know him. "He's Pindar," Tom said helpfully, "Pindar Falconer."

Terence's odd face turned deathly pale. "What kind of cruel joke is this? My poor Pindar is dead!"

"Terence, I swear it's me—I mean, I swear I'm Pindar! I ran away from my parents and fell into a vat of handsome-mixture—but I'm just the same old me underneath—achoo!"

"That sneeze—I'd know it anywhere!" Terence burst into tears. "My dear boy!"

He threw his arms around Pindar and hugged him hard. Tom felt like cheering; he had never seen his cousin so happy.

"I thought you'd been sent to the mines," Pindar said, half laughing and half crying.

Terence wiped his big, shiny black eyes with his sleeve. "I was in the mines, but I escaped. Oh, this is wonderful! I can see past your handsomeness now—you really are the same old Pindar!" He smiled at Tom. "And it's a pleasure to meet you, Tom. I used to share a flat with your dad when we were in college."

"Oh." Tom was having trouble keeping track of all his dad's old college friends.

"And I remember your godmothers very well—hello, girls. Let's go to Clarence."

"I don't like leaving poor old Milly. It doesn't seem respectful," said Lorna.

"Don't worry," Terence said. "The guards will stay with her."

He led them out of the clearing into a part of the forest where the trees grew close together. Pindar walked beside him. Tom was just in front of the three godmothers, and while they walked, he heard them whispering.

"Lorna—do you remember him from college?"

"No, I've never laid eyes on him. What about you, Iris?"

"If he's close to Clarence he must be all right," Iris whispered. "But no, I don't remember him. Jonas shared his flat with that awful little bat."

"The one he used to bring to the pub," Lorna whispered. "Who was always dragging on about animal rights, and going off to demonstrations with tiny little placards."

"Watch your heads!" called Terence.

They all had to crouch down so that they could get through a narrow opening in a sheer rock face, and there were some uncomfortable minutes of crawling along a stone tunnel.

"My nails are ruined," Dahlia sighed. "And I don't suppose there's a decent magi-manicure for miles!"

They finally emerged in a shadowy underground cavern. At first Tom thought the walls were covered with special insulation; then he saw that it was rows and rows of small brown bats, squashed tightly together like a furry duvet.

Terence lit a lantern and led them into another stone tunnel. There were no bats here, and the light caught at the glittering veins of gold in the rock.

"Keep together," Terence said. "This mountain's riddled with tunnels, and a stranger can easily get lost."

They walked out into a large underground chamber lit by a single orb of ghostly white light. Two masked guards with machine guns were stationed outside a metal door.

"Halt! Who goes there?"

"Agent Five," said Terence, "Terence Banshee."

"Password?"

"Dear me, what is today's word? Oh, yes—'figs.'"

"Pass, friend."

The metal door opened and they went into Clarence Mustard's secret office.

Tom didn't know what he had expected—an army ops room, maybe, or a wizard's cave hung with cobwebs. He hadn't expected this cozy sitting room full of flowery sofas, with a big round table laid for tea. Tom caught smells of toast and warm cake, and he and Pindar made faces at each other to show how hungry they were.

"This is more like it!" Lorna plumped down in one of the soft chairs. "He's hiding out in the middle of a mountain, but he knows how to make things snug. I'm starting to think my uncle Clarence must be quite a decent sort!"

"Thank you," said a deep voice.

Tom nearly jumped out of his skin. A tall, thin man with close-cropped white hair was suddenly standing beside the tea table. Where had he come from?

"You're my niece, Lorna Mustard."

"Y-yes . . . ," stammered Lorna.

"How very nice to meet you; I'm sorry we haven't met before. Your father and I had a bit of a falling-out over the affair at Quong."

Tom couldn't stop staring. Clarence Mustard was very, very old, with skin like cracked leather. Yet his bright-blue eyes were young and sharp. He had a way of looking at you like a spider sizing up a fly.

"Agent Twenty-Three reporting!" Iris said importantly.

"Hello, Iris. How are you?"

"I'm ready to give my report on the nude ball."

"Oh, that can wait." Clarence's piercing eyes fixed on Tom and Pindar. "Well, well, the Harding demisprite—and you seem to have brought me a runaway Falconer."

"Something wonderful has happened," Terence told him. "This runaway Falconer is none other than my dear boy Pindar—not dead after all! And he's just told me he wants to join us!"

175

"Indeed?"

Pindar's face turned red. "If you'll have me."

"Your father is Tiberius Falconer," Clarence said sternly, "the most corrupt and evil member of a corrupt and evil family. Your mother is Dolores Harding Falconer—and I can't think how a nice family like the Hardings ever came to produce such a frightful woman."

"But I'm not like them!" Pindar said fiercely. "What's more, I've never been like them—Terence will tell you. I'm different."

"I can see that," Clarence said. "I've been expecting someone like you for a very long time."

"Er . . . sorry?" Pindar was puzzled. "Did you know I was going to run away?"

"My boy, I know the ancient prophecy: *One Good Falconer shall come / To kick the others up the bum!* The message in the stars is that the One Good Falconer is here at last. You must be him, the one who will lead the Realm after his family's downfall."

"ME?" Pindar was horrified.

"Steady on," Terence said. "Pindar's the best boy in the world, but I don't think he's cut out for that sort of job."

"And Pindar can't stay in the Realm," Tom said boldly. "We've already decided he's coming to live in the mortal world with me."

"Thanks, Tom," Pindar said.

Clarence was not annoyed by the interruption. He smiled down at Tom, and his piercing eyes were kind. "Welcome, Tom. You've decided, have you?"

"He's my cousin and he saved my life."

"You have your father's gift for friendship. Let's sit down before the tea gets cold." He sat down by the big silver teapot and began pouring tea.

Tom was incredibly hungry and it was some time before he could think about anything except eating. The food was brilliant—cakes, toast, muffins and sandwiches. He hoped Clarence would forget about this One Good Falconer business. Pindar belonged with him, and if his cousin had to stay in the Realm, the flat above the deli would seem horribly empty when all this was over.

Clarence Mustard ate nothing, but kept up polite tea-party conversation. He introduced himself to Dahlia, and recommended his own magi-manicurist ("She's a miracle worker!"). He asked Lorna about Mustard Manor ("Dear old house! Does the back door still stick?").

When everyone except Lorna had stopped eating, he said, "Now we'd better think how to get you all home. It really isn't safe here—why on earth did you come?"

"We had to steal Milly's body as evidence," Dahlia said. "I'm Jonas's lawyer."

"Ah, you're defending him, are you?"

"Yes, I qualified as a fairy lawyer just before I ran off with my first husband."

"Prepare yourself for some bad news," Clarence said. "He's going to be tried under Rule Four."

Tom had no idea what he was talking about, but Lorna gasped through a mouthful of jam tart, and Pindar muttered, "Oh no!"

"It means," Clarence said, "that if Jonas is condemned to death, his lawyer will be killed with him."

"Thank you, darling," Dahlia said coolly. "I know what it means."

"Nobody would expect you to take such a risk. If you want to drop out, we'll quite understand."

Everyone looked at Dahlia. Tom hardly dared to breathe. This was the godmother he was least sure about—there was a decidedly selfish side to Dahlia— but she was very clever, and if she did drop out, who would defend his dad in court?

"Oh, I'm not dropping out," Dahlia said, giving Tom a much kinder smile than usual. "Nobody's going to be killed. I'm in it to win it—that cow Dolores is about to get the bum-kicking of her miserable life!"

"Hooray!" yelled Pindar and Lorna.

"Thanks," Tom said. "My dad hasn't got anyone else to speak up for him."

"It won't be an easy job," Clarence said. "But Jonas told me how clever you are, Dahlia. He has the greatest faith in all his son's godmothers."

"You've seen him!" Tom cried.

"Yes, we met just before his arrest."

"Was he OK?" Tom's chest felt tight.

"He's in excellent health," Clarence said. "He's being very well fed in prison because the trial's going to be televised and they want him to look fat."

"I saw him too," Terence said, pouring more hot water into the teapot. "He was hiding with some cousins of mine."

"But . . . I thought Dad was hiding with a colony of bats!"

"Yes," Terence said. "My cousins—on my mother's side."

"Terence is a demifur," Pindar said helpfully.

"What's that?"

"I'm a demi, just like you," Terence said. "My father was a fairy—though sadly not nearly such a nice fairy as yours—and my mother was a bat."

"Oh." Now he understood why Terence's face looked odd; he was half-bat. This was the nearest Tom had ever been to having a conversation with an animal.

"It must sound very strange to a mortal," Clarence said. "You see, Tom, us fairies are able to change ourselves into certain animals. Sometimes, a disguised fairy falls in love with an animal, and they produce a half-animal, half-fairy."

"We can choose which one to live as," Terence said. "Most of us choose our fairy side—I'd be the first to admit a bat's life is rather limited. When I was in college, however, I chose to live full-time as a bat."

"Of course!" cried Lorna. "Sorry I didn't remember you—but you weren't called Terence in those days, were you?"

"I used my bat name, but Jonas couldn't pronounce it, so he called me—"

"SQUEAKY!" cried Dahlia. "Now I know you!"

"You still owe me money," Iris said. She was looking at Terence as if he were a bad smell under her little dinosaur nose. "Why did you want to live as a bat, anyway?"

Terence sighed. "I decided I hated my fairy side. I never met my father—he was just a drunken lout who changed himself into a bat for a laugh, and tricked my poor young mother into falling in love with him. Some fairies"—he glanced at Iris—"are very unkind about demifurs. Jonas was never like that."

"No." Iris sniffed. "He had the most extraordinary collection of friends."

"Thanks for helping him," Tom said.

Terence smiled, but he was serious. "Your father is a great man, Tom. He left the Realm because he couldn't stand the wickedness. He didn't want to live in a place where demifurs were treated like dirt. It was Jonas's daring escape, on the night before his wedding to poor old Milly, that inspired me to join Clarence."

"We never found out who helped him," Iris said. "I bet it was you."

"Me? I always thought it was you!"

"We don't have time for arguments about the past," Clarence said. "There's still the problem of getting you all back to the mortal world. I was going to smuggle you over the border, but it's too risky. You'll have to go through our special escape hole in the membrane. If you've all had enough to eat, I suggest we set off."

Tom was rested now, and full of food, as he and Pindar straightened each other's wings.

"The Realm's great," Tom told Pindar, "but it's dangerous. I'm looking forward to being back in the mortal world."

"Me too," Pindar said. "I like the mortal world. The light's so soft and peaceful, and nobody's trying to kill me."

"If you come to live with us," Tom said impulsively, "will you miss all the magic?"

Pindar lowered his voice. "No—I was never very good at magic, and I'm allergic to most of it anyway."

"And—and you're not going to stay to be the One Good Falconer, are you?"

"I don't think Clarence will want me when he finds out about my record," Pindar said, and they both laughed.

The escape hole in the membrane was near the summit of Hopping Hill. Ten strong men in masks carried Milly's glass coffin, and the others followed it along steep, winding paths through the thick forest. It was a long walk, through darkness that somehow felt and smelled different from the darkness at home.

After nearly an hour of solid climbing, they reached a flat clearing. Tom's legs were tired and he would have loved to rest, but Terence called, "Time to hand over the coffin, lads!" And before he had a chance to sit down, Tom was back at his place by Milly's feet.

"We'd better make for Mustard Manor," Lorna said. "I had it double-sealed to hide from my ex-husband."

"One day," said Dahlia, "when we're not fleeing for our lives, remind me to ask you what on earth that genie did to you. Tom—hold very tight, this won't be easy for you. We're about to enter the mortal world through an illegal tear in the membrane."

He was alarmed. "I won't disintegrate, will I?"

"No, but it's a lot harder than going the legal way, and I'm not a hundred percent sure you'll be able to stand the cold, though it won't last long—oof, this wretched thing's heavy!"

"Good luck!" called Terence. "And if you see Jonas

before I do, tell him the Hoppers of Hopping Hill are right behind him!"

Tom was finding the flying spell easier every time; it had sunk into his memory like riding a bike. Tired as he was, he gabbled out the words and snapped his fingers (very awkward when you were hefting a coffin), and they rose slowly into the air.

There was a tremendous ripping sound, loud as a clap of thunder, and a feeling like being sucked down a giant plughole. Tom was suddenly bitterly cold—the coldest he had ever been. His hair turned to ice, his fingers stuck to Milly's coffin and his teeth froze together in his mouth. It was agony.

But Dahlia was right; the freezing didn't last long. There was a sudden gust of warmth, so delicious that it took Tom several minutes to notice they were flying again. There were no sirens, no shouts, no police. They were cruising in the warm darkness, above a carpet of orange lights. The air smelled of gasoline, grass, summer, mortal cooking and HOME.

They circled slowly over Lorna's scrapyard, and Tom thought the broken trucks were absolutely beautiful—the ordinariness of the mortal world had never looked so good. Hector barked a loud welcome.

"Phew!" said Lorna. "I haven't had a cup of proper mortal tea in days! And I can't wait to put down this blooming coffin!"

"Achoo! Achoo!" Pindar sneezed violently.

The coffin jolted as Tom lost his grip.

"ARRRGH!" screamed all three godmothers.

The glass coffin had dropped onto the concrete and shattered into a thousand pieces.

16

The Adored

Tom, Pindar and the godmothers hovered for a moment in horrified silence, before landing one by one on the carpet of broken glass in front of Lorna's disguised house. The body lay in a heap of glittery white material—Tom didn't want to look at the ghastly thing, but couldn't help it.

"She'll go moldy now that she's been exposed to air," Iris said. "We'd better put her in the freezer."

Tom shuddered at this—but it was nothing compared to the shock that hit him next.

The corpse sat up.

Milly Falconer brushed bits of broken glass off her

dress. "Hello," she said. "Where am I? Are there any more of those crab pastries?"

"I told you Tom's mother was right," siad Dahlia. "For a mortal, she's really quite intelligent. It's Snow White all over again!" She added, "Hello, Milly."

"You were poisoned," Iris said. "And you've spent the last fifteen years in a glass coffin."

Tom made himself take a couple of deep breaths. He was getting used to weird and scary sights, but seeing a corpse sit up and talk was truly incredible. In dumb amazement he watched while Pindar and Lorna helped the stout, dazed fairy to her feet. There, in the middle of the scrapyard, stood the famous Milly Falconer, in her huge white dress and glittering wings, with the dingy orange light catching at the jewels in her crown.

She stared round at them all in absolute bafflement. "Who are you? Will someone call my flying coach? And what's the point of all these broken mortal machines? Is this a new kind of theme party?"

"Keep calm, Milly," Iris said soothingly. "Your memory's still a bit dodgy."

"There's nothing wrong with my memory! And who are you, anyway? You look very much like my flatmate from college—only years older! Are you her mother?"

Iris frowned. "I AM Iris Moth! And I'm trying to tell you that you've missed the past fifteen years!"

"Iris? What happened to you? How did you get so wrinkled? I was at a nude ball—why am I wearing the dress I bought for my wedding?"

Milly thought she was still at the ball where she had been poisoned. Tom felt sorry for her—it must be tough, suddenly waking up to find you've missed the past fifteen years. How would he feel if he woke up thinking he was still eleven, and Charlie was twenty-six?

"You'll feel better when you've had a nice cup of tea," Lorna said, searching through her big bunch of keys. "I know I could MURDER one—whoops—sorry, Milly."

"Lorna Mustard!" cried Milly. "How's dear old Abdul?"

Lorna frowned. "We're divorced."

"Divorced? You and Abdul? But you adored that genie! What on earth happened?"

Tom would have liked to hear the answer to this, but Lorna shook her head. "I'd rather not tell you exactly what he did, if you don't mind. Let's just say we were—incompatible."

"Achoo!"

The sneeze made Milly look sharply round at Pindar, seeing him in the dim light for the first time. "Jonas?"

It was very strange, the way people kept looking at Pindar and seeing Dad.

"Don't be daft," Lorna said. "Jonas is as old as the rest

of us. This is his nephew, Pindar Falconer. I'll explain what he's doing here when I've made us all some tea."

"He's your nephew too," Tom said. "His dad's your brother Tiberius."

Milly looked at Tom and cried, "Great garters—another Jonas lookalike! Who are you, boy? You're no fairy!"

"I'm a demisprite," Tom said proudly. "Jonas Harding is my father."

"Your fa— Garters and gussets! I'm in shock! How old are you?"

"Eleven."

"And you—" She turned back to Pindar. "I'm amazed that my brother and his wife finally managed to have a baby—I thought nothing in the whole Realm would lift that curse!"

"You have a lot of catching up to do," Dahlia said. "Let's go inside."

"Dahlia Pease-Blossom!" Milly did not look pleased to see her. "Well, well. Are you sure it's healthy to be that thin?"

"Milly, darling, you haven't changed!" The way Dahlia said this made Tom feel it wasn't a compliment.

Across the yard Hector let out a series of sharp barks. Lorna, unlocking Mustard Manor, barked something back. "Nothing to worry about—he's just reminding me to pick up my mail. I'll do it later. Do come in, Milly."

"What—into this horrid little hut? Oh, my mistake—it's a magic house. Didn't I come here for your wedding reception?"

"Tom," Lorna said, "leave us old fairies to bring Milly up to date. Take Pindar up to Uncle Clarence's room."

Tom suspected she wanted them out of the way, but he didn't care. He was eager to show Clarence's old bedroom to his cousin. For Pindar, it was like entering a museum. He walked around slowly, examining each object one by one. Being a fairy, he could explain a lot of things that had puzzled Tom.

"That's a very old-fashioned diagram of a flying coach. They're more streamlined nowadays. My first job after Terence left was driving one." Pindar grinned suddenly. "Total disaster, of course."

"Don't tell me—you sneezed?"

"Yep. I was allergic to the weightless paint they use on the chassis. Nobody was hurt, but I wrecked nine coaches." They both laughed.

"What about this?" Tom picked up a long fossilized bone from the top of the chest of drawers. "Is it a dinosaur bone?"

"No, it's a dragon's."

"A dragon's? Seriously? I thought dragons were just made up."

"You thought fairies were made up too," Pindar

reminded him. "Dragons are extinct now, but they definitely existed once. That's where we get the design for our wings."

"So they died out, like the dinosaurs? What happened to them?"

"Terence said they were hunted to death—in the olden days fairies used real dragons' wings. Thousands of dragons died every time they raised an army." Pindar added, "It's great to know that he's all right."

"He's really nice." Tom knew how much Terence meant to Pindar—far more than his evil parents did. "And it was amazing to meet a demifur—nobody mortal would believe it. We—I mean mortals—are quite horrible to animals."

"It's a bit better for them in the Realm," Pindar said, folding up his wings, "but not much. Fairies think animals are lower class. Most of them work as servants in return for food."

"I suppose that's more or less the same as here," Tom said, "if they're farm animals. But what about wild animals, or really tiny creatures—like rats and mice?"

"They can work too, but they mostly live wild. There's a lot of trouble with gangs of rats—they're behind most of the organized crime in the Realm. My father's always cracking down on them, but he never manages to wipe them out."

"Are the animals in the Realm sort of fairy animals?"

"No—there's nothing magic about them, unless they're demifurs like Terence. But animals are a lot cleverer than mortals think."

"We can't talk to them," Tom said. "Maybe that's the problem. You're so lucky that you can—if I could talk to an animal, I could make friends with it, like your dad did with Terence. Do you have any friends who're animals?"

"Well, I used to have some great pet lizards. And I did get quite close to one of the elephants at the circus," Pindar said. "She was the one who told me the rumor that Terence had escaped."

"Oh." It was odd to think about hearing a rumor from an elephant. "Maybe you could teach me how to talk to my cat, when you come to live at the deli."

"Look, Tom—I'd love to live with you," said Pindar. "I'd love it so much that I hardly dare to hope for it. But we haven't asked your parents."

"I know they'll say yes." Tom was very confident about this. How could they say no? Now that he had found Pindar, he refused to think of letting him go. And surely nobody would expect Pindar to be the One Good Falconer if he didn't want to. "Let's see if they've finished briefing Milly about all the terrible changes."

Downstairs in the kitchen Milly sat at the table, eating chocolate biscuits and dabbing at her eyes with a lace handkerchief. "Hello, boys—Iris, please tell me more about my Adorers. Did you see any of their faces?"

The three godmothers looked embarrassed.

Iris said, "We definitely saw Derek Drapton."

"Dear, faithful Derek!" sighed Milly. "What about Brian Flitting? Was he there?"

"He got married a couple of years back," Lorna said.

"Oh. Well, what about Hamish Ptarmigan?"

"He's married too," Dahlia said. "To his fourth wife."

"Christopher Trout? Any of the Boot brothers?"

"Well . . . no," Lorna said. "The fact is, as we keep trying to tell you, things have changed."

"I haven't," Milly said. "I'm not nearly as wrinkled as you three. I suppose now that I've woken up I should marry one of my Adorers—it seems only fair. Is there anything else to eat?"

Far away in the gatehouse, Hector barked twice.

Lorna stood up. "He says the food's here—I ordered us a mortal Indian takeaway."

She went out to pay for the food and fetch her mail, and Tom and Pindar helped Iris to set the table. Dahlia made a jug of a cocktail called Rheingold Rocket (mostly orange juice and Kaulquappe, as far as Tom could see) and there was ordinary Coke in the fridge for the boys. The huge white skirt of Milly's wedding dress billowed around her chair and it was hard not to tread on it— particularly for Pindar.

"Great garters, boy—stop trampling on my gown!" Milly snapped the fourth or fifth time it happened. "You might not look like my hideous brother, but you've certainly inherited his gigantic feet!"

"Sorry."

"I think you should call me Auntie Milly."

"OK . . . er . . . Auntie Milly."

Milly looked closely at Pindar. "You know, you remind me of someone else—but who? Someone in my family who had gigantic feet and was always sneezing—oh, my memory's in as many pieces as my coffin! Perhaps food will help."

It wasn't long since tea, but maybe food eaten inside the Realm didn't count, because Tom was starving again and the Indian food was wonderful. They all ate enormously, especially Milly.

"Mortal food is so yummy!" she sighed. "Somehow, food inside the Realm never tastes quite so delicious!"

"You should meet my late husband Mr. Ghopal," Dahlia said. "He makes a terrific saag aloo."

Now that he was full, Tom realized how tired he was. What a day he'd had, and he couldn't even remember when it began. He and Pindar both kept yawning till their eyes watered.

"I'll make you boys some cocoa, and then you can go to bed," said Lorna. "Pindar can have the camp bed in Tom's room. Dahlia and Iris, you can sleep in the two rooms at the back—please don't open the windows, or there'll be no hot water tomorrow. Milly, you'd better have my mother's old room at the front. It's got a lovely four-poster bed, if you don't mind a bit of woodworm."

"But I've only just woken up!" Milly said crossly. "I'm not going straight back to sleep!"

Iris refilled the godmothers' glasses with Kaulquappe. "I'm in the mood to stay up for a bit." She had relaxed, Tom thought; her hair wasn't so stiff, and her little T. rex eyes were sparkling. "Tell you what, who's up for a game of electric poker?"

"Good idea," Milly said. "How many volts?"

"Count me in," Dahlia said with one of her wicked smiles. "I warn you, I can take a lot of electricity—it's going to cost you! Are you in, Lorna?"

"No." Lorna was frowning. "I don't hold with gambling. And don't you dare start playing that stupid game before Tom's safely out of the room!"

She made the cocoa in a huffy way, while the other godmothers set up their game of cards—didn't the old bags ever sleep? Tom wondered. Iris shuffled cards as Dahlia set out bowls of chips and nuts.

Lorna, helped by Tom and Pindar, dragged an old dusty camp bed from the cupboard under the stairs. The three of them managed to heft it up to Clarence's old bedroom, and once Lorna had put on sheets and blankets, it looked really comfortable.

"Sleep well, you two," Lorna said. "I'm not one for making fancy speeches—but you were both brilliant today. Good night!"

Climbing into bed felt wonderful. Tom waited for the wave of sleep to crash over him. He was glad to be back in the safety of Mustard Manor, with Hector guarding the scrapyard outside. He was on the point of falling asleep, when . . .

"ARRRGH!" A tremendous scream rang out downstairs.

Tom sat bolt upright in bed, his heart thudding. "What was that?"

Pindar sleepily raised himself on one elbow. "It's the electric poker. You see, if you don't want to bet money, you can agree to be electrocuted if you lose."

"But—but—doesn't it kill them?"

"They're a lot tougher than mortals."

"ARRRGH!" Another terrible scream rang out downstairs.

"That's Iris—she's either losing, or she's very mean."

They both chuckled over this, and Tom immediately started dreaming.

It was a warm afternoon in summer, and he was standing beside a shallow pond, gazing at a man in a horse-drawn cart, and a pretty cottage surrounded by trees. His mother sat in a wicker chair with a cup of tea. She wore a flowered dress and looked very happy.

"Hi, Mum." In the dream, they were not at all surprised to see each other.

"Hello, Tom. If you see your dad, tell him I've moved, but he's not to worry—I'm safe and sound in one of my table mats."

"OK," said Tom. He didn't ask her what she meant, and just fell deeper into a dreamless sleep.

17

Mothers

Early the next morning Lorna went out to the super-market. By the time Tom and Pindar came down-stairs, there was a big mortal fried breakfast of eggs and bacon sizzling in the kitchen. For a second Tom thought there was a stranger at the table, but it was Milly, wear-ing one of Lorna's blue jumpsuits. It looked a bit odd because she was still wearing all her jewelry, but it was a relief not to have to walk around her huge white dress.

When they had all (even Lorna and Milly) finished eating, Iris cleared herself a space on the table among all the dirty plates and took her little notebook out of her handbag. "Right, Milly. Let's have another crack at your memory."

"Oh dear, it's no use. All I can remember is arriving at the ball, taking off all my clothes and putting on my jewels." Milly patted her crown. "The very jewels I'm wearing now—aren't they splendid?"

"Paste," said Dahlia.

"What?"

"They're false, darling."

"Don't be ridiculous! These are the finest jewels in the Realm!"

Taking a jeweler's eyeglass out of her pocket, Iris snatched one of Milly's wrists and looked closely at her bracelet. "She's right—these are fakes."

"FAKES?"

Tom thought Milly seemed more shocked by this than by anything else. "Perhaps one of the Adorers nicked the real ones?" he suggested.

"My Adorers would never do such a thing!" Milly snapped.

"It was probably my father," said Pindar. "He made my mother sell her moon-diamonds."

"But . . . But why would Tiberius do that? He's rich!"

"Not anymore. The Realm's falling apart." He looked round at them all. "Didn't any of you wonder why none of the police managed to kill us? Half their lightning bolts are blanks. They have to rent their own guns and take turns with the helmets."

"You'd better prepare yourself for a shock, Milly old

girl," said Lorna. "These days the Realm is blooming chaos!" She picked up her pile of mail from the previous day and began shuffling through the envelopes and catalogs. "Hello—what's this?"

She held up a brown padded envelope with something hard and heavy inside it. "I wasn't expecting any parcels!"

"Achoo!" sneezed Pindar.

"Careful!" Iris pulled out her lightning-gun. "If Pindar sneezed, that means it's magic."

Tom edged round the corner of the table, bracing himself for an explosion.

Lorna opened the padded envelope with trembling hands and took out a small, stumpy black bottle. "OW!" She dropped it on the floor. "It's burning hot!"

The cork popped out of the bottle and the kitchen filled with purple smoke. A moment later the smoke had pulled itself into the outline of a short, fat man in a turban.

"Abdul!" cried Lorna. "Good grief—what happened to you?"

Her ex-husband was blackened and scorched, and his clothes were smoking as if he had just been plucked off a barbecue.

"My cafe!" He was breathless. "My beautiful cafe—they have burned it to the ground!"

Lorna turned so deathly pale that her lips were

gray. "The jar!" She grabbed Abdul's singed satin tunic. "For pity's sake—where's the jar of sun-dried tomatoes?"

Tom couldn't understand why she was in a state about a stupid jar of tomatoes. "Don't—he might be hurt! Are you OK, Abdul?"

"Yes, I'm fine." Abdul caught his breath and took Lorna's hand. "And the jar is safe, my flower."

"Where? Where did you put it?"

"Hussein took it. He was arrested—but not before he hid the jar somewhere extremely safe." Despite the fact that his turban was smoldering, the genie looked dignified. "Those Falconers destroyed my cafe, but they didn't get what they came for!"

"Blimey, you gave me a nasty turn!" Lorna's face turned back to its normal color. "Poor old Hussein! I was so wrong about him—he risked his life to save that jar!"

"I wish I knew what's so special about those tomatoes," Tom said impatiently. "You've been fussing about them since we left the deli!"

"You might as well know the truth," Iris said briskly. "I suppose Lorna didn't tell you because she didn't want to worry you. The fact is one of the tomatoes in that jar is your mother."

"What? What do you mean?" Tom thought he was used to shocks by now, but this was like a punch in the stomach. He turned to Lorna, so stunned that he could hardly get the words out. "You turned my mum into a . . . a sun-dried tomato?"

"I had to think fast," Lorna said unhappily. "I didn't want to scare the poor woman, and I knew the Falconers would be after her. So I put her to sleep, shrinking and hiding her in the nearest thing I could find, which was that jar of tomatoes."

"But—did it hurt her?"

"No!" Lorna put one hand on Tom's shoulder. "I swear, Tom—please believe me! It's an old genie trick that Abdul taught me—I had no idea they'd find him and burn down his cafe!"

"So where is she?" It was truly horrible to think of his innocent mortal mother being tortured by Falconers. "You said Hussein hid her?"

"Yes, my brother got wind of the attack a few minutes before it happened. There was just enough time for him to save the jar, put me in a Jiffy bag and mail me here." Abdul took a few more deep breaths and plumped down on the sofa. "What a day!"

"Hello, Abdul," said Milly.

Now it was Abdul's turn to be shocked. "Milly—Milly Falconer? Is this a dream?"

The three godmothers and Milly all began explaining at once, until Tom's head swam, but somehow they

201

managed to bring Abdul up to date. Lorna made him a mug of tea (very strong genie tea, with two tea bags and condensed milk), and he told them about the attack on his cafe.

"There I was, just wiping down the counter—and in comes Hussein, shouting about a Falconer raid—oh, we were all in an uproar—genies falling over each other and crashing through windows—Hussein grabbed the jar and told us all to get out—we turned ourselves to smoke and took cover wherever we could—Cassim hid in the tea urn—and then a huge ball of fire came shooting in from the top of a passing 134 bus, and everything was smoke and flames."

"Didn't the police notice anything?" Tom asked. "The mortal police, I mean."

"The mortals thought it was a gas explosion," Abdul said. "Thanks to Hussein, nobody was hurt."

"Your brother is a very brave genie," Milly said. "If he's single, I might marry him."

"Hang on," Lorna said. "Don't forget poor old Derek Drapton—he's been your Chief Adorer since the Chapel was built!"

"Oh yes," Milly said vaguely. "But does he still have those spindly legs?"

"Excuse me—but WHERE did Hussein take my mother?" Tom couldn't believe they were all chatting about Milly's Adorers while his mother's life was in danger. "And shouldn't we go and get her? I mean, wouldn't she be safer with us?"

"Shh!" Lorna was suddenly still. "Listen—that's Hector!"

Across the yard Hector's loud bark grew louder, and ended in a kind of roar.

"INTRUDER!" yelled Lorna. "Action stations!" She grabbed the first weapon she could find—a big soup ladle—and ran out of the room like a tornado.

Iris and Dahlia had cooler heads. They quickly armed themselves with their lightning-guns before dashing out of the room after her.

"What's going on?" cried Milly, wobbling on her white satin heels (which looked odd with her borrowed jumpsuit).

Even in high heels, fairies and genies can run a lot faster than mortals—unnaturally fast, like speeded-up film. Tom had no hope of keeping up. Pindar, Abdul and Milly streaked past him as he sprinted as fast as he could out of Mustard Manor and through the twisted remains of trucks and vans.

The gatehouse was a small wooden building, not much more than a hut, beside the big metal gate of the scrapyard. White light flashed inside it, as if someone had filled it with fireworks. Tom heard shots and screams—Lorna's voice yelling, "Bog off out of my scrap-yard, whoever you are!"

A tall figure dressed in a fairy police uniform ran out of the gatehouse, leaping into the air. Lorna was right behind it, and gave its leg a whack with her ladle. Dahlia fired a bolt of lightning, but the intruder whizzed off into the gray summer sky and was swallowed by a cloud.

There was an eerie silence while they all recovered from the shock.

Tom looked inside the gatehouse. Everything was scorched and smoldering, and there was a huge hole burnt in the front of Pindar's T-shirt.

"Pindar, are you OK?"

"It's only my shirt."

"Help me up!" Milly lay on her back on the floor, with her white satin shoes sticking in the air, as the two boys ran over to help her up.

"Hector! Where are you? Hector!" Lorna looked around frantically. "What has that fiend done to my dog?"

Tom heard a scraping, scuffling sound near his feet. Down on the floor a scrap of paper moved, and a small mouse hopped onto his sneaker. But it wasn't a mouse—when Tom picked up the little creature, he saw that it was Lorna's Rottweiler, shrunk so small that his barks were squeaks.

"Oh, you poor thing, I'll put you right at once." Lorna

took him outside in the palm of her hand, set him carefully down on the concrete and mumbled a spell. Hector instantly grew to the size of a cart horse.

"Allow me," said Dahlia, turning the startled dog back to his proper size.

"Thanks," Lorna said. "If he stayed that big, I could never afford to feed him. Where's Iris?"

Tom glanced round, seeing for the first time that Iris wasn't with them.

"My shoes are killing me," Milly said. "I must sit down." She started to sit down on the only chair.

"NO!" Pindar yelled suddenly, pulling the chair away from under her.

"OW!" Milly's bottom landed heavily on the floor. "What do you think you're doing?"

"Sorry, Auntie Milly but look!"

On the seat of the chair lay a little doll—no, it was Iris, shrunk to the size of a little doll and lying very still. Milly had nearly sat on her.

"Good thing you saw her, darling," Dahlia said, giving Pindar a smile that made him turn red. "Poor old Iris—she'd have been as flat as a pancake!"

"Is she OK?" asked Tom.

"Just stunned." Dahlia snapped her fingers and there was a flash of intense blue light.

The normal-sized Iris stood up, briskly wiping dust off her skirt. "Thank you. Was anyone killed?"

"I think we're all OK," Tom said. "Oh—I don't see Abdul."

"He's probably hiding somewhere," said Lorna. "You can come out now!"

Purple smoke seeped out of one of the drawers in the desk, and the rather sheepish genie appeared—he really was a bit of a wimp. "I thought we were all going to die! How did they find us?"

"I can't imagine," Dahlia said. "But we're not safe here."

They all trooped back to Mustard Manor. The godmothers were very serious and quiet, and Tom was afraid. If they weren't safe here, where could they go?

"I think we all need another cup of tea," Milly said. "I'll make it." She bustled about in Lorna's kitchen, making tea and putting Jaffa Cakes on a plate. Tom had thought this semiroyal fairy was a bit spoiled, but she suddenly seemed nice. She patted Lorna kindly on the shoulder. "Chin up, old thing! It's not so bad!"

"Yes, it is." Lorna was very gloomy. "If Tiberius gets Tom or his mother, our case will be ruined."

"If only you could remember what happened, Milly!" Iris said. "You must've seen who poisoned you!"

"Sorry, it's only coming back in little bits. I was at the ball . . . I danced with Derek . . . he asked me to marry him again—that's it."

"We must go back to Hopping Hill," said Dahlia. "The

Falconers know we're here now. It's only a matter of time before they send someone even more dangerous. Iris, can you get a message to Clarence?"

Tom had the cold feeling he got when he didn't know if Dahlia was basically a good fairy or a bad one. "What about my mum? We can't go without her! We can't just leave her alone in the mortal world!"

Dahlia's chilly eyes swiveled towards him. "Drat, I suppose not—my case will certainly be a lot stronger if we have her AND you."

"But I'm afraid it's quite impossible," Iris said (as usual sounding rather pleased, Tom thought). "The three of us are marked fairies now. If we try to rescue her, they'll just follow us."

"Let me rescue her," said Tom.

"Are you CRAZY?" groaned Lorna. "They'd spot you in a second and vaporize the pair of you—and then what would I say to your father?"

"I know they're after me—but they think I look like a bald chimp! It's got to be worth a try!"

"Quite mad!" said Iris, with a smirk.

"I'll go," Pindar said loudly.

Everyone turned to look at him, and his face became as red as Dahlia's lipstick, but he was frowning with determination. "I'm officially dead, so nobody's marking me. I should be the one to rescue Tom's mum."

"I admire your spirit," Iris said, "but it's out of the question. Your magic isn't up to it."

"We have to take the risk!" Pindar was firm, and Tom felt a bit less scared and hopeless.

Could the accident-prone Pindar really rescue Mum?

"Ahem." Abdul cleared his throat (he had been very quiet since they caught him hiding in the desk drawer). "My carpet is at the bottom of that bottle. I could fly Pindar to the hiding place—it's Hussein's house in Holloway."

"Oh, I know!" Lorna cried. "24 Pickle Grove, N7! I'm still sending him Christmas cards."

"I've been to Holloway," Tom said. "There's a big cinema; it's not that far from my house—let me go with him. I know my way around better than Pindar does."

All three godmothers shook their heads.

Dahlia put her hand on Tom's shoulder, and her eyes were kind. "You're a very brave boy, Tom. Your father would be proud of you. But it would be crazy to let you go—a demisprite, fighting the forces of the Realm! I'm afraid you must come with us back to Hopping Hill. It's the best way you can help now."

Tom hung his head so she wouldn't see how close he was to crying with frustration.

"But I don't see why Pindar shouldn't go," she went on. "Thanks to his dip in the handsome-vat, nobody will recognize him."

"I know all the genie flight paths," Abdul said eagerly, "and the secret way into the Realm. Once Pindar has the jar of tomatoes, we will meet you at Hopping Hill."

"Hmm, I suppose it's worth a try." Iris sniffed.

"You're both jolly brave," Lorna said, smiling at Abdul.

"It's really nice of you," said Tom. "I wish I could come with you!"

"Well, you CAN'T!" Lorna said firmly. "It's no use arguing with me!"

Tom saw there wasn't any point in taking it further—but he hadn't given up. He kept quiet while Abdul shook his carpet out of the bottle and unrolled it on the strip of concrete outside Mustard Manor. He listened in silence while Lorna rumbled out instructions to Pindar about the mortal world. "You mustn't let them see you flying—or shrinking—you mustn't kill anyone—or drop litter—"

At the same time Iris was giving instructions about the magic. "If you smell burning mugwort, say the protection charm AT ONCE."

Pindar looked at Tom. "Sorry you can't come—but you know I'll do anything to save her."

"Thanks, Pindar." The two cousins hugged briefly and everyone went outside.

Pindar and Abdul sat down on the carpet. Abdul

209

began his incantation, and the carpet slowly began to rise off the ground.

Tom never knew what made him do it—but on a sudden impulse he flung himself at the carpet and grabbed the edge, just as it whisked away towards the clouds.

"TOM!" screamed all the godmothers. "COME BACK!"

Too late. He was already hundreds of feet above them, hanging by his fingers from the edge of a magic carpet.

18

Pickle Grove

This was scarier than holding on to the coffin, though Tom at least had his wings with him. They were currently tucked in his bag. He scrunched up his eyes, terrified he would fall. What have I done? I must be mad—I don't do brave stuff!

A hand grabbed the back of his belt. "Let go," Pindar said. "I've got you." He dragged Tom up onto the smooth, flat carpet. "Wow—you gave me a shock!"

"Sorry—I don't know what got into me. I just had to be on this mission."

"Lorna will blame me for this!" moaned Abdul. "I should turn straight back!"

"Please don't!"

"Let him come with us," Pindar said. "After all, it's his mother." He moved along the carpet, so that Tom had room to sit down beside Abdul. "Auntie Milly made me some cheese sandwiches—do you want one?"

"No, thanks," said Tom, shifting himself into a more comfortable position. It was a murky day down in the mortal world. He tried to work out where they were, but could see nothing below except a bank of thick gray cloud.

"Tom, please tell Lorna this wasn't my fault!" said Abdul.

"Of course I will. You'd like to get back together with her, wouldn't you?"

"Oh yes! I have known from the moment I saw her that Lorna Mustard was a queen amongst women. I was a mad fool to let her go. The fault was all mine. Do you think I still have a chance with her? Can she ever forgive me for the terrible thing I did that made her divorce me?"

"She wouldn't tell me what you did," Tom said. "Was it something really bad?"

"Yes, Tom, very bad indeed." The genie let out a deep, sorrowful sigh. "I . . . I sold her mother."

"You WHAT?"

"I put her to sleep and sold her at the genie slave market."

"Wow, Abdul—that really was a bad thing to do."

"I know!"

"What did you do with the money?"

"I bought a novelty horn for the carpet," Abdul said. "It plays the first few bars of 'My Desert Is Waiting.'" He snapped his fingers and a horn blared out a tune. "Lorna was furious."

"So was her mum, I'll bet." Tom didn't want to offend the kindly genie, but he really couldn't help laughing— no wonder Lorna found it so hard to forgive him.

"It's a good thing my father didn't know there was such a thing as a genie slave market," said Pindar, "or he would've sold Mother and me years ago."

"When the old lady woke up she had to buy herself back," Abdul said, "and she tried very hard to kill me. Lorna had to divorce me to save my life. But that was many years ago, and her mother has passed away. We could try again."

"I'm sure she still likes you," Tom said. "She's always going on about how handsome you are."

"IS she? Tom, you give me hope!" Abdul checked his watch. "Sit still, you two—we're starting our descent."

The carpet dropped down to the clouds, and it was like flying through a wet sponge; when they came out Tom's clothes were damp and his hair was dripping. They had landed on a scrubby patch of ground, strewn with rubbish, behind a high, sooty wall with broken glass along the top. After the serene silence above the clouds, the noise of traffic came as a shock—a busy road roared on the other side of the wall.

"This is Holloway Road." Abdul neatly rolled up the carpet and turned it into a puff of orange smoke. "I thought it would be best to do the last part of the journey on the bus, so that we can hide among the mortals. Come along."

"Abdul—hey, wait!" Tom grabbed his sleeve. "You can't go on a bus looking like that!"

He was still wearing his scorched genie costume. "Whoops, how foolish of me—thank goodness you remembered." Abdul's clothes suddenly changed into a normal, everyday shirt and trousers, and nobody looked twice when the three of them emerged into Holloway Road. There were hundreds of cars, and the pavements were crammed with people—mostly mums with buggies and old ladies with shopping trolleys.

The bus arrived, and Abdul made them stand near the doors. "It's only three stops, but I'm worried that my brother's house is being watched by Falconer spies."

Pickle Grove was a small street of terraced houses just off the main road. Tom thought it looked dull and shabby. It was completely deserted, except for a large tabby cat stretched out in a sunny patch on the pavement.

"I knew it!" squeaked Abdul. "They're lying in wait for us!"

"That's not a Falconer agent," Tom said. "It's just a cat."

"Are you sure?" The timid genie rang the bell of number 24.

Tom couldn't feel scared on such an ordinary London street, but Pindar was looking round sharply. "Who lives here?"

"Mrs. Baggs," said Abdul. "She's Hussein's tenant—very old and completely mortal, and she has no idea that her landlord is a genie. We must remember not to frighten her with magic."

Tom heard shuffling footsteps on the other side of the door. It was slowly opened by a stooped old lady with white hair and cloudy blue eyes. "Mr. Hussein? Oh—it's Mr. Abdul! How are you, dear?"

"Good afternoon, Mrs. Baggs," Abdul said politely. "I've just popped round with—er—my two nephews, to pick up something Hussein left here."

Mrs. Baggs gave a heavy sigh. "I'll tell you now, dear, unless you know what you're looking for, we'll get nowhere! As I said to the woman this morning."

"Woman?" Abdul gasped. "What woman?"

"I don't know who she was, dear. When I told her I hadn't a clue what Mr. Hussein had left here, she went off in a huff."

"What did she look like?"

215

"My eyes aren't so good," said Mrs. Baggs. "Quite young—but everyone looks young to me these days! Do come in and have a cup of tea."

Tom was glad to get inside the house. He didn't like the sound of that woman—who else would she be but a Falconer looking for his mother? Very luckily, she hadn't known his mother was hidden in a jar of tomatoes.

Mrs. Baggs led them down a dark, narrow passage, holding on to Abdul's arm. "I hope Mr. Hussein's all right—I haven't seen him for nearly a week."

The kitchen was small and old-fashioned, and a very good place to hide something. The shelves were crammed with packets, tins, jars and bottles and the cheerful yellow walls were covered with little pictures of animals wearing clothes. Among them was a big calendar with a picture on it that Tom had seen somewhere before—a swirly old painting of a cottage and a pond, and a man in a cart.

"Now," said Mrs. Baggs, switching on her kettle, "what exactly was it that Mr. Hussein left here? He only stayed for a minute."

"It's a jar of sun-dried tomatoes," Tom said.

"Eh? Sun-dried what? I've got a tin of tomatoes, would they do?"

Tom was starting to worry, but Abdul suddenly cried, "There!" He reached up to a crowded shelf beside the stove and grabbed at something. "Got it!"

216

"Oh yes," said Mrs. Baggs. "My granddaughter brought me back a lot of funny food from her holiday in Cyprus."

Abdul held the jar up to the light. "Thank goodness! Let's take this back to Hopping Hill as fast as we can!"

"Hopping where?" asked Mrs. Baggs. "Is that near Archway?"

Tom was distracted by something moving on Abdul's shoulder—a ladybug, which was crawling down his sleeve. While he watched it, smoke began to rise from underneath its tiny body and a tiny jet of flame shot out.

"OUCH!" yelped Abdul.

He flicked the ladybug off. It hit the floor—and there was a loud BANG that knocked Tom off his feet.

Where the ladybug had landed, there now stood a tall, thin woman with long black hair, dressed all in black leather.

"D-Dolores Falconer!" squeaked Abdul. "We are lost!"

Tom stood up on legs that wobbled with fear. He had never met a truly wicked person before. The darkness he saw in Dolores's face was all the more horrible because she looked like Dad.

"Thank you!" She snatched the jar of tomatoes from Abdul.

"No!" Tom shouted desperately.

Dolores turned her wicked eyes towards him. "What

have we here? How very convenient—my brother's mortal hussy AND his demisprite spawn!"

"Put it down," Pindar said. He was pointing his lightning-gun at Dolores. "Achoo!"

She spun round sharply. "Who are you? Your sneeze is familiar—"

"I'm your son, Pindar—and if you don't put that jar down, I'll kill you; I don't care if you are my mother!" He held the gun steady, aiming at her head.

Dolores burst into a ghastly laugh. "I'M NOT YOUR MOTHER!"

She held up the jar of tomatoes mockingly for a second, before vanishing into thin air.

"Who was that? Isn't she staying for tea?" said Mrs. Baggs.

"This is a disaster!" whispered Abdul. "How was I to know she could change herself into a ladybug? Tom—I can't tell you how sorry I am! Oh, this is dreadful!"

Tom drew a long, shaky breath. He felt better. The bad fairy had gone, and he had seen the jar. He patted Abdul's shoulder. "It's OK—she took the wrong one."

"Wh-what?" Abdul gasped.

"That wasn't my mum's jar. Hers has a black top, and that one was green. And there's a different picture on the label."

"Really? Truly?" Abdul clutched Tom's hand. "Oh, joy! That means the magic jar is still here!"

Pindar was very pale. "Did you hear her? She said she's not my mother."

Tom didn't know what to say. On one hand, it was surely a good thing if the nasty Dolores was not Pindar's real mother. On the other hand, it would mean that he wasn't Tom's cousin anymore, or Dad's nephew—and that might stop him coming to live with them.

"Sit down, dear," said Mrs. Baggs. "You look as if you've seen a ghost!"

She gave them all mugs of strong tea and opened a packet of ginger biscuits; delicious and comforting if you've just been frightened out of your wits.

"I will make a proper search of the shelves and cupboards as soon as my knees have stopped trembling," said Abdul.

"If she's not my mother," Pindar said, "I wonder who is. It must be one of my father's mistresses—he has hundreds of them."

"Perhaps Dolores was lying," Tom suggested.

"It feels true."

"Then how come you look like my dad?"

"I don't know." Pindar hung his head. "I don't seem to belong to anyone."

"You still belong to us," Tom said firmly. "I don't care if you're not my biological cousin."

Pindar smiled. "We'd better find that jar. Do you mind if we search, Mrs. Baggs?"

219

"No, dear, you go ahead."

Pindar, Tom and Abdul began to go through Mrs. Baggs's kitchen shelves, cupboards and fridge. They found every kind of jar—pickles, peanut butter, strawberry jam, mustard—but there was no sign of the sundried tomatoes.

"I don't understand it!" Abdul sighed. "I know he hid it here!"

They searched every corner of the kitchen for nearly an hour, and finally sat down for a rest and another cup of tea.

Tom was very tired, and very worried about his mum. He thought about her, and suddenly remembered his dream—could it mean something, like the first time she had sent him a dream-message?

"I had another dream about my mum," he told the others. "It sounds a bit mad—but she was right last time, so maybe it means something." Pindar and Abdul looked at him eagerly. "She said she was safe in one of her table mats."

There was a silence.

"Table mats?" Abdul echoed. "What have table mats got to do with anything?"

"I don't know." Trying hard to concentrate, Tom found himself staring at Mrs. Baggs's calendar. Suddenly he remembered. "Wait . . . that picture . . . I know where I've seen it! Mum's National Gallery table mats!"

He jumped up. "And in my dream, she was sitting inside it!"

The three of them crowded round the calendar. The writing underneath the picture said it was *The Hay Wain*, by John Constable. It showed a pretty house, swirly green trees and a horse and cart in the middle of a pond. Tom's cye was drawn to a little speck of bright red, next to the man in the cart. If you looked really, really closely, you could see that it was—

"A jar of tomatoes!" Abdul cried joyously. "My clever brother—no wonder Dolores didn't see it!"

It was enormously odd to think of Mum inside a famous painting; would the real one in the National Gallery now include a small jar of sun-dried tomatoes, or was it just this one? And how would they ever get her out?

Abdul took off his shoes and socks and rolled up his trousers. "I'm going in."

"Do you know how?" Tom asked.

"I studied history of art in college." Abdul neatly rolled his socks into a ball. "I've entered some of the greatest paintings in the world."

Tom was so interested that the dreadful, gnawing worry about his parents sank to the back of his mind. He and Pindar watched as Abdul vanished in a puff of smoke and suddenly appeared in the painting.

"He's in there!" Tom gasped.

Constable's famous painting now included a stout man in rolled-up trousers, who waved at them like a painted cartoon. Tom and Pindar burst out laughing. The figures in the picture—the horse and the man—stayed still, like wax figures, but the painted genie splashed through the shallow pond, climbed up beside the painted man on the cart and picked up the jar of tomatoes.

Inside the picture, Abdul held up the red jar like a trophy, and the boys cheered and did high fives.

Another puff of smoke—and a second later Abdul stood on Mrs. Baggs's linoleum floor in a puddle of pond water.

"You got her—that was brilliant!" Tom hugged Abdul.

"We'd better go," Pindar said. "My mother—I mean Dolores—will be back."

Abdul sat down and hastily dried his feet with a tea towel. "You're right—she'll soon find out she got the wrong tomatoes." He stuffed his feet back into his shoes and socks and slipped the jar into his trouser pocket. "Your mother will be quite safe here."

"Well, thanks for popping in," said Mrs. Baggs (who didn't seem to have noticed anything at all unusual). "Give my love to that smashing brother of yours!"

The doorbell rang.

"That's funny," said Mrs. Baggs. "I'm not expecting anyone."

She shuffled out of the kitchen, not noticing that Tom, Pindar and Abdul were frozen with fear.

"Achoo! It's my mother again—I can smell her!" said Pindar, grabbing at Abdul in a panic. "What shall we do?"

The genie's face was pale and terrified, and Tom could see that he was making a huge effort to be brave.

"We can still make a run for it." Out of nowhere Abdul conjured his carpet—the colors were shockingly clear and pure on top of Mrs. Baggs's old red flooring. "Sit behind me—link arms and hold on to the back of my belt!"

Abdul (back in his genie clothes) sat down on the carpet as Tom and Pindar hastily took their places behind him. Tom linked one arm through Pindar's, and they both took hold of Abdul's belt.

Outside the kitchen door they heard Mrs. Baggs say, "The gas meter's down in the cellar, dear."

"Huh!" Pindar said scornfully. "That's no mortal gas man—achoo!"

Something terribly strange was happening to Mrs. Baggs's kitchen. At first Tom thought it was growing, and then he realized they were shrinking. Suddenly, they were hovering above a sink the size of an Olympic swimming pool—and still they were getting smaller, until he was afraid they would disappear.

"Sorry about the smell," Abdul said as the tiny

shrunken carpet zoomed down the plughole. "Two thousand years ago the genies of the Roman Empire built a secret path along a beautiful London river. Unfortunately the river has now been covered up and turned into a sewer. There might be quite a bit of poo."

19

The Mountain Is Quaking

The sewer part of the journey was short and disgusting. The shrunken carpet twisted and turned along a spaghetti of pipes and tunnels, dodging sudden rushes of soapy water and enormous boulders of poo. The smell was terrible.

"Hold tight!" Abdul yelled.

There was a ripping sound, so loud that it made Tom's ears sing, and a flash of intense white light. He felt a chill in the marrow of his bones as if someone had filled them with toothpaste, and then a blast of deathly cold, and knew he had entered the Realm—crossing between the dimensions was quite uncomfortable for his mortal molecules.

The carpet juddered to a halt.

"Achoo! Hey, we're back!" Pindar gave Abdul a slap on the back. "Nice work!"

The smell wasn't as strong now, and Tom could look around properly. He was his normal size again, and they were at the bottom of a drain, with daylight showing through a grating above them. He could hear a confused babble of shouting and chatter. The carpet they sat on was half covered with dirty water, yet the beautiful colors still shone eerily in the semidarkness.

Abdul was pale with relief. "That was the bravest thing I've ever done—I don't think I like being brave!"

"Lorna will be impressed," Tom said encouragingly.

"Oh, I hope so! Now, if I took the right exit we should be in Hopping Hill, in the heart of Genietown."

"Genietown? You mean like Chinatown in London?"

"Yes, it's where the exiled genies live when they don't like the mortal world." Abdul brushed something brown off his shoulder with a deep shudder. "I'll go up first and take a quick look."

There were iron footholds set in the damp walls. Abdul rolled up the carpet, putting it over his shoulder, and climbed up to the grating. "Safe!" he called. "Come up!"

Tom and Pindar climbed out of the drain and emerged in a busy market. After the darkness of the sewers Tom's senses whirled at the explosion of light and color.

The narrow street was lined with stalls that sold all kinds of genie stuff—lamps, bottles, jewels and gorgeous magic carpets. He also saw stalls piled high with sticky sweets and luscious dates. The air was full of shouting and music, and they were in the middle of a crowd of bustling genies.

Nobody took much notice of three people climbing out of a drain (though two lady genies wrinkled their noses when they walked past). Tom saw then that though most of the people around them were genies, quite a few were fairies, strolling about in sunglasses and taking photographs.

"Tourists," Abdul said.

"I thought people weren't supposed to come to Hopping Hill."

"Not officially," Pindar said, "but nobody takes much notice—it's only a Falconer law, not the old law, so you don't die if you break it." He added, "There are some great restaurants here—achoo!"

"My friend Cassim from the cafe is staying with his sister, who has a house on this street," Abdul said. "Someone there will know where to find Clarence and your godmothers."

"Get away from my stall!" shouted a nearby genie. "The stench of poo is putting off my customers!"

Tom and Pindar snorted with laughter, suddenly noticing how filthy they were, but Abdul cried, "A thousand pardons! Come, boys—I can't do a cleaning spell here, or it'll make the food taste of soap."

He led them through the jostling, noisy crowd to a wooden door in a white wall.

The second they were through the door, something swooped down on them out of the air and knocked off Abdul's turban.

"Iqbal, you little monkey!" shouted a woman's voice. "Stop mucking about!"

Tom and Pindar had thought they were under attack, and they started laughing when they saw that the "attacker" was a cheeky little genie of about four years old, zooming around a courtyard on a little magic carpet the size of a doormat.

The heavy door shut out the racket of the market. The courtyard was quiet and very pretty, with flowers and fruit trees and a small fountain with a lazy-sounding splash. Tom counted four—no, five—little genie children, dressed in gaudy satin, playing in midair like hummingbirds.

"Ha ha—they smell of POO!" cried the cheeky little boy.

"I'll do that cleaning spell," Abdul said. "Keep your mouths shut."

He babbled out a spell and Tom was glad he'd shut his mouth—for a few seconds he was covered in thick white foam. The foam evaporated a moment later, leaving the three of them incredibly clean and smelling of roses.

"Well?" A cross-looking woman with a baby had come out into the courtyard.

Abdul bowed low. "Madam, we are searching for Cassim."

"CASSIM!" yelled the woman. "It's MORE of your friends!" She added, "He's on the roof."

"May we fly up?"

"I can't stop you." She flounced back into the house and smartly shut the door.

"Oh dear," said Abdul. "Cassim's sister doesn't seem very pleased to see us!"

He unrolled his carpet to take the three of them up to the roof of the house—very slowly, because the flying children kept getting in the way.

Tom hadn't understood why Cassim would be on the roof. When they got up there, however, he saw that the flat roof was like a large and comfortable room. A big awning kept the sun off, and there were low sofas and tables. And it was crowded—no wonder Cassim's sister hadn't exactly been welcoming. There had to be at least twenty genies sitting cross-legged on the cushions.

One of them jumped to his feet to greet them, and Tom recognized Cassim from the cafe.

"Abdul, my old friend! I got a message from Clarence's

men that you were coming!" He bowed to them all. "Please sit down and relax, before the next stage of your journey."

He sat them all down on a long sofa, and another genie gave them glasses of a lovely cool drink that tasted like candy.

"What is the next stage?" asked Tom. "I have to find my godmothers."

"They will be very worried about him," Abdul said. "He's a stowaway—he wasn't meant to be on this mission."

"But it's a really good thing he came with us," Pindar said. "We'd never have found the jar without him."

Tom had been wondering how he was going to face his godmothers after jumping on the carpet, and he smiled gratefully.

"All this is known," someone said, from the middle of the crowd of genies. "Dolores Falconer told her husband, and we have a top spy in Tiberius's private office— she's a woodworm in his desk, so she hears everything."

"The end is coming for the Falconers," Cassim said, passing round a plate of fresh dates. "Their foes are gathering on Hopping Hill, waiting for the moment they twist the old law too far—then we will swoop down and take the Realm by storm."

"You seem very sure about all this," someone else said, in a grumbling tone. "But if it doesn't happen soon, I'll have to go back to the mortal world—I own a pastry factory on the North Circular Road, and it doesn't run itself."

"Yes, and I have to get home to Macclesfield," someone else said. "My wife's a mortal and I told her I'd given up magic. If she finds out about this, she'll go berserk."

"Patience!" cried Cassim. "Clarence wouldn't have summoned us all unless he was sure the time had come. And the mountain is quaking! Didn't you feel it last night?"

Several voices broke out at once.

"Rubbish—that wasn't a quake!"

"Yes, it was! It shook my alarm clock right off the shelf, and it hit me on the head!"

"It threw me out of bed!"

"It was nothing but a hiccup!"

"Shut up, all of you," snapped Cassim. "You'll wake the baby, and then my sister will kill me. Clarence says the mountain is quaking, and you know what that means." Seeing that Tom was puzzled, he added, "It's one of our ancient proverbs—*When the mountain quakes / The Falconer shakes*. It's a sign that the One Good Falconer is among us at last."

Tom's heart sank—here was that One Good Falconer stuff again, when he wanted to take Pindar back to the mortal world.

Pindar's face turned bright red, and then very white.

"It's not me!" he said loudly. "I wish people would stop saying it's me!"

Several of the genies laughed.

"Well, if it's not you," Cassim said, "who is it? Do you know of any other Good Falconers?"

All the genies laughed now.

"But I'd be useless at leading the Realm!" Pindar argued, "and there have been good Falconers before—why didn't any of them kick the others up the bum?"

"The young Falconer is quite right." An elderly genie with a white beard spoke out in a solemn voice. "There have been decent members of his cursed family in the past. I am old enough to remember Tiberius's second cousin Trajan, and how bravely he spoke up for the gnomes when there was that cruel fashion for making gnome-bombs. But he wasn't in the direct line of Tiberius, Vespasian, Cassius or Seneca, the four sons of Julius Falconer. That's where the One Good Falconer must come from."

Pindar said, "Dolores isn't my real mother."

The crowd of genies gasped.

"Your mother is of no consequence," the old genie said. "It is well known that Tiberius has many mistresses. When Dolores couldn't have children, he used one of them to get himself a son. You are that son. Therefore the mantle must fall upon you."

"But what if I don't want to lead the Realm?"

The genies laughed softly and muttered among themselves.

"They are saying 'kismet,'" the old genie said. "That word means something like 'fate' or 'destiny.' It is kismet. You cannot argue."

Pindar looked so dismayed that Tom gave him an encouraging nudge, and whispered, "There must be some way we can get round it—I'm not giving up!" But he was worried too.

It's no use, he thought—I don't care about the Realm as much as I care about Pindar, and I don't want him to be the One Good Falconer; I want him to live with us at the deli. But if Dolores wasn't Pindar's mother, Pindar wasn't his cousin. It was very puzzling, when he looked so much like her.

"I don't want to hurry anyone," said Abdul, "but the boys must move on to somewhere safer—the market is swarming with Ali Kazoum's spies."

"It is all arranged," Cassim said cheerfully. "My sister has provided perfect disguises to get them through every checkpoint!" He picked up a Sainsbury's plastic bag and pulled out yards and yards of pink and mauve chiffon, two little sequined caps and two pairs of pink satin shoes.

"Hang on," Tom said suspiciously. "Those are girls' clothes, aren't they? I mean, I know you guys like quite girly colors . . ." His cheeks were hot. He didn't want to offend anyone, but he really didn't want to wear pink satin shoes.

"Ali Kazoum is expecting two beautiful dancing slave girls," Cassim explained. "He doesn't know we've already intercepted them and told them their booking's canceled. You two will go in their places, and Clarence's Hoppers will pick you up on the way." He held up one of the sequined caps. "You see, it has this rather sweet little pink veil to hide your face."

"You're JOKING!" Tom was horrified. How could he ever face Charlie or his other mortal friends again, knowing he'd once dressed as a girl?

He caught Pindar's eye, and they couldn't help laughing at each other's shocked faces.

"They're a bit thin for dancing girls," Abdul said doubtfully. "Especially Ali Kazoum's—his girls have such magnificent figures that people call them the Pillows of the Desert."

"We will stuff them!" someone cried. There was another ripple of genie laughter.

Tom and Pindar looked at each other.

"Oh well," Pindar said. "It can't be worse than flying through the sewers."

The godmothers and Milly giggled so much at their disguises that they forgot about being angry with Tom for jumping on Abdul's carpet.

"What pretty eyes you both have!" Milly cried. "Those dinky little veils really set them off!"

"Yeuchh!" said the two boys, tearing off the veils and cushions and pink slippers as if they'd been red-hot, and that made the godmothers giggle harder.

These curvy dancing girls had left Genietown in a white Rolls-Royce that had been stolen from Ali Kazoum. They had driven up into the deepest part of the forest, and Clarence Mustard's men had bundled them into a cart and set fire to the Rolls-Royce. They were now back in Clarence's flowery sitting room.

Tom had wrapped the jar of sun-dried tomatoes in two cushions and a scarf. Thankfully, since his mother was magically sealed in the jar, she'd survived the journey to the Realm. Taking it out carefully, he handed it to Clarence for safekeeping. He noticed that Lorna looked unusually smart. Instead of her jump-suit, she wore a blue skirt and matching jacket. Iris wore white gloves and a feathered hat, as if she were off to a wedding. Milly had put her huge white dress back on. And Dahlia wore her barrister's wig and gown.

Suddenly he knew why they were all dressed up. "It's my dad's trial, isn't it?"

"Yes, it's tomorrow." Lorna patted his shoulder. "We're setting off after supper."

"I'm very glad you managed to get hold of these

tomatoes," Delia said. "Well done. We should be all right, if only Milly can remember who murdered her."

Milly shrugged crossly. "I've told you until I was blue in the face, I CAN'T remember any more! It was probably my brother Tiberius. He's always killing people."

"But he's got an alibi, and so has Dolores! At the time of your murder everyone was watching them open the ball with a nude waltz. Who was working for him?"

"Sorry to keep you waiting." Clarence was suddenly in the room, in front of the fireplace.

"Good grief!" Lorna gasped. "Stop doing that!"

"I beg your pardon, but it's the fastest way to travel. I've been giving a rousing speech to my troops—enjoy yourselves, by all means, I said, but don't leave too much of a mess. Ah, my dear boys!" Clarence smiled at Tom and Pindar. "Well done, both of you."

"We saw my mother," Pindar said. "And she says she's not my mother."

The legendary outlaw was solemn. "So my contacts told me. It must've been a terrible shock."

"Do you . . . do you know anything about my real mother?"

"I'm afraid not. And neither does Terence."

"What about you, Auntie Milly?"

Poor old Pindar, Tom thought; I'd hate it if I suddenly didn't know who my real mother was.

"No, I don't," Milly said. "But—"

She stopped. They all looked at her.

"Something's niggling at me, that's all—oh, what is it? I see a face—hear a voice—then it's gone."

The floor suddenly shifted under Tom's sneakers, and he fell over. The ornaments on the mantelpiece danced like puppets. A flowered vase toppled off and shattered in the fireplace.

"The mountain's quaking, all right!" Clarence yelled joyfully. "I've never known anything like it!"

The quaking stopped, and the boys and fairies picked themselves up. Tom brushed plaster dust off his T-shirt. A few days ago, he thought, I'd have been terrified by an earthquake; now I'm hardly even shocked.

"It's been rumbling ever since Pindar came to Hopping Hill." Clarence snapped his fingers a few times to tidy the wrecked room. (Tom thought how humans would love to be able to do this.)

"Please don't say I'm the One Good Falconer!" Pindar blurted out. "I'd be totally useless at leading the Realm!"

"You'll soon get the hang of it," said Clarence.

Tom and Pindar gave each other despairing looks— why wouldn't anyone listen?

"Knickers!" muttered Lorna. "I've got a run in these stupid tights! I still don't see what's wrong with my jumpsuit!"

"The High Fairy Court is not a scrapyard," Dahlia said. "We have to look smart."

"Sit down, everyone!" Clarence called. "Supper's ready!"

The round table where they'd had tea was now spread with a hearty supper of stew and roast potatoes. Tom and Pindar made pleased faces at each other. But Pindar was sad and quiet during the meal and Tom wished he could offer some comfort. All day, since seeing Dolores, he'd been thinking about what Mum had said in his dream, about Pindar's mother. "She loved him very much" sounded as if Pindar's real mother might be dead—and that was the last thing he needed to hear now.

After apple crumble and cups of tea Clarence said, "Right, girls—time for you to start out for the trial."

It was a long journey from Hopping Hill to the High Fairy Court. The three godmothers and Milly were traveling by flying coach, and despite being so anxious, Tom was very interested to see one of these. It looked like a small mortal coach with no wheels, and hovered a few centimeters off the ground outside Clarence's hideout.

"This is like the one I drove," Pindar told him. "They're light to handle, but I never got the hang of the steering."

Lorna, who was driving, squeezed herself in behind the wheel. "I'm glad you're staying here, Tom—you'll be much safer and you can watch the trial on television."

"The entire Realm waits with bated breath," Iris said solemnly. "Tomorrow could be the day the Falconers' power crumbles—Milly, I told you to sit in the back behind the smoked windows! You're supposed to be a secret!"

Dahlia shook hands with Clarence and kissed Tom and Pindar.

"Good luck," said Tom. "And when you see my dad . . ." He wanted to say, "Tell him I love him," but the words wouldn't come out.

Dahlia smiled kindly. "I know. Don't worry, Tom!" She jumped into the flying coach and slammed the door just as Lorna started the engine.

"Oh my GARTERS!" Milly's voice shrieked suddenly, in the middle of takeoff. "I REMEMBER!"

20

Big Screen

"Excellent," said Clarence. "I can see that tomorrow's trial is going to be splendid entertainment."

Tom thought this was a rather heartless way to talk about it, when his dad might be condemned to death. "If Milly's memory has come back, does that mean Dahlia will win?"

"Yes, of course," Clarence said in a surprised way, as if this was a silly question. "We'll need to set out early so we get to the big screen in plenty of time." He led the two boys back into the hideout and to a small room with two single beds. It was windowless, but the lamplight made it look comfortable, and it was great to get into bed—Tom had only just realized how exhausted he was.

"This day has been like three days for the price of one," he said, with a mighty yawn. "I hope Milly's remembered who really killed her. If she has, they'll have to free my dad."

This hadn't hit him until now—by this time tomorrow, he could be back at home with his parents. For a moment he was filled with intense, painful longing.

"Tom," Pindar said from the next bed, "I've been thinking."

"What about?"

"I hate to say this, but I don't know if I should go back with you."

"What?" Tom sat up, forgetting about being tired. "Why not? Don't tell me it's this One Good Falconer thing!"

"Everybody seems to think it's me," Pindar said sadly. "I've a horrible feeling I should . . . I don't know . . . . do my duty."

"But you don't want to?"

"No. You know I'd much rather live with you."

"Then let someone else lead the Realm!"

"Look, Tom, you have to admit it's different now. If Dolores isn't my mother, you're not my cousin."

"But . . ." There was nothing to say to this. The

thought of going back to his old life without Pindar was incredibly disappointing. Tom had secretly set his heart on Pindar coming with him to his new school, and helping in the deli on Saturday mornings.

"And there's something else," Pindar said, his face reddening. "I need to stay in the Realm to find my real mother."

"Oh—I mean, of course."

"I'd love to know what she's like," Pindar said. "She's bound to be nicer than Dolores."

He sounded so wistful that Tom wanted to cheer him up. "Maybe my dad will be able to help you. All the godmothers say he's really brilliant at magic. And you could still come and visit us, couldn't you?"

"That'd be wicked—if your parents wouldn't mind." Pindar brightened. "So what if we're not cousins? Nothing can stop us being friends."

"No way," said Tom, grinning and suddenly feeling a lot better. "Not when we've been covered in sewage and disguised as two fat dancing girls, all in one day. That sort of thing makes you friends forever."

"I swear that policeman at the last checkpoint fancied you!" said Pindar.

"Bog off!"

The two of them shook with laughter, and Tom was still smiling when he fell asleep.

*

The big screen was set up on Dragon's Lawn, the largest open space on Hopping Hill. After a breakfast of tea and porridge cooked over a campfire, Tom and Pindar walked there with Clarence. The road was crowded with every kind of magical creature.

"The word has gone out," Clarence said, smiling. "The anti-Falconers are gathering from all over the Realm, and from the mortal world." He nodded towards two nearby fairies in mortal nurses' uniforms. "Those foolish Falconers have gone too far this time. They seem to be the only people who don't know they're doomed!"

"Nobody will have told them anything," Pindar said. "My father kills anyone who brings him bad news. You can't even tell him when it's raining."

It was a cloudless morning. The silvery sunlight of the Realm made the woods and meadows of Hopping Hill look beautiful, and everyone was in such high spirits that Tom couldn't help feeling optimistic. Fairies jostled around them, laughing and singing, carrying large picnic baskets, as if they were on their way to a football game or an outdoor concert.

He saw wiry goblins with semitransparent ears. He saw a group of tiny pixies in bright emerald green, packed into the back of a cart—they called and waved to Clarence as they passed. There was a large party of white-bearded gnomes, far less goofy-looking than the ones you saw in mortal gardens. He was a little nervous when two fierce-looking leopards went by, pulling a large cooler on wheels, until they raised their paws in a salute to Clarence, and he explained that they were demifurs, like Terence.

"Wow, this is amazing," Tom said to Pindar. "I'll never be able to talk to anyone about this when I get home. They just wouldn't believe a word of it!"

"I wish I knew why those girls keep pointing and tittering at me!" Pindar muttered. "Do I look weird or something?"

A group of girl fairies were following them in a tightly packed huddle, all giggling and gaping at Pindar.

"Not weird," Tom said, "just handsome."

"You mean they're acting like this because they think I'm handsome?" Pindar shook his head. "I'll never understand girls!"

The thick forest opened out into an enormous clearing, packed with the creatures of the Realm.

"Wow!" breathed Tom.

A huge white screen stood at one end of the open-air arena. As the leader of the outlaws, Clarence was led to a special roped-off section near the front; they would have a wonderful view of the trial. The outlaws (no longer wearing their masks) set out comfortable chairs and served coffee and pastries. Everyone had brought food— the warm, bright, still air was hazy with the smoke of a thousand campfires and barbecues.

Tom was still very worried about his parents, but the party atmosphere was infectious. There was a flash like lightning, and the big screen flickered into life—not showing the trial, but pictures of the crowd. Just like mortals at a football game, people kept seeing themselves on the big screen and going crazy. It was all very entertaining.

The screen suddenly showed a group of genies, and the boys yelled, "Abdul!"

Abdul was in the middle of eating a kebab and it took him a couple of minutes to realize he was on the screen— his shocked expression when he finally saw himself made the boys fall about laughing.

And a moment later they were on the screen themselves. When Clarence appeared, the great crowd broke into a roar of cheering.

"WELCOME TO DRAGON'S LAWN!" a voice boomed out over the sound system, "BEFORE THE BIG TRIAL, A SONG FROM A BIG STAR—GIVE IT UP FOR JAY TRE-BONKERS!"

There was screaming, and a surge of teenage fairies towards the stage in front of the screen. Dahlia's rock-star son walked on with his band (all dressed in black leather jeans and amazing shoes like the claws of an eagle) and launched into his latest big hit, "Old Fairies Suck."

The music was deafening, and Tom couldn't make out

much more than "*Old fairies suck | They're always trip-ping balls* . . . ," but the atmosphere was electric; Pindar was on his feet stamping in rhythm and waving his arms. The next song was called "Up Yours, Falconers" and even Tom joined in the chorus, which was simply "*Up Yours, Falconers! | Bog off and don't come back!*" roared by the crowd over and over again.

"Isn't he fantastic?" gasped Pindar. "Didn't I tell you?"

"He's great!" Tom yelled back over the cheering.

Jay Trebonkers gave a special bow to Clarence, and mouthed, "Hi, guys!" to the boys before he left the stage.

"Good," said Clarence. "I can take my earplugs out— he's a nice young man, but rock music is wasted on me. I fear I am one of the old fairies who suck. Shall we have lunch?"

It was a very good lunch of chicken pie followed by ice cream, which had magically been kept cold. Clarence had coffee and cheese, and posh chocolates were passed round. Lorna was right, Tom thought. He certainly knows how to make himself comfortable.

The noise in the arena had quietened down to a seeth-ing murmur like the sound of a strong wind.

"Tom, bring your chair close to mine," Clarence said, "and I'll do my best to explain anything you find puzzling. Would you care for a glass of really excellent fairy port?"

"No, thanks." Tom's eyes were fixed to the screen.

It showed a courtroom full of polished wood and very smart people in robes and wigs—just like a court in the mortal world.

A deep male voice boomed, "The High Fairy Court is in session—let the song begin!"

"Song?" The trial hadn't even started, and Tom was already bewildered.

"It's called the Tiberius Anthem," Clarence said. "It has to be sung before every public occasion."

"You mean, like a national anthem?"

"Pretty much—the words are all about Tiberius being wonderful."

On the screen everyone in the court stood up and began to sing, but it was impossible to make out the words—everyone in the arena broke into loud boos and catcalls. In the packed court Tom saw Lorna and Iris looking nervous but very excited, and Terence Banshee opening a packet of mints and chatting to a bat on his shoulder.

"That's one of his cousins," Pindar said. "And there's my ex-mum—the nude one in the front row."

Tom saw his wicked aunt Dolores, stark naked except for a chunky necklace. "Why isn't she wearing clothes?"

"She's too stuck-up," said Clarence. "In the Realm, being nude is a sign of being posh."

The screen was suddenly swamped by a huge wrinkled face with little black eyes like sour currants and a terrible Falconer nose. He wore a red robe and long white wig.

"That's Judge Plato Falconer," Clarence told Tom, "the greatest legal mind in the Realm."

"Let's get on with it," said Judge Plato, up on the screen. "This is the case of the Ten vs. Jonas Harding—what idiot agreed to defend him?" A court official whispered something in his ear. "Who? Speak up! Ms. Pease-Blossom?"

"Yes, my lord." Dahlia appeared, elegant in her wig and gown, and the Hopping Hill audience broke into cheers and whistles.

"You're aware of Rule Four? You know you'll be killed along with the prisoner?"

"Yes, my lord."

"SHAME!" someone shouted in the court. "It's a setup!"

"Silence!" the old judge snapped crossly. "Pease-Blossom—that name is familiar—you were one of my students at the university."

"Yes, my lord," said Dahlia.

"Hmmm—you were rather bright, until you ran off to get married. What've you been up to?"

"This and that," said Dahlia.

"Well, I admire your courage. But I warn you now, you are pitting your wits against the full might of the Realm—Tiberius Falconer himself is speaking for the prosecution."

"BOO!" yelled the crowd on Hopping Hill.

"But that's so unfair!" cried Tom.

"Indeed it is," Clarence said, taking a sip of port. "When we throw out the Ten and have proper elections, my slogan is going to be 'Vote the Fair back into Fairy.' Quite snappy, don't you think?"

Tom wasn't interested in elections. Another face had appeared on the screen—a face that looked like that of a duck-billed platypus with ears and a mustache. Dahlia's description of Tiberius Falconer had been spot-on. Tom would have known him at once, even if the crowd on Dragon's Lawn had not erupted into howls of rage.

"My father," Pindar said bitterly. "And that's the rest of the Ten with him."

Tiberius and the Ten were all nude. Tom counted the rest of the nasty-looking bunch. "There are only seven of them."

"Two were changed into beetles, don't forget," Clarence said. "They're inside the matchbox on that cushion."

"OK, Plato," Tiberius began, "I'll keep it short. He's guilty—end of story."

Judge Plato was stern. "You have to address me as 'my lord,' and you have to follow the rules."

"But I'm Tiberius Falconer! I don't follow other people's rules!"

"When you're in my court, you follow MINE! Bring in the prisoner."

The prisoner—Tom could hardly breathe. He was about to see Dad for the first time since his disappearance.

To his disappointment, the screen showed a large police fairy holding something furry in the palm of his hand.

"Why is he still disguised as a BAT?" shouted the judge. "This court can't be bothered with the translation spell. Change him back!"

"Well, you see," Tiberius said, "he was cheaper to feed as a bat, and he'll be much easier to execute—I can just walk on him."

"I don't care! For one thing, this court doesn't have a truth-globe small enough."

"Who cares about the truth?"

"Change him back," rasped Plato, "or I'll throw out this case!"

"OK, OK—keep your wig on!"

Suddenly, there was Dad—a bit thinner despite the fattening diet, but otherwise looking just the same and perfectly healthy in his familiar mortal clothes. Tom's heart leapt with relief, and it was hard not to burst into tears.

"You see, Tom?" Clarence gave his arm a reassuring squeeze. "Fit as a fiddle!"

He really did look fine—Tom's spirits lifted as he saw his dad smiling at his friends while a court official hung a truth-globe around his neck.

On the screen Judge Plato said, "Read the charges."

Tiberius cleared his throat and read from a piece of paper. "Jonas Harding, you are charged with heartbreaking with intent to kill, unlawful marriage with a mortal, kidnapping a dead body and producing a demisprite. How do you plead?"

Jonas stood up very straight, and looked boldly at the judge. "NOT GUILTY!"

21

A Small Job

There was tremendous cheering on Dragon's Lawn. The court stayed silent—most people looked scared of Tiberius's quivering nude fury.

"NOT guilty?" he snapped. "Do you DENY that my sister Milly was in love with you?"

"Excuse me, my lord." Dahlia leapt smartly to her feet. "I hate to interrupt, but Jonas is wearing a truth-globe—he can't lie."

"TELL THAT WOMAN TO SHUT UP!" roared Tiberius.

Tom held his breath, afraid that Dahlia had gone too far and was about to be vaporized.

But Judge Plato said, "Certainly not. 'That woman'

happens to be the counsel for the defense, and Ms. Pease-Blossom expresses herself very elegantly."

"Thank you, my lord!" Dahlia smiled. "I had a very good teacher."

"Too kind! Too kind!" For a moment the judge's wrinkles creased into something like a smile. "Your hair's different—it suits you."

"Look, this man broke my sister's heart and killed her!" Tiberius said, stamping his foot. "He violated the old law, which means this court must sentence him to death! Now can we please execute him and start blowing up Hopping Hill?"

Pandemonium broke out—in the court on the screen, and on Dragon's Lawn.

The screen suddenly flickered, and the picture changed to a lot of nude fairies doing a folk dance.

"BOO!"

"Bring back the trial!"

Tom tugged at Clarence's sleeve and shouted above the din, "What's going on?"

Clarence was calm. "I expect they've broken into a massive fight. They'll restore the picture when they've cleared up the mess. Let's all have another cup of tea."

Though he was frantic to know what was happening to his dad, Tom was forced to be patient. He ate a slice of fruitcake and watched the folk dancing on the big screen.

At last, after about half an hour, the picture of the trial came back, and there were more deafening cheers. The courtroom looked exactly the same, but most of the people there had torn and dirty clothes. Some had black eyes and swollen lips. Lorna had lost a sleeve of her jacket, and half her hair seemed to be covered with green ink. Iris's feathered hat was squashed out of shape.

The only person to come out of the fight looking better than before was Judge Plato, who had changed into a smart new white wig and pinned a large scarlet carnation to his robe.

"Ms. Pease-Blossom, please carry on with the case for the defense."

"WHY?" cried Tiberius. "Who cares about his so-called defense? Let me kill him—I've got a ring of bulldozers around that wretched Hopping Hill, just waiting to move in!"

Again the crowd around Tom burst out in angry booing—and this time the ground beneath Tom's chair shuddered, tipping a couple of glasses off the picnic table.

"The mountain's on our side!" Clarence said, chuckling.

"Are we safe here?" asked Tom.

"Quite safe, dear boy—no Falconers for miles!"

"That wasn't what I meant," Tom muttered to Pindar. "Isn't he scared of being in an earthquake?"

"He doesn't look scared," Pindar said doubtfully, "but let's put our wings on, just in case we need to make a fast getaway."

"Good idea." Tom took his wings out of his backpack and quickly buckled them on.

Clarence was glued to the screen. "Why isn't Plato allowing Tiberius to speak? And why on earth is he wearing that fancy wig?"

In the courtroom, Judge Plato went on: "I warn you, Tiberius, I have the power to seal up your mouth with sticky tape—and I won't hesitate to use it if you interrupt Ms. Pease-Blossom one more time!"

"My lord," Dahlia said, "you're being absolutely sweet—thank you so much!"

"Take your time, Ms. Pease-Blossom. It's a pleasure to watch you."

The crowd in the arena whistled and made kissing noises—and even people within the court were trying not to giggle. Tom caught a glimpse of his dad, openly grinning.

"How convenient," Clarence said. "Old Plato's fallen in love with Dahlia! Look at Tiberius!"

Tiberius's nude body was scarlet and trembling with anger. He looked so funny that Tom and Pindar burst out laughing.

"Wait till his medals fall off," Pindar said. "They're only stuck on with Blu Tack!"

Judge Plato leaned over his desk towards Dahlia. "Do you have many witnesses to call, Ms. Pease-Blossom?"

"Yes, my lord—I hope that won't be a nuisance."

"Not at all! But I think we'll take a long break for supper first. There's a lovely little French place beside the river, where the quails' eggs and champagne—"

"OBJECTION!" shrieked Tiberius.

"Objection overruled," said Judge Plato. "This court is adjourned for at least three hours. All rise!"

To the general astonishment of Tiberius, the people in the court and everyone watching on the big screen, Judge Plato sprang out of his chair and the screen suddenly went blank.

"Oh well," Clarence said. "That will give us a nice break to make our own supper. It's a Lancashire hotpot." Something bleeped in his pocket. "Excuse me."

He took out his phone and Dahlia's face appeared on the little screen (fairy mobiles were powered by magic and showed the person's face). "Hello, Dahlia. What's the matter?"

"This is an emergency; I need your help."

"My dad!" Tom looked over Clarence's shoulder. "Is he OK?"

"Oh, this has nothing to do with Jonas," Dahlia said. She had removed her barrister's wig, and seemed to be wearing something blue and gauzy. "In about twenty minutes I'm meeting Judge Plato for a cozy little supper beside the river. The only problem is, he's very prim and proper about fairies who . . . er . . . bend the law to exploit mortals."

"I know what this is about," Tom said. "You don't want him to find out about your husbands."

"No, Tom, he wouldn't understand at all. I was careful never to break the old law—obviously, because I would've been killed if I had—but I did twist it about a bit."

Clarence chuckled. "Twist it? You MANGLED it!"

On the phone, Dahlia looked pained. "This isn't a laughing matter, darling. Plato won't approve at all. I'll confess, of course—but I have to get rid of them first."

"We can deal with it after the trial," Clarence said.

"It has to be now. I remember him from college—I can't let him anywhere near me if there's the tiniest hint of bad magic!"

"I'm surprised you want him anywhere near you," Tom said. "He's not much of a looker."

"Darling, what are you talking about? Plato's one of the most attractive men in the whole Realm." She seemed to mean this, and Tom had to avoid looking at Pindar in case they started laughing.

Clarence frowned. "Sorry, Dahlia—but I'm waiting for the fall of the Falconers, and I don't see how I'm supposed to help your romance."

"It's quite simple," Dahlia said. "I want Tom and

Pindar to nip into the mortal world and set my husbands free."

Tom felt like cheering—Dahlia's enslaved husbands had been the main thing that had stopped him from liking her properly.

"But the boys will never be able to cope with the magic," Clarence said. "Undoing such spells is a complicated matter—they must be unpicked word for word, and by a real expert."

"You're an expert, Clarence, darling! You can easily do the magic from your end. And it's a perfect little job for the boys. Who'll take any notice of them?" Dahlia glanced at her watch. "I must go! The wallets and passports are in the cupboard in the hall." She sighed heavily. "And before you say anything, I know it means giving back all their money—thank goodness my son's a rock star!"

"Won't it look a bit weird?" Pindar asked. "I mean, if all those dead guys come back to life at the same time?"

"He's right," Clarence said. "They'll all need to have good solid reasons for losing their memories—the backup magic alone will take my whole supper break!"

"Clarence, I beg you!" Dahlia cried. "If this date doesn't go perfectly, think what he might do to Jonas! It might stop him from being on our side!"

Tom was alarmed; it was terrible to think of Dad being sentenced to death because old Plato disapproved of

Dahlia's behavior. "We have to do it," he said to Clarence. "And I know we can—can't we, Pindar?"

"Yes, and we should start as soon as possible," Pindar said. "How much time do we have?"

"You wonderful boys! Thank you! I do wish you could see me properly to tell me honestly how I look—I've changed into a ball gown."

"You always look lovely," said Tom.

"My dear Tom, you really are so like your father!" She blew a kiss and the screen on the phone went blank.

Clarence tutted and shook his head, though he was smiling now. "Oh well, I'd better do as she says. I'll perform an emergency transfer to my secret lab to work on the magic—but first I'll get you two out of the Realm."

"Wait a sec," Tom said. "If you're not coming with us, how will we get back?"

"A very good question," said Clarence. "It won't be comfortable for your demisprite molecules—illegal entries and exits are far more punishing—but I'll have to do a trampoline spell."

"Sorry?"

"Don't worry, there's no bouncing involved. I simply set a timer, and when the alarm goes off you and Pindar will shoot back into the Realm. I can only let you have an hour, but that should be enough. All you have to do is get the husbands out of Dahlia's house and scatter them before their memories come back."

"OK." This didn't sound too difficult.

Tom was prepared for another long flight to the nearest illegal exit, but Clarence's magic was very advanced. He pointed his finger and drew an invisible door in the air.

"AAARGH!" yelled Tom. A great icy blast of cold hit him, freezing the blood in his veins. A few seconds later he was lying on a dirty London pavement, thawing like a bag of frozen peas.

Pindar helped him to his feet. "Are you OK?"

"Y-yes, I think so." Tom took a few breaths of delicious mortal air, thicker and more nourishing than the air of the Realm. "Wow, that hurt! Didn't you feel anything?"

"Not really; I don't have any mortal molecules. This is the right place, isn't it?"

Tom took a proper look around. They were in a Chelsea square, posh and leafy and peaceful. "Yes, this is Dahlia's house, but I don't know how we're meant to break in."

"That'll be easy. Even I can do that spell. Come on."

"Wait!" Tom grabbed his arm. "If anyone sees us, we'll be arrested—and that's all we need."

The square was deserted. The boys ran up the front steps of Dahlia's house, and nobody saw them except a fat gray pigeon perched on a gatepost.

"Achoo!" Pindar sneezed violently, pulled out his lightning-pistol and shot the pigeon.

Tom stared at the little pile of ash where it had been. "What are you doing?"

"It was an enemy agent—one of Dolores's spies. I smelled it. My allergies are useful sometimes."

"So it was a disguised fairy?" Tom was shocked.

"No, just a normal pigeon."

"Oh."

"I had to act quickly, before it killed us."

"How was a pigeon going to kill us?"

"It was probably armed."

"What? With a tiny little invisible machine gun?"

"Yes, actually." With a frown of deep concentration, Pindar mumbled a spell, and sneezed again. The front door swung open.

Once they were safely inside the hall, both boys relaxed. Tom slightly loosened the straps of his wings, which were starting to rub his shoulders. The house was still and silent. They waited for a few minutes, and the silence stretched on.

"Well," Tom said, "if they're not going to come out by themselves, we'll have to look for them." He glanced at the only piece of furniture in the hall. "This must be the cupboard with the wallets and passports."

He opened the doors and found three drawers. The

top drawer contained a neat bundle of different-colored passports and a box of leather wallets. The middle drawer was a jumble of expensive car keys, and the bottom drawer was stuffed to the brim with cash.

Pindar whistled softly. "She's a master criminal—no wonder she doesn't want that old judge finding out!"

"A Rolls—a Jaguar—a Ferrari—two Bentleys—another Rolls . . ." Tom shuffled through the car keys. "They probably don't remember that they ever had cars, so it won't be any good trying to give these back. But we can give them their wallets and passports and a good bit of cash. That'll be useful when they suddenly wake up."

Pindar gathered everything up. "So where are they?"

"I think she keeps them downstairs. She said they had luxurious quarters."

Tom had never been to the basement of Dahlia's house. They went down a narrow staircase to a huge, gleaming kitchen, achingly clean and totally deserted.

"Maybe we should try calling them." Pindar dumped the bundles on one of the polished counters. "Er . . . hello!"

They waited, and the silence went on.

"Husbands!" Tom called—and they both snorted with laughter at how daft it sounded.

Three doors opened off the kitchen. Pindar tried the nearest and found a broom cupboard. The next door led to a utility room with a washing machine, and the third—

"Bingo!" said Pindar. "She's got a funny idea of luxury."

The third door belonged to a square, windowless closet. Two rows of elderly men in white jackets sat on facing benches, like two rows of wax figures. Tom was horrified—how could Dahlia leave these poor old tycoons sitting in the dark?

"That mean old cow! She's been treating them like— she's the one who should be locked up!"

"I think she's quite cool," Pindar said. "She's risking her life to defend your dad, don't forget."

"But to do something like this. What's her problem with mortals, anyway?"

"Look, we're running out of time. How does Dahlia talk to them?"

Tom said, "I'll try calling a name—Mr. Grisling!"

Inside the dark closet, the late Mr. Grisling stood up and droned, "Yes, sir?"

"You're free," Pindar said. "You can go home."

Mr. Grisling stared blankly at the wall.

"It's no use," Tom said. "He's still under the spell. Come out, Mr. Grisling."

Mr. Grisling walked out into the kitchen. "Yes, sir."

"Hey, I know," Pindar said. "Let's call out the names

on the passports—then we'll know for certain that we're giving them to the right people."

This was an excellent idea. Tom called out the names on the husbands' passports as Pindar gave each husband his rightful wallet and a wad of cash, and in a few minutes all eleven husbands were standing in the kitchen in a respectful half-circle.

Tom looked at them helplessly. "Now what?"

"I don't know," Pindar said, "but we'd better get them well away from here before they wake up."

"Clarence said to scatter them." Tom groaned softly. "We'll have to call out all their names, or they won't do anything."

"Do you remember them all?"

"We'll just have to keep checking those passports."

It took the best part of fifteen minutes to get the whole group of husbands upstairs. Tom and Pindar circled them like a pair of sheepdogs—the narrow stairs kept getting jammed with husbands, and then they had to start all over again.

"Upstairs, Mr. Grisling!"

"Mr. . . . er . . . what does this say? Mr. Hochen-hammler, go upstairs!"

"Upstairs, Mr. Chang-Wu!"

At last the hall of Dahlia's house was packed with eleven very quiet elderly businessmen. Tom squeezed through them to open the front door and a summery breeze blew into the house, but the husbands stayed as still as wax statues.

"Shoo!" cried Pindar.

Nobody moved.

"We'll just have to do it again," Tom said. "Mr. Ghopal!"

"Yes, sir?"

"Go out of the house and keep walking!" To Pindar he added, "I hope he doesn't walk straight into traffic, but it's the best I can do."

One by one, the husbands heard their names and slowly walked out of the house into the fresh air (very luckily, there were no other people in the square). It was a strange and moving sight—as their gray locks stirred in the breeze, they raised their heads and stared in wonder at the sky. One by one they plodded away along the street.

Pindar and Tom watched from the front door.

"They should be singing," Tom said, "like freed birds."

The last husband disappeared round the corner and Pindar shut the front door.

22

Milly's Memories

"Phew," Pindar said. "I must be getting less incompetent—normally I'd mess up something like that. Now I suppose we just wait for Clarence to trampoline us back to the Realm. D'you reckon Dahlia's got anything to drink?"

The two boys returned to the kitchen. Dahlia's huge fridge was stuffed with food and drink. Tom handed Pindar a can of Coke and took one for himself.

Just as his hand closed around the can there was a blinding white flash that froze Tom's heart in his chest. The agonizing cold was back, and a moment later he was lying on grass with the icy can of Coke frozen to his fingers.

"Ow! Ow!" The agony didn't last long—warmth blasted back into his bones, and his fingers loosened.

Clarence's face looked down at him. "Well done, Tom. I'm sorry about your molecules. Can you stand up?"

Pindar helped him to his feet. "You turned blue just then—it was freaky."

"Yeuch!" Tom shook the feeling back into his arms and legs. As he got used to the sweet, giddy-making air of the Realm, he became aware of the noises that swirled and seethed around them. The crowd on Dragon's Lawn was lively after the supper break. People were settling themselves on cushions and refilling their glasses.

"Sit down, Tom," Clarence said. "You'll be glad to hear that those poor husbands are safe now—it took simply huge amounts of backup."

Tom was tired, and it was pleasant to sit in a comfortable chair beside Clarence, sipping sweet tea and eating egg sandwiches.

The big screen flickered and the crowd on Hopping Hill cheered loudly.

"This is going to be great fun," Clarence said. "The mountain was quaking like a jelly while you were gone!"

Tom was alarmed. "Is it safe?"

"All will be changed and many will be dead!"

"Oh." This wasn't his idea of fun.

"It'll be the end of Tiberius—unless he submits to the One Good Falconer."

"Excuse me," Pindar said politely, "but it really can't be me. I'm rubbish at everything and allergic to magic."

"You must be good at something," Clarence said.

"Well, I'm not—OK? I'm NOT the One Good Falconer. I'm the guy who wrecked nine flying coaches!"

"Nobody's perfect. Your destiny will reveal itself. Have some popcorn." Clarence handed each boy a large carton of warm, sugary popcorn.

Tom and Pindar shrugged at each other helplessly— what was the point, when nobody wanted to listen?— and settled back to watch the rest of Jonas's trial.

Judge Plato appeared on the big screen. "Silence in court!"

His words were drowned by a barrage of catcalls and whistles from the crowd on Dragon's Lawn. The crabby old judge was wearing a grand new robe of deep purple encrusted with gold.

"Looks like the date went well," Tom said. "We freed those husbands in the nick of time."

"Maybe he'll marry Dahlia now," Pindar said. "I hope a thirteenth husband's not unlucky."

On the screen Judge Plato said, "Get on with it, Tiberius."

Tiberius—stark naked except for his medals—jumped to his feet, and the crowd at the big screen booed loudly.

Tom was sure he felt a slight tremor in the ground beneath his trainers.

"I'm bringing in a witness," Tiberius said, "just to show you I know how to handle the old law. Call Derek Drapton!"

Tom nudged Pindar. "Hey, it's the chief sobber!"

Derek Drapton stood in the witness box, meek and nervous in his long black robe.

"OK, Derek," Tiberius began. "You were at the ball where my sister died of her broken heart."

"Yes, sir."

"Take us through the events of that fateful night."

"I arrived at your palace," Derek Drapton said. "I removed my clothes in the undressing room, and as soon as I was decently nude I went to the ballroom. I danced once with your wife, Dolores Falconer, and once with . . . with . . ." Drapton broke down in tears. "With your sister Milly."

"And how did Milly seem to you?"

"Pale and sorrowful and dying of a broken heart."

"RUBBISH!" a voice yelled out in the court.

"Iris!" both boys cried.

There on the screen was Iris Moth, her tiny eyes flashing with anger. "That's rubbish, and you know it, Drapton! I was at that ball— Milly was stuffing her face with cake and leading a conga line! Does that sound like someone with a broken heart?"

"Silence!" snapped the judge. "Go on, Mr. Drapton."

"I asked her once again to marry me"—Derek Drapton was trembling—"but she refused."

"Did she give a reason?" Tiberius asked.

"Yes, sir, she said it was my spindly legs."

There was a roar of laughter, in court and on Dragon's Lawn.

"No, you great twit!" shouted Tiberius. "The REAL reason!"

"Oh—sorry—because Jonas Harding had broken her heart."

"Was that the last time you saw my sister alive?"

"Is this leading to anything?" the judge interrupted crossly.

"Of course it is!" Tiberius stamped his foot hard and the row of medals dropped off his naked chest. (Another roar of laughter at the big screen—and a couple of giggles in court.)

"Well, get on with it. I'm bored."

"You'll be sorry for this, you miserable old git! I don't care if you are a High Court judge and my fourteenth cousin!" Tiberius said. "OK, Drapton—tell him what happened next."

"I went into the conservatory," Derek Drapton said, in a trembling voice, "and found Milly lying dead. I knew then that she must've died of her broken heart."

"Right, you can sit down, Tiberius," said the judge.

"I haven't finished!"

"I don't care, I need to look at something beautiful. Ms. Pease-Blossom, have you any questions for this witness?"

Dahlia stood up—she had changed into a slim, shell-pink cocktail dress that looked elegant with her gown and wig. "Just one or two, my lord. Mr. Drapton—are you sure you asked Milly to marry you BEFORE you went to the supper room?"

"I . . . er . . . I—yes." The Chief Adorer was very nervous.

"I'm prepared to call three waiters who remember giving you a plate of crab pastries. Did you eat any crab pastries that evening?"

"Er . . . I might have. . . ."

"Could you possibly have been holding the plate when you talked to Milly?"

"Right, that's it!" Tiberius leapt to his feet. He snatched up his lightning-pistol, aiming it directly at Dahlia, and pulled the trigger.

Tom caught his breath—but Dahlia did not catch fire and disintegrate into ash. There was something wrong with Tiberius's gun. The bolt of lightning bounced off Dahlia's shoulder and into Tiberius's flabby stomach, making a noise like a loud slap.

"Damn these cheap guns!" screamed Dolores. She jumped up and took a shot at Dahlia. This bounced back too, knocking Pindar's ex-mother off her feet.

There was an uproar. People jumped to their feet, shouting furiously at Tiberius.

"SHAME!"

"Murderer!"

The screen suddenly went blank, and a moment later the nude folk dancing came on again.

"BOO!"

"BRING BACK THE TRIAL!"

Tom's heart was in his mouth. Dad was in the middle of a gunfight, and he had to watch a load of silly dancers.

"Oh dear," Clarence said. "I wish it wouldn't do that. More tea?"

The picture came back after fifteen minutes. Tom studied the screen anxiously, and was very relieved to see his dad in the dock, still safe and sound.

"Tiberius Falconer," Judge Plato said, "there's nothing wrong with your guns. They failed because this is a High Court of the Old Law, and you are IN CONTEMPT. Ms. Pease-Blossom, I'm so sorry you were interrupted. Have you any more questions for Mr. Drapton?"

"No, my lord."

"That's all then, Mr. Drapton."

The Chief Adorer hurried out of the witness box and sat down near Dolores.

"My lord," Dahlia said, "let's waste no more of this lovely summer evening. I'm going to prove that Jonas Harding hasn't killed anyone, stolen any dead bodies or broken the old law. I'm also going to reveal Milly Falconer's real killer." She left a pause for everyone to gasp and murmur. "I call my star witness—MILLY FALCONER!"

The door of the court opened and in sailed Milly, stately as a galleon in her huge white dress.

The court erupted into pandemonium.

Derek Drapton fainted.

This time it was a nude choir singing fairy sea shanties—which could hardly be heard above the booing.

"This is getting ridiculous!" Clarence said. "Do the Falconers really think they can hide their crimes by blocking the airwaves? No— here it comes!"

Milly stayed splendidly calm. She hung the truth-globe round her neck and waited in the witness box until the court had quietened down.

"It's impossible!" croaked Tiberius. "That can't be my sister!"

"Shut up," said the judge.

"Ms. Falconer," Dahlia said, "tell this court where you met Jonas Harding."

"We met in college," Milly said, "when a few of us formed a punk-rock band, and I fell in love with him."

"Did Jonas return your love?"

Milly sighed and smiled at Tom's dad. "Poor Jonas, we were all in love with him; every single one of us except Lorna, who was engaged to a genie! But no, he didn't love me. I spent the next few years trying to forget him and move on—my brother and his wife kept nagging and nagging me to marry someone else."

"Did you have any other offers?"

"Hundreds!" Milly said. "But no other man was good enough."

Derek Drapton started to sob again.

"What's up with him, anyway?" Pindar said to Tom. "I thought he'd stop crying when he saw Milly again. You'd think he'd be pleased after all those years adoring a corpse."

"Tell the court what happened next," Dahlia said.

"My brother and his wife suddenly changed their tune." Milly shot a scornful look at Dolores. "All of a sudden they desperately wanted me to marry Jonas."

"Do you know why?"

"Oh yes. They wanted Hopping Hill. It was full of outlaws—and gold."

Inside the court there were gasps. At Dragon's Lawn the great crowd roared with fury.

"As soon as Tiberius found out the core of Hopping Hill is made of molten gold, he was consumed with greed. The wedding was announced," Milly said. "Tiberius declared a public holiday and bought me this lovely dress. But the day before the wedding, Jonas escaped into the mortal world."

"Darling—I mean, my lord," Dahlia said, "I'd like to remind the court that Jonas's escape was considered impossible. He was a marked man and couldn't even make an illegal tear in the membrane without instant detection. There was only one person who could have helped him to escape—wasn't there, Milly?"

"Yes," Milly said. She held up her head proudly. "Me."

"YOU!" screeched Iris, leaping up so quickly that her squashed hat fell off.

"YOU?" cried Lorna.

"Yes. Jonas flew in through my bedroom window disguised as a wounded bat and begged me to help him—his life was in terrible danger. And he had to ask me because I could get hold of the Falconer Seal."

"The Seal's a special Falconer pass in and out of the Realm," Clarence explained. "Well, well! She must be more intelligent than she looks."

"You great stupid girl!" Dolores Falconer was on her feet in the court. "You let my brother slip through your fingers! Didn't you WANT power? Didn't you WANT gold? Didn't you LOVE him?"

"Of course I loved him," Milly said, "but not in any way that you'd understand, you horrid, cold-hearted woman! I loved Jonas so much that I didn't care about power, or gold. I loved him so much that I wanted to help him—even if that meant letting him go."

In the dock, Jonas dabbed his eyes with his handcuffed wrists; Tom had never seen him so moved.

"And anyway, I knew that I could never marry him," Milly added.

"Why not?" asked Dahlia.

"Because," said Milly, "Jonas was married already!"

23

One Good Falconer

For one moment a shocked silence hung over the court and the crowd watching on the big screen. Tom heard whispers rustling around him. He gaped at his dad up on the screen, too stunned to move.

Married? Dad had another wife before he met Mum? Tom wasn't sure how this made him feel. He didn't like finding out that his dad had so many secrets.

"He was married to my poor cousin Clover," Milly said. "I wasn't sure exactly what happened to her after the arrest, but my brother had put Jonas in prison, ready for our wedding."

"Clover Falconer—I've heard the godmothers talking about her," Tom said. "She's the one who sneezed and

277

had big feet!" It was incredibly weird to think of this unknown girl as his dad's wife.

"Was Tiberius angry when Jonas escaped?" Dahlia asked.

"OBJECTION!" yelled Tiberius.

"Oh, shut up," said Judge Plato.

Milly gave her brother a look of scorn. "Tiberius went ballistic—and he suspected me, though he couldn't prove it. So he arranged to have me murdered."

This was a bombshell—the crowd burst into furious shouts.

"This is it!" cried Clarence. "Caught red-handed breaking the old law! Nearly time to open the champagne!"

Tiberius shouted, "It's a LIE!"

"He didn't do it himself," Milly said. "He thought he could get round the old law if he paid one of his lackeys to poison me."

"Who was it?" Dahlia asked. "Do you see him in this court?"

"Yes," Milly said. "It was Derek Drapton."

"WHAT!" Tom and Pindar gasped. Milly had been poisoned by her own Chief Adorer.

"Milly, forgive me!" Derek Drapton wailed. "Tiberius made me do it! I've spent fifteen years in agonies of remorse!"

"You TRAITOR!" shouted Iris. She jumped over to

Drapton and started whacking him with her feathered hat. "You slimy lying BEAST!"

"I've heard enough," said Judge Plato. "Jonas Harding, this case is dismissed and you're free to go."

"Free!" Tom grabbed at Pindar's arm. "He says my dad's free!"

"Not so fast!" Tiberius's nude body was scarlet with fury. "Who cares about the old law? If you refuse to kill him, I'll do it myself!"

He raised his gun, and for one sickening moment Tom thought he was going to shoot Jonas.

But before he could fire, Milly did an extraordinary thing. She pointed a finger at her brother and screamed, "NO-O-O-O-O-O-O!"

The scream went on and on, getting louder and louder, until everyone in the courtroom was covering their ears. The big screen on Dragon's Lawn suddenly went blank— and still the scream rang on like a great fire alarm, until it seemed to rip through the entire Realm and pierce to the very heart of Hopping Hill.

Tom was flung off his chair onto the grass. The picnic table fell on top of him, covering him with cheese and biscuits.

"Earthquake!" yelled Pindar.

The grass beneath them rocked violently and rose up around them like great grassy waves in a stormy sea.

Milly's supernatural scream died away and Tom began

to hear the shrieks of the crowd around him. The mountain stopped quaking and he struggled giddily to his feet. The front half of the arena was a chaos of upturned picnic furniture and shocked fairies, but no one seemed to be hurt.

The big screen—now blank and white—shifted, and something suddenly erupted right through it.

Tom was rooted to the ground with amazement. He wanted to run away, but he could only stand and stare. The thing that had smashed its way through the screen was—incredibly—the large head of a genuine dragon.

A dragon.

The shrieks and cries of the crowd hushed into silence. For the fairies this was as strange a sight as a living dinosaur would be to mortals, and they were very nearly as flabbergasted as Tom was.

"Oh joy!" whispered Clarence. The old outlaw's eyes were full of tears. "It was TRUE! They're not extinct after all! Oh—isn't she splendid? You can tell it's a female from the shape of the nostrils."

The dragon shook her huge head impatiently and the screen shivered into fragments. Tom could see all of her now. Her scales were knobbly and dark gray, except where her sides glowed a dull red. When she moved she clinked and clanked like a gigantic iron stove.

His mouth was dry. She was too close. He could feel the heat blasting off her—but he didn't dare to move a muscle. She was the size of a removal van. The expression in her little black eyes was old, old, old—and perhaps not good.

The dragon made a rumbling sound deep in her chest, and the edges of her nostrils glowed red-hot.

"This is awkward," Clarence said quietly. "I don't want to annoy her, but I haven't a clue how to do any kind of language spell. All dragon languages died out eons ago. I don't know how we're supposed to communicate."

"She's trying to tell you something!" Pindar blurted out.

Clarence shot him a look of surprise. "Don't tell me you understand her!"

"I . . . I think I do, sort of." Pindar was bright red, but stood his ground. "I used to keep pet lizards, and a couple of the words sound the same."

"You mastered the reptile language spell? My dear boy! Even the greatest fairy scholars find that one nearly impossible!"

"Do they?" Pindar was bewildered. "I thought it was quite easy."

"Well, for goodness' sake, say something nice to that dragon before she starts breathing fire!"

So dragons really did breathe fire. Tom looked at Pindar. Could he talk to her?

Pindar bravely walked right up to the dragon. A

deathly hush fell upon the crowd as his lips moved silently, muttering a spell. It was very weird indeed when he suddenly let a deep rumble out of his chest and the edges of his nostrils flickered.

The dragon turned her head sharply towards Pindar. When he had finished speaking she rumbled something back at him.

"Well?" hissed Clarence.

"Er . . . I said hello and welcome in Lizardish. She answered me in Old Reptile, but I can just about follow it. She said . . . well, she's quite angry."

There was another rumble from the dragon—longer this time, and ending on a growl.

"She says she's had it up to here with fairies," Pindar translated. "She says that thanks to fairies she's been living all alone in the depths of the hill for the past eight hundred years. She says fairies destroyed her brethren and we're a load of stupid, smelly, evil—er . . . er . . ." He was embarrassed. "And a lot of very rude words—do I have to say them?"

"No, dear boy," Clarence said. "I get the gist. Tell her we're all frightfully sorry, and find out why she's here."

"OK." Once more Pindar rumbled, and twitched his nose (a strange and fascinating thing to watch). "She says she was driven out of hiding by the Falconers' shameful disrespect for the old law. Now the old legend has come true and she was summoned by the One Good

Falconer, so that the new era could begin. And that just proves it's not me," he added to Clarence. "I certainly didn't summon her!"

"Yes, but you can speak to her," Clarence said. "That must be a sign. Ask her what she'd like us to do now."

Pindar turned back to the dragon. He rumbled something at her, and her answer was long and detailed—and less fierce, Tom thought. To his surprise, Pindar suddenly smiled, and then he and the dragon exchanged some lively rumbles; and Tom could have sworn he saw a glint of humor on the ancient creature's wrinkled, snouty face.

"What's she saying?" Clarence asked eagerly.

Pindar grinned. "She says she wants to meet the guy who sang 'Old Fairies Suck.' She thinks it's the only decent fairy music she's ever heard."

Shocked laughter rippled through the crowd, with a few screams from Trebonkers fans.

"Trebonkers!" groaned Clarence. "Are you sure?"

"Oh yes. I was just telling her about his latest album— that's another thing she wants now. She'd really love a signed one."

Clarence whispered to one of his bodyguards, "Go and find that ghastly young noisemaker—tell him all our lives depend on his being nice to her."

Tom found that he was a lot less scared. Pindar was now very relaxed with the dragon, and she looked less angry. And she couldn't be all bad if she liked Jay Tre-bonkers.

Luckily Jay was still at Dragon's Lawn. He came to meet the dragon, and if he was afraid of her, he didn't show it; he shook one of her claws, handed her a complete set of all his albums and posed with her for photographs.

"Tell her she's cool," he told Pindar.

"OK," Pindar said, "though I'll have to use another word. Dragons think anything cold means death."

Jay said, "Wow, man—you're clever."

Tom remembered Pindar telling him it was easy to talk to animals—it was the sort of spell that didn't make him sneeze. He remembered how easily he'd made friends with the elephants at the circus. He had mastered the fiendishly difficult lizard language spell, and he could understand the extinct language of a dragon.

"Yes," he said, "Pindar's really clever. Talking to animals is his special talent."

"Is it?" Pindar was doubtful. "I suppose I have always been quite good with that sort of spell." He grinned suddenly. "Hey—I am good at something after all!"

"Ask her what we must do next," Clarence said.

Pindar said something to the dragon and she rumbled back a detailed reply.

"She says she must bow to the One Good Falconer. And—" He listened a little more, fired off a question in dragon-language, and then his face lit up. "Tom! It's NOT ME!"

"What?' Clarence asked sharply.

"I'm NOT the One Good Falconer! I'm just an ordinary bad one!"

Tom and Pindar burst out laughing and did high fives, and Tom was so happy that he almost forgot he was standing uncomfortably close to a very hot dragon.

"But . . . ," Clarence said. He was astonished. "If it's not you, then who?"

"Of course!" Tom shouted. "Don't you see? It's MILLY!"

24

Justice

"Wow, that was such a relief," said Pindar. "When that dragon said Milly was the One Good Falconer, I could have kissed her!"

"It's so great that you can talk to her," Tom said. "When do you have to go back?"

"Clarence said they wouldn't need me until she's finished eating."

The two boys lay in the long grass on the edge of the great arena, drinking Coke while the dragon ate her supper. Finding the right food had not been easy. She had asked for a thousand live goats and two hundred live human slaves. When told this wasn't possible, she had asked for a hundred tons of top-quality coal. Finally she settled for hamburgers, and Clarence had appealed to the crowd for help. Hundreds of fairies all over Dragon's Lawn had relit their barbecues and made heaps and heaps of burgers, which were now being collected in wheelbarrows and shoveled down the dragon's throat.

"They won't make you stay in the Realm to be her interpreter, will they?" asked Tom.

"Hope not. She's OK, but I don't want to spend my life with an ancient dragon. I've always wanted to go to a proper school. That's what made me try so hard to talk to my lizards—I didn't have any friends my own age."

"You'll just have to teach someone else to talk to her," Tom said firmly. "Look—Clarence is waving, we'd better go over."

"She probably wants to ask for seconds," Pindar said, grinning.

They hurried back through the crowd. The dragon had polished off her hamburgers and now sat, stuffed and red-hot, on a burnt patch of grass, occasionally burping and sending out clouds of sparks.

There was nervous excitement in the air as people tidied up picnic stuff and strapped on wings. The boys passed two television crews, and Clarence was surrounded by reporters and photographers.

"Ah, Pindar—I think she's finished." Clarence looked years younger, and seemed to quiver with impatience.

"Ask her if she's ready to go—I've had a call from Milly to say everything's prepared. Tell her the whole Realm is waiting."

Pindar and the dragon talked for a few minutes.

"She says the burgers were great," Pindar said. "Now she wants to meet Auntie Milly."

Tom knew that he would never forget being part of the triumphant procession from Hopping Hill to the High Fairy Court. The dragon took off first, and they had to clear a space on Dragon's Lawn so that she could spread her enormous wings. Clarence, Pindar and Tom flew in close formation behind her, and following them flew a huge crowd of fairies, elves, goblins, pixies, genies, gnomes, demifurs and every kind of magical creature.

The dragon flew at a slow, dignified pace, and kept low so that the crowds of fairies on the ground could get a good look at her. The news had traveled fast, and the entire Realm was celebrating the fall of the Falconers. Every village and town they flew over had its big screen up to watch the ceremony, and when they saw the dragon the crowds cheered loudly.

The High Fairy Court was surrounded by an enormous crowd—there were no less than four huge screens up, and as they lost height Tom saw picnics, more television crews and stalls selling food and dragon T-shirts. Directly outside the court, however, a very large green space had been cleared. Milly waited there, in her big white wedding dress.

Police fairies patrolled the air above the clearing, and most of the crowd following the dragon were directed to the big screens, but Clarence, Pindar and Tom were waved through.

"Touch down somewhere behind her," Clarence called. "The dragon will need plenty of room."

Tom hardly heard him. A little way behind Milly stood a man with curly gray hair.

"Dad!" Tom was so overjoyed to see him that he landed in a clumsy heap at his feet, and Dad had to untangle his wings before he could hug him.

"Tom! You're safe—and you've learned to fly!"

"Are you really OK?"

"I'm absolutely fine—and incredibly sorry that I didn't warn you about any of this; I know I've got a lot of explaining to do, but it'll have to wait till after the ceremony."

The dragon landed on the grass and a deep hush fell. Dad took Tom's hand and squeezed it tightly. They watched in silence as the dragon shuffled towards Milly and bowed her head to the ground.

"It's all right, Pindar—we've found someone else who

can talk to her," Milly said. "This is Professor Bunty Goodfellow, from the Institute of Extinct Languages."

A tall, thin lady with gray hair and gold-rimmed glasses stepped forward and rumbled something at the dragon. Tom was very happy to see her—now nobody would try to keep Pindar in the Realm as a translator.

He looked round for his ex-cousin and saw him standing shyly a few meters away. "Hey!" He grabbed him and pulled him over. "Dad, this is Pindar—he's my best friend and he saved my life!"

"I used to be your nephew, but Dolores says she's not my mother," said Pindar.

"That doesn't matter," said Dad, giving Pindar a friendly smile. "It's great to meet you, Pindar—Squeaky's told me lots about you. Thanks for saving Tom's life."

"Squeaky? Oh, you mean Terence!" Pindar suddenly spotted Terence waving to him in the crowd, and waved back.

Milly kissed one of the dragon's claws, and the great crowd burst into deafening cheers.

"She's going inside now, to give her verdict," said Dad. "Justice has returned to the Realm!"

They went into the court, where Judge Plato was waiting to formally give up his place. He bowed to Milly and went to stand beside Dahlia. Milly squashed the white billows of her dress into his chair, while everybody else crammed into any seat they could find. Tom,

Pindar and Jonas managed to find places beside Lorna and Iris.

Lorna hugged the boys. "I'm so glad you're all right. Isn't this thrilling?"

Tiberius and Dolores Falconer and the rest of the Ten were now in the dock, looking very sulky.

"Silence in court!" Milly's voice was strong and loud. "On behalf of the last dragon, I formally accept the leadership of the Realm and will now settle any outstanding business."

"This is NONSENSE!" shouted Tiberius.

"Since you can't keep quiet," said Milly, "I'll deal with you first. According to the old law, you should be killed at once—but this is the beginning of a new era and there will be no more cruel punishments. I'm sending you and Dolores and the rest of the Ten to work at the Home for Retired Donkeys."

"What? Milly, you can't be serious! Give the leadership back to me!"

"Certainly not!" Milly angrily tossed her ringlets. "Don't you get the message, Tiberius? You're not the leader anymore. You're an ordinary worker at a donkey sanctuary."

"You fat cow!" shrieked Dolores. "You'll be sorry for this!"

"And a few years shoveling donkey poo will do YOU a world of good," Milly said. "Goodbye." She pointed a finger at the dock, and Tiberius, Dolores and the rest of the Ten vanished.

There was polite clapping inside the court, and loud cheering from the crowd outside.

"Next," Milly said, "the case of Derek Drapton."

The Chief Adorer—still sobbing, and wiping his eyes on the black sleeves of his robe—stepped into the dock. "I don't care what you do to me—I deserve to be punished. I've spent the past fifteen years wishing only for your forgiveness!"

Milly sighed impatiently. "Oh, Derek, do stop that sniveling! Of course you can have my forgiveness—on the condition that you disband the Adorers and get married to someone else."

"Milly, thank you!" gasped Drapton.

"Now listen, everyone," Milly went on. "I declare an end to all Falconer rule and influence."

Huge cheers as the public gallery did a wave.

"I declare that all prisoners are free."

More cheers. "That means Hussein!" Lorna shouted above the din.

"I declare that all taxes are abolished."

This time the cheers were loud enough to shake the building, and bits of plaster rained down from the ceiling.

"I declare that the mountain known as Hopping Hill

is the property of the Fairy State, and protected as an area of outstanding magical beauty—is that OK by you, Jonas?"

"I think it's wonderful. I don't want it. Hopping Hill belongs to the Hoppers."

The cheers were incredible now. Tom felt very proud of Dad.

"Finally, I declare five days and nights of feasting, and with my new powers I shall cast one of the oldest spells from the old law—the same spell the blabbermouth Shakespeare let out to the mortals—the PUTTING-RIGHT." Milly stood up. In a loud voice she declaimed, *"Jack shall have Jill / Nought shall go ill / The man shall have his mare again / And all shall be WELL!"*

Rays of sunlight streamed through the tall windows of the court. And suddenly everyone was smiling and shaking hands and hugging and kissing, as if it were Christmas morning.

Dad hugged Tom. "All shall be well," he said shakily. "I really believe that now."

Tom had hundreds of questions for his dad, but these had to wait until they had all flown back to Dragon's Lawn. Parties were breaking out all over the Realm, but this was where Milly had decided to hold hers, with the dragon as guest of honor. Jay Trebonkers was going to give a free concert, and Dahlia rode off splendidly with Judge Plato, in a flying gondola drawn by sixteen swans.

Tom flew beside his dad; after that botched landing he wanted to show off how well he could manage Clarence's old wings. He secretly hoped that there would be some way of doing a bit of flying back in the mortal world.

Dragon's Lawn was a magnificent sight: a great carpet of campfires and colored lights, under a sky filled with stars (Tom wasn't sure he recognized all of these). Clarence's bodyguards set out tables and chairs, and a selection of drinks and snacks. It was very hot. The summer night was warm and still, and the dragon was glowing like a furnace. A well-wisher had sent her a hundred tons of coal, which she ate with fiery greed. Professor Bunty Goodfellow didn't dare to stand too near to her because of the sparks.

It was a fantastic evening. Tom and Pindar listened to Jay's free concert, ate a delicious meal and finally lay yawning on big cushions beside the campfire.

Milly was making a stately procession around Dragon's Lawn in her big white gown. She shook hands, kissed babies, gave television interviews and posed for photographs.

"She's enjoying leadership," Jonas said, chuckling. "I always told her she'd make a good prime minister."

"And look at Iris!" said Lorna. "I've never seen that old dinosaur-drawers so jolly!"

Tom looked at Iris, half hidden behind the white billows of Milly's dress. Her hair was ruffled, her hat was still bent out of shape and her little eyes sparkled with happiness. "If Dahlia can give up her husbands," he said, "maybe Iris will stop making her schoolgirls steal for her."

"I can't believe those two let themselves get so wicked," said Jonas.

"A bit of tough godmother duty was just what they needed," Lorna said. "They're a lot nicer now, thanks to Tom." She grinned at him. "And thanks to Tom, I've remembered how to fly."

"Tom," his dad said softly, "I really am very sorry I didn't tell you about your fairy heritage."

"That's OK, I'm over the shock now."

"I will explain everything, but if you don't mind, I'll wait for Milly to tell the whole story." A shadow crossed his face.

Dahlia joined them in time to hear this. "You mustn't blame yourself," she said softly. "You couldn't have saved her." She looked elegant in her off-the-shoulder ivory silk.

Judge Plato was right behind her, wheeling a trolley full of bottles. He had changed into a white dinner jacket with a black bow tie. "Cocktail, anyone?"

"She'd have wanted you to celebrate tonight," Dahlia said.

Dad tried to smile. "You're right, I mustn't spoil the mood. Thank you, my lord; I'll have a small Rheingold Rocket."

"Call me Plato—ice and lemon?"

Terence had a guitar, and he began to sing a plaintive love song he had translated from the bat language. The great crowd was quieter now. Hundreds of fires glowed in the darkness. Tom sat on the grass, leaning against his dad. Jonas was thrilled to be back with his son, but while he listened to the song, he was far away, thinking about something that made him very sad.

He snapped out of it when Milly finished being a politician and joined them at the campfire. She had changed out of her wedding-and-burial dress back into her borrowed jumpsuit, and Jonas poured her a glass of fairy beer.

"I think the Realm's got a decent leader at last," he told her. "No offense, Pindar—but Milly's the perfect Falconer for the job."

"There were no other Falconers," Milly said. "When my memory came back I knew that it couldn't be Pindar. Oh, I remembered all sorts of things!" She smiled at both boys, making her face very pretty and sweet in the firelight. "Have you told them about Clover?"

"No," Jonas said, very quietly. He bowed his head. "I couldn't bear to."

"Clover Falconer was my second or third cousin," Milly said, "and my very dear friend. Her father, Trajan Falconer, was a decent man who fell out with my ghastly brother."

"Oh yes," Lorna muttered. "The gnome-bombs!"

"After Tiberius killed her father," Milly went on, "Clover was very poor—she worked as a governess for the children of one of Tiberius's mistresses. When she had any time off, she used to visit me in college—I was sharing digs with Iris."

"Clover was very pretty," Iris said. "Luckily she didn't look like her father, who had a terrible Falconer nose. Her mother was a Cobweb and they're a much better-looking family."

"Anyway," Milly went on, "Clover and Jonas fell in love. Of course I was disappointed that he hadn't fallen in love with ME, but I couldn't hold it against her—poor thing, she was so happy! But my brother's vile wife had already decided to sell her handsome brother to the highest bidder, and she didn't want him to marry a poor governess. So they married in secret."

"Good grief, I didn't know you actually married Clover!" Lorna gasped. "You should've told me! I would've sent you a present!"

"Your head was too full of Abdul," Milly said, smiling. "And it would have been too risky. I knew about it because I helped them."

"You were a very good friend to us," Jonas said. Tom couldn't see his face, but his voice was choked.

"For a few years they were very happy," Milly said. "They had a little cottage in Hopping Hill, where they ran an excellent delicatessen."

"Another deli!" Tom cried.

"Yes, he was always great with food. And the kids loved Clover's exploding buns. But then Dolores and Tiberius decided to get their wicked hands on Hopping Hill. They ordered me to marry Jonas, and thought I'd go along with it because I was in love with him. Then they found out about the secret marriage. Jonas was taken off to prison, and Clover—" She broke off to sigh. "Well, when I asked Dolores what had happened to Clover, she just showed me her wedding ring and a lock of hair, and said she'd been vaporized."

Dad made a coughing sound that could have been a strangled sob. In the darkness Tom felt for his hand, and Dad squeezed his fingers gratefully.

"So I helped Jonas escape to the mortal world."

"You took a huge risk," Iris said. "I had no idea you loved him that much!"

"You're a typical fairy, Iris; you don't understand about love. I wanted Jonas to be free."

Dad murmured, "I've never thanked you properly."

"I haven't finished!" Milly said. "You went to the mortal world and opened your shop, eventually meeting your mortal wife."

"Sophie," Jonas said sofly. He reached out to stroke the jar of sun-dried tomatoes. "I thought I could never be happy again, and then I found her and we had our demispritc." He smiled at Tom.

"I didn't get round to telling the court the real reason for my murder," Milly went on to say. She gazed round at them all solemnly. "He did it because I found out about the baby."

There was a silence.

"Baby?" Jonas whispered.

"Brace yourself, my dear Jonas. Clover wasn't vaporized."

"She . . . survived the lightning storm?"

"Yes, because she sneezed just before the attack and fell into the fridge—poor dear, she was always tripping over those enormous fect! She survived and went into hiding. And then she found out that she was pregnant."

Lorna spluttered on her beer. "Pregnant?"

"She told me," Milly said, "because we were still in contact. I'm so sorry, Jonas—we couldn't let you know! It would've been instant death for both of us! A few months later one of Terence's bat-cousins brought me a message; the baby had been born, and poor Clover had died—oh, Jonas, my poor dear!"

In the shadows, Tom blinked away a tear. His dad was crying softly, and he wished he could comfort him; the Realm was a cruel place.

"Dolores and Tiberius couldn't have children of their own," Milly said. "They brought a curse on themselves by stretching the old law too far. They tried everything, including things I won't talk about in front of these boys, but nothing worked. And then Dolores heard that Clover was still alive and about to have a child."

"Did they hurt her?" asked Jonas.

"The bat who brought the message was with her when she died." Milly's voice was gentle. "She had time to bless her baby boy and cover him with protection-charms. She loved her baby very much, and that's the best protection there is."

They were all quiet. The fire crackled as Tom's dad wept. The three godmothers were crying too. Tom tried to digest this incredible story. His dad's first wife had had a baby boy, and that meant he had a half brother. That explained why he'd always had a sense that some-one was missing.

"My son!" Dad cried suddenly. "What happened to my son?"

"I just told you." Milly blew her nose and refilled her glass with beer. "My brother and his wife stole him."

Suddenly it was all so obvious that Tom almost laughed. "Pindar!" he cried. "Dad—it's Pindar!"

Jonas and Pindar gaped at each other, their mouths hanging open in identical looks of amazement.

Lorna chuckled. "Well, now we know why you two are peas in a pod! The old Pindar looked like Clover's dad—didn't I say that dip in the handsome-vat brought out his Harding side?"

"My boy!" Jonas murmured. "My first boy! Now I know why I had that sense that I'd left something behind in the Realm!" He hugged Pindar. "Forgive me, Pindar—I wish I'd known. I should have been there to take care of you—I loved your poor mother so much!"

Pindar was trying hard not to cry, but happiness began to dawn in his astonished face.

"I'm so proud of you," Dad said. He put one of his arms round Tom and hugged his two sons hard. "Both of you!"

Tom felt a huge balloon of happiness swelling inside him. "Now he has to live with us! And if he's living in the mortal world he'll have to go my new school! And help out in the deli—arggh!"

Something suddenly swept him off his feet and whisked him upside down, and Tom nearly landed in the fire. He was so happy that he had automatically turned a somersault in midair.

It made everyone laugh.

"Sorry!"

"Oh, don't apologize—I feel exactly the same!" Jonas shot into the air and did a showy triple flip. "Wow, I didn't know I could still do that!"

"You'd better forget it again," Iris said. "It won't go down well with the mortals."

"Oh garters!" Jonas swore suddenly. He looked at Tom. "What on earth are we going to tell your mum?"

"That needn't be a problem," Clarence said. He had nodded off the minute Jay had stopped singing, and Tom had almost forgotten he was there. "I can arrange it so that she knows just enough when she wakes up to set her mind at rest."

Tom thought about the meetings he'd had with Mum in his dreams, when she had been so happy and so wise. He was longing to see her. "I think she might know a bit more than you think."

Jonas caressed the nearby jar of sun-dried tomatoes. "I wish I could see her now, but her molecules would never survive in this atmosphere. I'm sure she'll understand why I never told her about my fairy background."

"She's been sending Tom some very useful messages," Lorna said thoughtfully. "The fact is, mortals can be jolly clever. And they're such a lot nicer than fairies."

"You're a nice fairy," Tom said. "She's been a great godmother, Dad."

"Oh, go on!" Lorna said gruffly, though she looked pleased. "My magic wasn't up to much."

"I chose you because you had something else," Jonas said. "A kind heart."

"Quite right, darling," Dahlia said graciously. "I would never have got involved at all, if it hadn't been for Lorna."

"Neither would I," Iris said stiffly—she was always stiff when saying something nice, as if it had to be pulled out of her with tweezers. "Thanks to Lorna and Tom and their mortal values—well, I started to feel bad about my school. I'm going to sell it and move back to the Realm."

"Iris has agreed to be my private secretary," Milly said cheerfully. "We'll be sharing a flat, just like in the old days."

Iris giggled suddenly. "I feel twenty years younger!"

"Girls," Dad said, "you've all been fantastic. I'd like to propose a toast." He raised his glass. "To Lorna, Iris and Dahlia—the best godmothers in the universe!"

They all drank and the three godmothers looked very pleased, even Iris.

A massive explosion ripped through the air above them—but it was an explosion of fireworks, the most spectacular display Tom had ever seen. The crowd broke into ooohs and aaahs of wonder as the fireworks made huge bouquets of fiery flowers, in colors so bright that they almost hurt.

"It's a gift to the dragon from the genies," Milly said. "To thank her for freeing the prisoners in Ali Kazoum's desert fortress."

The climax came with a brilliant firework dragon and the word WELCOME. The cheers in the arena were tremendous.

More words blazed across the sky: LORNA, WILL YOU MARRY ME AGAIN?

"Great garters!" gasped Lorna. "Abdul!"

People in the crowd started to chant: "Lorna! Lorna!"

Her craggy face turned bright red, though she tried to frown. "Impossible!"

Another message flashed into the sky. SORRY I SOLD YOUR MOTHER.

"Oh, THAT'S what he did!" Dahlia cried. "My dear Lorna, don't you think you should get over it?"

"He still loves you," Tom felt he should say. "He thinks you're a queen among women."

Lorna turned a darker shade of red. "I'll think about it."

"It's a very good time for getting married," declared Judge Plato. "Dahlia, will you marry me, and make a springtime in the barren winter of my life?"

"Yes, darling, like a shot," Dahlia said. "My son

will be so relieved that he doesn't have to support my luxurious lifestyle! We all know he thinks old fairies suck."

"Well, I don't," Tom said, smiling round at his three godmothers. "I think they rock."

About the Author

Kate Saunders has written lots of books for adults and children. She lives in London with her son and her three cats.